# GIFTWITCH

# GIFTWITCH

## *The Magic of Keb, Book 1*

### CHRISTOPHER I. HANKS

Everthink Publishing
Fishers, Indiana

An Everthink Book

ISBN: 069282894X
ISBN-13: 9780692828946
Library of Congress Control Number: 2017900111
Everthink Publishing, Fishers, IN

# CONTENTS

# CROZADA ON THE WORLD OF KEB

Kaoric Ocean

N

Bay of Mirth

Caves & Grottoes

Vanig Bay

Calimygna

Keras Bay

Buscade

Severlandon

R. Nina

Duchy of Nydia

R. Lyria

Drozza R.

Porvatis

Forest of Ard Shaab

R. Lynd

Vinglandon

Haggle Bay

Janni Lake

Mudon Inlet

R. Merlin

Tantahir Lake

Lyric Mnts.

Pangerean Sea

Rockhis Mnts.

Akhdiria

Rashida

Walid

Qadir

Khada's Pass

R. Tyria

Ard Alabia

Intolia

Xenrali

Menuha

Ukbawa

Qoto

Domus Viho

Trigoti Bay

Trigoti

Tyenese Mnts.

Crescent R.

Grolandon

Crescent Bay

Orbalese Mnts.

Kewu

Kivuli Falls

Surbal R.

Tuskawa

Chayl

Riven Mnts.

R. Masai

Surbalese Mnts.

Wall of Wukoa

Burúji

Monestary of Kila

Cliffs of Kusma

Norwood Marsh

Bay of Danu

Mbúso

Nyango

Sacn Bay

Gulf of Kusma

Omo Islands

Kiriti Island

Andyric Ocean

BGM17

# PROLOGUE

Sand. She hated the sand. It had killed her once—or very nearly—so perhaps *hate* was not even a strong enough word. She detested the sand. She loathed it.

She loathed the village as well. Rashida, it was named, which meant "righteous" in the old language of the Holy Scripture. She had died a child in the desert and been reborn in Rashida as Adia Varani, a young woman with dark secrets easily hidden under a veil of righteousness.

After three years, she had left Rashida to pursue him, and she'd thought she would never return to the village of her rebirth. But, after she'd spent a year watching him, the opportunity had called to her in the secret spell underneath the surface of a group prayer. She could finish the journey where it began, and such perfect symmetry did not exist outside the divine will of Sabar. It appeared that her righteous mission had, indeed, been blessed by the Almighty.

So, she returned to her second home and planned her revenge. *No*, Adia thought, *she should not call it revenge, for Sabar did not support vengeance.* It was justice. It was the protection of innocents. It was holy work, the seed of which had been planted in the inhospitable sand of Rashida and would finally bear fruit after four years of careful cultivation.

So, she prepared, and she waited in the shadows until he appeared, silhouetted in the light of the autumn moon. Despite the darkness, she was certain of his identity as he left his camel and strode to the door that bore his evil mark. She was afraid, she admitted to herself, because he was more powerful than she could hope to be. But her strategy was solid, so she succeeded in suppressing her anticipation and fear, careful not to reveal her concealment in the shadow. Still, she could not prevent her hairs from rising, pushing against the surface of her skin as if they feared to remain attached.

Adia watched closely as the tall stranger rubbed his hand over the sign of the beast, a bull's head crudely carved into the wooden door. She smiled in satisfaction when the stranger shook his head in confusion upon finding the door locked, but she closed her eyes, steeling herself against that which was certain to follow. Predictably, he activated his Gift Magic, and the energy of sorcery erupted from his body, nearly stealing her breath in its intensity. Oh, the depth of his power was something to behold. But, refusing to be intimidated, she opened her eyes to see him shining like a star in the night sky, sparkling with tongues of lightning snaking around his body and electrifying his hair, suddenly as white as the heart of a flame.

The sorcerer pointed a long finger at the door handle and sent a bolt of energy streaking from his fingertip, scorching a hole in the door where the handle once had been. However, when he pushed the door and found it had been barred as well as locked, he cursed and spat in frustration. Adia smirked. Her victory lasted but a moment, for a thick bolt of kinetic energy burst from his hands, striking with a grand explosion and blasting the door inward.

Glowing like a candlelit evergreen at Winterfest, the sorcerer entered the modest little home with a growl. Despite the distance, the light from his crackling energy was sufficient for Adia to watch the owner of the home lurch from its shadows, just as she had instructed, and attack from behind. Wielding a common ax, the man aimed to split the intruder's skull but, misjudging the stranger's height, succeeded only in slicing into a shoulder. As a roar of pain sprang from the sorcerer's lips, so, too, did a ball of fire spring from his hand, striking the assailant full in the chest. As the ax rattled to the floor, the man's burning body struck the edge of the doorway, igniting the frame before falling into a smoldering heap on the sand outside.

She was saddened by the man's death, perhaps even moved, but it was not unexpected. He was a casualty of war, in her mind—an unfortunate necessity. Still, listening to the sounds of the Gifted infant within the house, ignorant of his father's violent death but crying and screaming nonetheless, Adia was haunted by her own memories. Like the boy, Adia Varani had been born Gifted, and her father, like his, had been murdered by the tall sorcerer. Her mother and foster mother each had been killed by the sorcery of Gift Magic, too, she recalled, one by her own hand.

She would not weep, however, and her memories were silenced by a primal scream that ripped through the night, eloquently conveying the inexplicable anguish and indomitable strength that could only be possessed by a desperate mother. Focusing her eyes through the dark and the still-burning doorway, Adia gasped as the mother's body crashed through a wall into the night. Abandoning her discipline, Adia rushed across the road, only to find the woman with a sunken chest and an unbeating heart.

Her cold resolve replaced with rage, the young Gifted woman rose to her feet and leveled her incendiary gaze at the sorcerer, visible through the gaping hole in the wall, his stark white hair raised on end. His back to her, he raised the crying infant aloft and began to chant:

A newborn babe with hair milk-white,
with eyes as black as a moonless night,
upon my soul, I claim this child
with power strong and spirit wild!

With a chaotic rush of noise, like the great waterfall of Kivúli, an enormous flow of energy erupted from the child's body and smashed into the sorcerer, sending him reeling and loosening his grip on the delicate infant. The unfortunate child fell lifeless to the ground, a slow stream of blood trickling from his mouth and sinking into the packed dirt floor.

Feeling the fury and power building inside her, Adia watched as the sorcerer stumbled through the same exit the child's mother had taken, gripping the ax wound in his shoulder and grimacing in pain at every step. His crackling energy had dissipated, and his hair had returned to its natural colors of brown and gray. He muttered to himself, wondering how a simple peasant and his wife could have found such courage, foolish as it was.

"I can tell you," Adia said softly as he stumbled near. "I gave it to them."

The sorcerer looked up at her, startled from his mumblings. "Who...who are you? Gave them what?"

"Courage," she responded, spitting the words.

"Courage?" he asked, confused. "To resist the Angel of Mercy?"

"Ah, yes," Adia responded, laughing bitterly. "You call yourself the Angel of Mercy, because murdering helpless infants makes you *merciful...*" Her eyes narrowed and her sarcasm fled, angry bitterness replacing it. "But I *know* you, and you are *not* an angel!"

She finally allowed herself to release, exploding with the rage, energy, hatred, and vengeance so long restrained. She had no time to smile at his shock when her body was surrounded by the familiar crackling energy, and the black from her hair evaporated, for she was already attacking, alternating between blasts of concussive force and balls of fire.

"I *know* you!" she shouted, advancing upon him. "Angel of Mercy? Ha! You are a man! You are Gifted! You are Ixodis!"

Her initial torrent had driven him back into the stone house, collapsing it upon him. When she finally pulverized the obscuring rubble, she found him surrounded by a thin energy shield, wrapped around his broken body in a desperate cocoon. He bled profusely, and his breathing was short and ragged. Adia towered over him, triumphant, and prepared the final blow.

Before she could deliver it, Ixodis coughed. "I believe *I* know *you...*"

Adia froze in fear and confusion. He could not possibly...

"It was in a small Alabian village, much like this one...Intolla, I think, near Khada's Pass." Ixodis choked, spitting blood before continuing, his voice rambling. "I found your parents kneeling at the door when I arrived. They died quietly before I absorbed your soul."

"Not *my* soul," Adia whispered, her voice tinged with pain.

"It was weaker than I expected, your soul, weaker than usual…" The confused words tripped and stumbled out of his mouth.

"Not *my* soul," she echoed, her cold resolve returning in time to prevent the tears.

Finally, the sorcerer's strength failed, and his shield slipped away, preceded by a small, defeated whimper.

The young sorceress raised her hands. "For my sister," she whispered as she delivered a massive blast.

"Your *twin* sister!" he shouted with a sudden surge of strength, managing to resurrect his shield just as the heat of the blast stung his face.

Adia stood frozen, yet again, flames licking her palms in aggravation.

He frowned at her questioningly. "But…I missed you. How did I miss you?"

"You saw what you expected to see," she replied in an icy voice. "One child, one victim."

Realization washed over his face, transforming his frown into a smile of awe and wonderment. "You hid! You were an infant, no more than ten days old, and yet you sensed the danger and managed to hide yourself. That would only be possible if you siphoned your sister's strength, which would explain why she was weaker than I expected."

He shook his head. Suddenly, his eyes brightened in another epiphany. "And you watched! Those many years ago, you watched me from your hiding place. You witnessed me performing the Spell Magic on your sister, so you knew what the absorption of a living soul does to me. And so, you waited. And then here, today, once again, you planned this, and you waited."

The young sorceress could not prevent her pride from forcing her chin to dip in a small nod of acknowledgment.

"But how did you know to be here?"

Adia snorted in derision. "When your gullible masses carved your symbol on the door and chanted the prayer you taught them, with the hidden spell that summoned you—"

"It summoned you, as well!" Ixodis finished. He nodded, fascination clear upon his burned and broken face. "So you convinced these people to attack me, not because you thought they could succeed, but because you wanted them to *weaken* me. And then you waited. You waited until I absorbed that demon-child."

"Demon-child?" she exclaimed. "How dare you insult him when he was merely Gifted, just as *you* are Gifted?"

"You misunderstand the word, my dear," he said, laughing in haughty condescension. "Gift Magic is evil, and the Gifted are witches possessed by demons. My magic is different, because it comes from the Almighty God."

Adia shook her head in disgust and disbelief. "It's almost as if you believe your own lie. You sicken me!"

"Sicken you?" Ixodis replied, feigning shock. "You, who could have tried to stop me from murdering those brave parents and did nothing? You, who waited and allowed me to murder that poor baby boy with my absorption spell so I would be further weakened? You, who *sacrificed* these innocents as *bait*? *You* are sickened by *me*?"

Her face as cold as her voice, the sorceress responded, "I do what I must."

He nodded. "Well, then, we are not much different, you and I."

It may have been the arrogance that triggered her response or, perhaps more likely, the truth that Adia stubbornly refused to accept. She pursued the work of Sabar, her god, but murder as a means to an end would never be easy to reconcile with her conscience; so, she chose to mask her discomfort with fury. Her entire body detonated in a blast that shook the nearby homes and forced Ixodis deeper into the rubble.

The young sorceress had abandoned her discipline, relentlessly flinging blasts of force and fire in her maniacal obsession with finally destroying the evil of Ixodis. She reminded herself that she was acting not out of guilt for the lives she had taken or had allowed to be taken; rather, she was acting for justice. She reminded herself of the sorcerer's crimes, including the coldhearted killing of her parents, the parasitic murder of her sister, and the ongoing slaughter of helpless Gifted infants. It was her God-given mission, she insisted to herself, and she refused to allow the deceptive voices of guilt to distract her heart from its holy purpose.

She doubled her efforts, raining attacks upon her enemy like hail from a thunderstorm, while defending her mind from the subtle tentacles of conscience. So strong were her defenses that she was unaware of the Mind Magic cry for help from an angel battling a demon. She was unaware of the devout villagers, eager to wake and respond to a heavenly servant of their god. She was unaware of the quietly advancing man or the heavy shovel he carried until a flash of pain burst into her head.

## Chapter 1

# AFFLICTION

It had been fifteen years, Hillian realized, since his mother had brought him to his first witch burning. Though he had been only a boy of ten, she'd felt it was imperative that he understand the pain and suffering the Church of Jalidinity had been inflicting upon his people. As Lady of Nydia, the largest and most powerful duchy in the nation, she felt it was her responsibility to use her influence to make the kingdom of Vinglandon a better place. When he inherited the lordship, she explained, he would also inherit the responsibility.

Hillian Drake's father, however, had vastly differing priorities. As the prime cardinal—the worldwide high priest of Jalidinity—Hydronimus Drake taught his son of responsibilities to the church, not the least of which was protecting the good people of Nydia, and all of

Vinglandon, from the demons of Lakis by burning their human hosts to send the evil spirits back to hell.

"You don't have to do this."

Startled by his traveling companion's voice, Hillian regarded his friend. A master innkeeper, Eryk Val Varen was a wealthy man, dressed in a rich black doublet, a long black cloak, and fine black leather boots. He sat atop his horse with the bearing of a nobleman, though his long hair marked him as a commoner in the tradition of Vinglandon's deeply ingrained class structure. The clasp at the back of Eryk's neck had failed in its purpose of containment, as it often did, and strands of dark-brown hair clung to the sweat on the man's bearded face, drawing Hillian's attention to the lines and subtle wrinkles that demonstrated the ten years between them.

"Do what?" Hillian asked. "Observe the burning of a Giftwitch? It is exactly what we have come to support."

"No, it is what *you* have come to support," Eryk replied dryly. "I am here to support *you*, but we have already established that I do not agree with human burnings. Not all of us are afflicted with your disease of religious faith."

"It is not an affliction to those of us who believe, Master Val Varen," the devout nobleman responded, his dark-blue eyes flashing with frustration, if not exactly anger.

"It is the belief itself that is the affliction, my friend, for it allows an otherwise logical and reasonable person, such as yourself, to support an activity so evil—"

"It is *not* evil!" Hillian shouted, drawing attention from the few travelers who populated the spellport station. "A Giftwitch is a human born with a demon soul—"

"Yes, and the only way to return the demon spirit to the eternal fires of Lakis is to burn the host," Eryk interrupted, his voice cruel with condescension. "I am familiar with the teachings, my lord, but the Church of Jalidinity makes no effort to explain why the human host must be alive and conscious at the time of burning."

"Because—" Hillian responded, but Eryk quickly interrupted him.

"Or how these demons can be so easily identified. How can you know for certain that this woman we are going to see is a Giftwitch at all? There was no trial and no evidence!"

"My World Council colleague, Rami Jaser, as an ordained dalil, judged her—"

"Yes, a Sabarist priest judged her after observing her battling the Angel of Mercy. But how could this Giftwitch possibly have grown to adulthood to fight the Angel of Mercy if that very same Angel of Mercy is murdering all the Gifted infants in their cribs?"

"It is *not* murder if an angel destroys a demon!" Hillian replied passionately.

"No, of course not, even in Mbúso, apparently, where angels and demons do not exist!"

"Oh, angels and demons exist everywhere, even in a nation that has outlawed religion," Hillian retorted.

Narrowing his eyes, the innkeeper challenged his lord with biting sarcasm. "Well, be sure they burn the fire extra hot, my lord, for this is a demon Giftwitch whom the Angel of Mercy has now failed to destroy *twice*, despite the fact that he wields the power of heaven and is guided by an omnipotent god."

Hillian hesitated, running his fingers through his short brown hair as he searched his memory for the church's relevant teaching but found only contradiction. Exasperated by the satisfied expression on his friend's face, the nobleman said, "Even with the power of heaven and the guidance of God, an angel is not perfect."

"Much like a man," Eryk replied, his voice steady and controlled. "Some say that's what he is: a man, born with the same Gifts as those he hunts."

"The Angel of Mercy...a *man*? A Giftwitch? Impossible!" Hillian said.

"Is it? You must admit the powers are similar."

"They are the powers of the eternal realm, but one is evil and one is good."

"Yes, my lord," the older man agreed, "an invisible distinction, impossible to refute, that would certainly work to his favor, would it not?" The nobleman frowned as Eryk continued. "There are people who accuse him of perverting the world religions into believing and supporting the Angel of Mercy mythology simply to justify his atrocities as religious necessities."

"Which people?" Hillian asked, animated in his fury. "Traitors? Heretics? Criminals like that assassin thief Rook?"

Shocked into an expression that teetered between insulted confusion and proud rebellion, Eryk prodded, "Why would you mention Master Rook?"

"Do not honor him with that title," the young lord commanded. "He is an enemy of the state, and his band of thieves, those Carrion Crows, do everything they can to turn the people of Vinglandon against the church. They are the ones spreading these rumors about the Angel of Mercy. Surely you, Master Val Varen, would not fall victim to such ridiculous propaganda!"

The words hung in the thick air of Mbúso as the two men exited the spellport station. Eryk Val Varen chose his words carefully. "Well, perhaps my mind has more room for ridiculous thoughts, my lord, as it is not quite so filled as yours with the unproven teachings of an unproven god."

Hillian choked, his throat tightening. "Such words suggest heresy and treason," he accused, breathless in his incredulity.

Eryk shook his head slowly, adding, "If my lord, who plans to defend witch burning on the grounds of religious freedom, wishes to persecute me for my free thoughts on our national religion, then I will loudly expose his hypocrisy before gladly submitting to the dungeon."

Before Hillian had time to construct a reasonable retort, Eryk excused himself, wishing to visit the inns and taverns he owned within the city. The Lord of Nydia rode on with only his retainers, and his thoughts grew ever more nervous. His eyes roamed the unfamiliar surroundings of Burúji for comfort but found none. Eryk's words haunted the young nobleman, pushing into his thoughts and preventing him from peacefully acknowledging his God-given mission. As the young lord finally arrived at the square in the capital of Mbúso, however, his eyes found a familiar, if not entirely reassuring, face.

"President Kesler," he greeted her in a friendly tone. "Your inauguration ceremony was splendid. I'm sorry I had to leave before I had the opportunity to congratulate you, in person, on your election to a second term."

"Thank you, Lord Drake," responded the President of Severlandon, who also served as her nation's delegate to the World Council. Her luxurious golden hair was pulled to one side, woven and wrapped with light-blue ribbons that perfectly matched the color of her stunning eyes, which sparkled as her famous smile erased Hillian's anxiety, if only temporarily. "I am truly pleased to see you again," she said, "though, after all of our success working together on the council, I do regret that these particular circumstances are clouded with such…" Her blue eyes drifted upward as she pondered the most appropriate word. "Contention," she said finally.

Hillian observed the shift in her expression, subtle while intentionally visible. Mona Kesler was famous for her beauty, but Hillian had learned that her clever mind was even more brilliant than her smile. The nobleman shook his head and chuckled. "President Kesler, while I respect your diplomacy, I do not believe you have any such regrets."

Her perfect lips curling into a smile, the Severlandi president nodded. "You speak truth, Lord Drake, and your wise words have amplified my eagerness to face you in tomorrow's council debate!"

The Vingish nobleman bowed his head, acknowledging her compliment. "Thank you, Madam President. I will endeavor to deliver a performance worthy of your enthusiasm."

She smiled, again infecting him with the vivid clarity of her eyes, before asking, "And will you be performing this evening, with your friend from Ard Alabia?"

She motioned to the center of the square, where a crude gallows platform had been hastily erected. Rising from the center of the platform, a tall wooden shaft swayed and creaked, straining against the angular supports that shackled it to the planks below and prevented it from pitching forward and delivering its captive to the hungry mob of Burúji. The captive, suspended from a chain threaded through a hole near the top of the post, was dirty, nearly starved, and streaked with blood. Her eyes were covered by a cloth tied around her head, presumably soaked in a spellcasted narcotic solution, a tactic commonly used to ensure the Giftwitch was conscious and able to feel pain, yet unable to muster the concentration required to perform her Gift Magic.

At the base of the post, below her swinging feet, a pile of logs and sticks eagerly awaited the burning arrows that would be loosed by archers posted on the small, square buildings lodged in the angled ground. Hillian counted six archers standing upon the red roofs, their stoic, black faces illuminated by blazing torches.

A dark-robed Sabarist priest stood on the platform, reading aloud from a book of scripture in the flickering torchlight that illuminated the city square as dusk surrendered to the darkness of night.

"He is not my friend, exactly, but my colleague—as he is yours," Hillian responded. "We are allies in our opposition to your proposal, but I believe Dalil Jaser will be the only speaker tonight."

"Perhaps not," she responded as she quickly strode away, leaping onto the platform.

"President Kesler, you cannot be up here," the dalil shouted, rushing to her, his hair flowing behind him like a cape. Though perhaps only half as long as the hair of his al'awwal, or high priest, Rami Jaser's dark-brown locks measured to the middle of his back, their length indicating his rank among the clergy, a rank that had led to his appointment as Ard Alabia's World Council delegate.

Mona ignored him. Turning to address the crowd of dark faces, the President of Severlandon asked, "How many of you have ever been wrongfully accused? Perhaps it was when you were a child, and your sister claimed you stole her favorite doll, or your friend insisted you broke his toy. Perhaps, as an adult, you have sold your wares to an angry customer who declared you a cheat. Or perhaps your wife, or your husband, has accused you of being unfaithful when you have done nothing but work your fingers to the bone to support your family!"

Her oratory talent was apparent and required only a handful of moments to turn the mood of the crowd. Dalil Jaser appeared to be crippled by shock, his dark-brown skin twisted in a horrified expression that made the hair on his lip and the hair on his chin seem even more misaligned than usual.

"Imagine," Mona continued, pointing to the frail and pathetic form dangling from the post, "this could be you!"

As Mona continued to plead with the audience, Hillian was reminded of Eryk's words. The Giftwitch had survived the Angel of Mercy twice, which was remarkably difficult to reconcile with Jalidin teachings.

"This woman is wrongly accused," Mona proclaimed, "and should be released!"

"No!" Hillian shouted, suddenly compelled to interrupt for the sake of religious freedom. "Rami Jaser is an ordained dalil of Sabarism," the nobleman said as he vaulted to the platform, "and it is his right to judge a demon from a human."

"Lord Drake, you cannot possibly—" Mona began.

"*Yes*, it is my right!" the dalil interjected, finding his voice. "Fire!" he commanded, flinging his right arm in the air.

"No!" Mona cried, as the archers lit their arrows. She rushed to the post, her arms extending as if she intended to protect the condemned witch with her own body, but she never reached the prisoner. As the first arrow struck the base of the post, igniting the sticks and logs, Hillian felt a violent lurching, followed by a dizzy sickness.

Suddenly, the nobleman was tackled roughly, knocked from the platform, his face driven into the dirt. As a hand grabbed a cluster of his short, brown hair and yanked his head back, he detected a vaguely anesthetic smell. Instinctively, he lunged backward, the back of his head sharply striking his assailant's nose. Thankful for the training he'd received from the master-at-arms of Nydia, Hillian grabbed the wrist of the hand that held the narcotic-soaked cloth and pulled it forward, expertly rolling his attacker over his own head. Quickly, the young lord drew his blade, a gleaming short sword, and swung forward, faltering only when his left arm exploded in agony. Dropping the sword and tumbling forward, Hillian began to comprehend that a knife had plunged into his shoulder. Casting about for understanding, the nobleman spied his friend, Eryk Val Varen, straightening from a throwing stance.

Confused, Hillian froze for just a moment, but it was long enough for his attacker to rise and put a knife to his throat.

"Wait," Eryk commanded. After a moment and a tortured sigh, Eryk shook his head. "Let him live and bandage his wound," he said.

"As you say, Master Rook," Hillian's captor responded.

Master Rook? Hillian's eyes widened in shock and disbelief. Surely he had not heard correctly, or perhaps he had misunderstood. His friend could not possibly be the infamous Grandmaster of the Carrion Crow Thieves Guild, enemy of the Vingish Crown and the Jalidin church. But Eryk's eyes betrayed his guilt as he glanced at Hillian before turning his back and walking toward the gallows platform.

Shocked and reeling, Hillian scanned his surroundings, desperate to make sense of his situation. As his shoulder was being dressed, Hillian noticed the darkness, with a single campfire the only source of light beyond the stars. The platform looked just as it had in the city square of Burúji, but the sticks and logs had been extinguished. The Giftwitch, no longer dangling on the post, sat upon the steps drinking from a flask that surely contained spellcasted medicinal fluids. Behind her, a large Búso man, with muscles rippling beneath his black skin, slung an unconscious Dalil Jaser over his shoulder. Jaser was enjoying a narcotic-induced slumber, much like the one to which he had subjected his prisoner.

"What should I do with him, Master Rook?" the large man asked, dropping the Alabian diplomat to the ground at Eryk's feet.

"Let us allow his victim to decide his fate," Eryk answered. He looked at the Giftwitch and asked, "What do you say, Miss Adia? Should we string him up? Burn *him* at the stake?" Hillian searched his friend's voice for the sarcasm, the joke, but there was no humor in the question. Eryk was truly willing, even eager, to kill the priest.

Adia was Alabian, her coloring much like that of Jaser, but the brown of her eyes was so light that it was nearly amber. Those eyes stared at her captor for only a moment before turning to her liberator. "String him up, but I want him awake before we light the fire." Eryk nodded to the large man, who deftly slung the priest back over his shoulder and climbed back up the steps.

Consumed by panic and concern for his colleague's life, Hillian blurted the first distracting thought that came to his mind. "Where is President Kesler?"

Visibly shocked, Eryk quickly scanned the clearing before breaking into a run. Lurching free from his captor, Hillian followed, trailed by several of Eryk's men. They rounded the corner of the platform just as a small, dark man dropped his trousers, preparing to take advantage of the beautiful woman lying unconscious before him.

The knife appeared in Eryk's hand as if by magic, but his momentum prevented him from throwing it; instead, he crashed violently into the smaller man. The blade found its mark, however, and when the master thief rose from the dust, the smaller man's throat gaped wide open, spilling his life's blood into a terrifying pond of filth.

"Rape is *unacceptable!*" the master thief shouted, the anger in his voice punctuated by the bloody knife in his hand.

"Oh, sure," quipped a large Búso man with hungry eyes set deep in a pitch-black face, "but if a bitch is *that* delicious—"

Reminding Hillian of a toymaker's kaleidoscope, the first man's blood splattered in a circular pattern as the knife spun through the air before driving into the skull of the sarcastic second man.

"No exceptions," Eryk clarified to his collection of dark-skinned Búso rogues as the second man's body dropped to the ground. "Any questions?"

There were no questions.

Having addressed the crisis, Eryk removed his cloak and carefully placed it over Mona's body. Slipping a vial out of a pouch that hung from his belt, he removed the stopper and placed his finger over the opening, tipped it, and then slipped his finger into her mouth.

As soon as her eyes opened, Eryk spoke to her in a soothing voice. "President Kesler, I am honored to have you as my guest."

She looked at him briefly, glanced at the cloak over her body, and then returned her eyes to him, squinting in expectation. When she spoke, Hillian's world began to spin, yet again.

"I should have known you would be involved, Master Rook," she noted casually, demonstrating a familiarity with the infamous criminal that Hillian found deeply disturbing. "Can you tell me, please, what happened here?"

"I sincerely apologize for your confusion and discomfort," Eryk replied, "but the man who attempted to dishonor you has been dealt with." He motioned to the dead would-be rapist.

She nodded approvingly, her eyes moving from one man to another, systematically assessing her situation. She reached under the cloak to adjust her dress, restoring her dignity, before gracefully rising to her feet, her eyes continuing to scan the faces gathered around her. She paused for an extended moment on Hillian before returning her focus to the master rogue standing before her.

"Thank you," she said with a short nod as she politely returned his cloak, "but may I ask how I came to require your rescue?"

"Ah, yes, well," Eryk stammered, flashing his mischievous smirk, "I do apologize for that, as well. I can only assume that you were standing upon the platform at the time it was ignited, an unfortunate and entirely unplanned complication. I did not realize you were on the platform with Lord Drake and Dalil Jaser when it was spellported."

"I see. I also see you are preparing the dalil for execution. You must understand that I cannot allow you to do the same with Lord Drake."

Thoughts swirled within Hillian's confused mind. Not only did Mona Kesler appear to have a close association with the master criminal, but she presumed to give him commands!

"Madam President," Eryk responded with an encouraging tone, "*Jaser* is my prisoner. You and Lord Drake are my guests."

"Begging your pardon, Master Rook," Adia interrupted, the Giftwitch's angry voice commanding attention, "but would not Lord Drake be an equally worthy candidate for burning?"

"No, he would not."

Adia shook her head. She was a passionate creature, Hillian noted, her every word and expression filled with unbridled hatred, unfettered enthusiasm, or a similarly powerful emotion. It was the hatred that seemed to prevail as she spoke of Hillian Drake. "But he exceeds even Dalil Jaser in his support of human burnings and plans to defend the practice to the World Council tomorrow."

Calmly regarding the passionate Giftwitch whose life he had saved, Eryk spoke in a steady, measured tone. "I am aware of his misguided philosophies, believe me, but such knowledge does not alter my decision."

"Very well," replied the frustrated sorceress. "If you are reluctant, for some reason, to kill him, I would be pleased to do so myself."

"Miss Adia," the master rogue replied quickly, the words seeming to thunder out of his mouth, despite no change in inflection or volume, "you are alive at this very moment only because of the protection I extend to you and have extended to you several times in the past." He paused, allowing her to acknowledge the truth of his statement, which she did with a reluctant nod. "Lord Drake is my guest and enjoys that same protection. I suggest you do not threaten his, lest you forfeit your own."

Grudgingly, Adia nodded again, satisfying Eryk enough that he returned his attention to the unfortunate Dalil Jaser. "Now let us wake our holy man, for we cannot have him sleeping through this perfect penance!"

*Chapter 2*

# TRUST

After leaving Dalil Jaser burning at his own stake, Hillian's objections ignored entirely, Eryk led his crew northeast, presumably toward Nyángo, the nearest city with a spellport. It took two full days for the nobleman to fully understand that, though not precisely a prisoner, he also was not precisely a guest. He was not shackled or bound, and certainly he was not threatened in any way. He was provided with food and shelter as well as a fine horse that served him well. In fact, Hillian enjoyed the journey, receiving friendly conversation and laughter from the thieves and thugs who accompanied him. But from Eryk Val Varen, the infamous Master Rook, he received not a word, not a glance, not even a reprimand. From the man to whom he had trusted his friendship, Lord Drake received only silence.

It had been nearly six years since Eryk had opened the Unicorn Palace Inn, located in the heart of Porvatis. He had declared it a "palace-class" inn, the first of its kind, and its potential had created quite the controversy in the capital city. The objective, Hillian had been quick to recognize, was to provide the luxury of royalty to the nonroyal, to offer a means by which commoners could live like kings, a concept that met with great distaste among the highborn society of Vinglandon's capital city.

Hillian had been Lord of Nydia for two years and, despite the contrary guidance of his father, the young nobleman had chosen to follow his instincts, and his mother's legacy, in championing Eryk's venture. While Porvatis was, indeed, the capital of the nation and seat of the king, it was also the seat of the Nydia duchy, and Hillian's support was sufficient to ensure the success of the Unicorn Palace Inn. Such support did not go unnoticed, of course, by the master innkeeper, and their business relationship had grown into a strong friendship.

Yet, his friend had also been his enemy. Eryk Val Varen was also Master Rook, a notorious criminal who had caused no end of trouble for both Hillian's father and his king. While it could be argued that a secret of such magnitude could not be shared even with one's closest friends, Hillian could not prevent an overwhelming feeling of betrayal.

On the morning of the third day, Hillian awoke to discover the Giftwitch standing above him, her expression a mixture of menace and confusion.

"Miss Adia," the young lord offered, reaching for his sword.

"Do not annoy me with your pathetic weapon, you miserable bigot," she spat, the fire in her eyes burning.

Abandoning his sword, Hillian quickly assessed his options. "May I stand?" he inquired, certain it was necessary but unsure what benefit it would bring. She nodded but did not adjust her position, forcing him to scuttle backward before rising.

"Master Rook strongly suggests I not kill you," she said.

"How ironic," Hillian responded, the words rushing out of him without warning. "He tells me the same."

"That *you* should not kill *me?*" Her amber eyes sparkled not with the fire of anger but with the light of amusement.

"That I should cease in my support—'vehement' support, I believe he said—of Giftwitch burnings."

"Why must you all use that word?" she asked. She glanced away, as if embarrassed at the degree to which she was affected.

"The word 'vehement' offends you?"

She sighed, clearly irritated. "Not that word."

With a sharp intake of breath, Hillian realized his mistake. "Is 'Giftwitch' a derogatory term? I am not aware of an alternative."

"I am Gifted, but I am not evil, and I am not a demon. I wield magic, but I am not a witch, just as Spell Mages and Mind Mages are not. I am a Gift Mage."

Hillian regarded her, brimming with power, yet laboring under the weight of her existence. When she returned her attention to him, mustering her confidence once more, he found he saw her for the first time. She was beautiful, the way a lightning storm was beautiful, with the same underlying danger. She had well-defined curves in the appropriate locations, but it was her eyes that most struck the young lord. Her bright, almost luminous amber eyes displayed a wildness and fearlessness that was only further highlighted by the shy nervousness that had passed through them, if only momentarily.

"Pray forgive me," he mumbled, embarrassed on several levels.

"Do you, in fact, pray, Lord Drake?"

The suddenness of her question caught him unprepared, and he stumbled over his response. "Yes, I...well, yes, of course."

"To the god your father represents?"

"Yes, I pray to Jalidus, who, in his grace and wisdom, has chosen my father as high priest."

"And does Jalidus tell you the Gifted are demons?" she asked, surprising Hillian with an utter absence of sarcasm. Her inquiry was entirely genuine.

"The church teaches—"

"But does Jalidus tell you?"

"As the chosen instrument of Jalidus, my father may have direct conversations with the Almighty, but I, myself, do not often receive a direct response to my prayers, Miss Adia," the devout Jalidin finally responded, sadly. "I am forced to follow my instincts, trusting that the spirit of God is guiding them."

"And what of me?" the sorceress continued. "What have your instincts to say about me?"

"That you are dangerous," he answered honestly, recalling his mental comparison of her to a lightning storm.

"You are right to trust that instinct," she agreed, nodding. "What else?"

"That you represent an opportunity," Hillian responded.

"What opportunity would that be?" the sorceress asked, suspiciously.

Regretting his words but finding himself mysteriously determined to forge ahead, the nobleman elaborated upon his awkward comment. "I do apologize, Miss Adia, but I ask you: What man has been blessed with the opportunity to learn about Gift Magic from an actual Giftwi…" He paused, correcting himself. "To learn about Gift Magic," he repeated, "from one who possesses the very magic he wishes to study?"

"You wish to *study* me?" She was offended, yet she obviously noticed his efforts to respect her terminology preference. The struggle reflected in her eyes, alternating between ferocity and appreciation.

Dropping his head in a sigh, Hillian made a final attempt to explain his position. "In supporting the full freedom of religion, I find myself in direct opposition to two of my closest allies, who strongly object to a religion's right to conduct witch burnings. You claim to be a mage but not a witch, and I find myself wondering if this may be the missing element that could bridge the gap."

Tentatively, suspicion clinging to her voice, Adia asked, "So in studying me, you hope to understand why human burnings should be abolished?"

"That would be one possible outcome."

Smoothly transitioning from suspicion to accusation, the sorceress inquired, "And what would be the other outcome, Lord Drake? That you would learn enough from me to convince your allies that I *am* a demon and that burning me would be a necessary step in protecting the human race?"

"That, too, is a possible outcome," Hillian admitted.

Shaking her head but gaining control of her anger, Adia declared, "Well, I shall pray to *my* god that you are guided to the appropriate conclusion by *your* god."

"Do you pray, Miss Adia?" the nobleman asked, surprised.

"Yes, I pray to Sabar, which I suspect a demon would not do."

Hillian frowned. "No, I suspect a demon would not. But if you are a follower of the Sabarism faith, why would you wield your powers in the presence of a Sabarist priest?"

Adia scoffed as she responded, bitterly, "I was not aware that a dalil was present, Lord Drake. I was focused on destroying Ixodis, and I very nearly succeeded."

"Ixodis..." the young lord responded, searching his memory. "That is another name for the Angel of Mercy, is it not?"

"He is *not* an angel!" the sorceress cried, her eyes flashing in anger. "He is a man, a Gift Mage like me, who has fabricated the Angel of Mercy myth to support his campaign of murder."

Hillian was instantly reminded of Eryk's similar words on the short journey to Mbúso. Unbidden, the question sprang to life in his mind, and he wondered how many others shared such a belief.

"My purpose in this world," Adia declared, "the only meaning to my existence, is to destroy him, thereby ending the bloodshed. That is *my* instinct, Lord Drake, *my* religious responsibility, guided by the spirit of *my* god!"

"Your God-given mission is to murder the murderer?"

Perhaps the young lord's pondering had sufficiently distracted him from common decency. Whatever the cause, he was unaware of the depth of his offense. His only warning was a nearly blinding luminescence as her hair blinked to white and her entire body was enveloped in a glow of energy. As her open hand struck his cheek, the panic caught his breath, but the pain nearly stopped his heart. He landed hard in the dirt, blood already pouring into his mouth. He started to rise, but pain rushed to the surface, and darkness engulfed his senses.

～※～

When his consciousness finally detected a window in the fog, Hillian managed to thrust his eyelids open. He was immediately overcome with vertigo and the associated nausea. Choking on his bile, the nobleman found the inspiration to force his aching body into a sitting position. As he wiped his mouth, a woman's hand offered him a glass of water.

"President Kesler?"

"Good morning, Lord Drake."

Frowning, Hillian sipped the water as he labored to sort through the thoughts and images that relentlessly clattered and crashed through his mind. Shaking his head, he asked, "How long?"

"Three days."

"Where?"

"You have been brought to the great monastery of Kila on the Cliffs of Kuúma."

"Why?"

"You needed medical attention," the beautiful politician replied softly, her eyes drifting to his left cheek. Unconsciously, Hillian's hand rose to his face, the tips of his fingers lightly stroking four long swollen wounds left by Adia's magical slap. "The monks were able to set your broken jaw, which healed quickly with their spell-induced medicines, but they were perplexed by the outer damage. Apparently, Gift Magic wounds are more difficult to heal."

"I suppose there is some logic to that," Hillian admitted, gripping his head as dizziness returned.

"They said the medication may cause some nausea and disorientation."

"Clearly," he agreed. After a moment, the room slowed enough that he could ask, "Why are you here?"

"I trust you will forgive any impropriety," she responded, "but I felt you should have a friend at your side when you awoke, to put your mind at ease." She smiled.

Remembering her apparently close association with Master Rook, Hillian was far from reassured. "*Are* we friends?" he challenged.

She laughed, shaking her head. "Hillian Drake, you fool of a man, of course we are friends," she answered, "though when we first met, I thought you an arrogant pig."

"So says my friend," he joked, largely to hide how much he was offended.

"Well, my impression of you began to change when you spoke in favor of my plans to connect the nations with spellportals. Do you remember? That was before my presidency gave me a voice on the World Council, and I truly believe the proposal would not have passed without the support of Vinglandon's popular delegate."

"You flatter me unfairly."

"Do be quiet, Lord Drake. You are ill, and I am not finished," she said, a smile softening her rebuke. "As I was saying, I grew to respect you, even more so when you approached me at my first inauguration and begged me to support you in pushing the council on women's rights. I had not even attended my first World Council meeting as a delegate."

"You were the first female head of state, and your spellportal network had become quite popular. You were a political advantage."

"Rubbish!" Mona said, laughing once more. "You never saw me as merely a political advantage. I will not believe that!" She squinted her brilliant blue eyes at him.

"Well, I certainly do not remember begging," the Vingish lord maintained.

"No, that is true. You did not beg, and you did not condescend. You treated me as your equal, despite my gender and my relative inexperience. After our first collaboration succeeded, you invited me to partner with you on prisoners' rights and ethnic tolerance, through which we grew to trust each other."

"And we became friends?" Hillian inquired. "Is that when it happened?"

"Perhaps, but I knew it for certain when you threw your trust and support behind my failed attempt to protect the rights of commoners, even though it would have served to erode the power of your nobility."

"What good is power if it is not used to serve the greater good?" the nobleman asked.

"There!" she said, pointing at him excitedly. "*That* is what makes you so unique. That is your greatness, and that is why you have accomplished so much."

Frowning, the Vingish lord shook his head. "I am not great," he said, looking away.

"Oh, but you are," she insisted, placing her hand on his arm. Her touch brought his eyes back to her, and he was startled at the look upon her face. "You are a great man, Hillian Drake, and I am confident that, one day, you will see it, as I do."

Her eyes drew him in, capturing and pulling at him like the tide of the Andyric Ocean. When she smiled, he could not avoid being affected, finally allowing a smile to join the turmoil etched upon his face. "Thank you for being here, my friend," he said, placing his hand upon hers. "I find myself confused and disoriented, and your presence has truly helped."

"She knocked you dizzy, didn't she?" the president quipped.

"She did, indeed." The nobleman laughed, before adding, "She and he both."

Mona nodded. "He is concerned about his friend."

"*You* seem to be friends with him, but I am certainly not," the nobleman replied, sadly.

"You cannot truly mean that," she said.

"He is not who he claimed to be, so how can I trust him?" Hillian responded. He gingerly attempted to stand, accepting Mona's hand for support. "And if friendship is based upon trust, as you suggest, then he and I cannot be friends."

"Is it feasible that he is *both* the man he claimed to be *and* something more?"

"Possibly," the young lord acknowledged, "but I am not at all certain that such a distinction is sufficient to restore my trust."

"He leads a double life, as two men. The man you've known, Master Val Varen, has proven to be your friend," Mona replied, smiling encouragingly as Hillian gained his balance and carefully exited the small room. "Perhaps I merely need to introduce you to the man I've known, Master Rook, who has proven to be *my* friend."

## Chapter 3

# RESPONSIBILITY

After a short walk, during which Hillian was often forced to pause as he battled the recurring nausea, Mona opened a heavy oaken door that creaked loudly to announce their arrival. As the Vingish nobleman tentatively stepped through the doorway, he had only a moment to notice the presence of Eryk and Adia before he was greeted by a dark-skinned Búso man dressed in the robes of a Mahalist priest, whose curly white hair and beard suggested advanced age but whose enthusiasm communicated an impressively youthful energy.

"Ah, yes, Lord Drake, welcome, welcome," he squeaked, grasping Hillian's head and twisting it to better examine the bruised cheek. "Astounding, but you will be fine." Then, pushing past Hillian, the old man embraced the Severlandi president, exclaiming,

"And Mona, my dear, you look radiant as ever!" After exchanging cheek kisses with Mona, the priest giggled. "And now we may finally begin!" he said as he sprang across the room, dragging Adia with him. "Right here, child," he said to her.

Placing her hands on the edge of a large hole cut in the wall, the sorceress sang her Spell Magic:

Oh, window in the wall, now be
transparent such that we may see
and hear all that transpires there,
but of us, keep them unaware.

The hole clouded, filling with a dark smoke that dissipated quickly, leaving the window as transparent as before. Adia and the old priest smiled at each other as they turned to a dark figure standing in the corner.

"I am but an amateur Spell Mage, Master Rook," Adia admitted, "but it should be sufficient."

"Oh, you did well, my dear," the old Búso priest declared with a small giggle as he danced out of the room.

Following the old priest with his eyes, Eryk's gaze came to rest upon Hillian. "Lord Drake," he said, "I am pleased to see you alive and well."

His friend, if such a word did still apply, had finally spoken to him, after several days with no acknowledgment of any kind, and yet there was no hint of apology or remorse. It was commendable while simultaneously irritating, Hillian thought, but was distracted by his own question. "What just happened?"

"I made the window appear to be a solid wall from the other side," Adia answered. "We can observe without being observed," she added, approaching the nobleman.

Recalling their altercation, Hillian instinctively retreated, nearly falling as he stumbled backward away from her.

"Lord Drake," she said, stopping her advance and holding up her hands in what must have been a gesture of peace, "I must apologize for striking you." Her voice was clear and seemed sincere; her eyes, however, betrayed her internal conflict, and the young nobleman felt sympathy.

Still somewhat dizzy, both from the medication and the confusing events that had transpired, Hillian stared without responding. In fact, it wasn't until Adia's head fell, in defeat, that he spoke. "Perhaps it is I who should be apologizing, Miss Adia," he said.

His apology was unexpected, apparently, for the sorceress cocked her head, looking at him for a moment before adding, "Perhaps, but..."

Inspired by a feeling or force he could not explain, Hillian smiled and offered more forgiveness. "Let us consider it a fitting punishment for a man who insults a Gift Mage."

"You said Gift Mage, not Giftwitch," Adia noted, smiling.

Hillian returned the smile. "Well, you have made clear to me that I cannot study you if I do not respect you," the nobleman replied, earning a smirk of approval from the sorceress.

Nodding to her before turning his attention to the magical window, Hillian watched as the old priest hopped into the sitting room, accompanied by a Golden Knight of Mbúso, whose gilded armor gleamed in the firelight. As the priest eased into a chair by the fire, the knight began to speak.

"I am—"

"No," interrupted the priest. "You sit," he commanded. "I will talk." His voice was calm, even quiet, but it carried a strength that demanded respect, and the knight obeyed without hesitation, sitting in a chair on the opposite side of the hearth and placing a turban-wrapped helmet on the table between them.

"My name is Galen Ziraili," the priest began. "For most of my seventy-two years, I have served Kila as a simple priest." As the knight shifted nervously, the priest smiled. "Yes, I am a banyan, a priest of the Kila Maháli church, the religion your government…and mine…has outlawed. And it is because of that law that our high priest, the malini, was forced to build this fortress of a monastery to defend our right to practice our faith."

"May I meet the malini?" asked the knight.

"You have already met him," the priest replied. "You see, the malini died shortly after completing the monastery, leaving behind a host of banyans with equal rank who, for some reason, looked to me as a leader."

The priest paused, leaned forward slightly, and said, "I am certain it had less to do with my age or experience and much more to do with my engaging personality." As a smile crept onto the malini's face, Hillian was certain, despite the distance and the dim firelight, that it was quickly mirrored on that of the knight sitting across from him.

Straightening in his seat, the old man went on. "So, no longer was I Banyan Ziraili, but Malini Ziraili, which gave me the responsibility of dealing with the issues, interruptions, irritations...such as a company of knights, armed for battle, arriving without notice at our doorstep."

The sudden change in direction, from playful to accusatory, seemed to startle the knight. Galen, clearly having established his control of the room, smiled and relaxed in his chair. "What brings you to Kuúma, Knight Captain?"

The knight recovered quickly and responded, "We are pursuing criminals who—"

"*Convicted* criminals?" the priest interrupted.

"One of them, yes, convicted," the knight captain said. Then, after a moment's hesitation, the knight added, "Well, convicted in Ard Alabia, but not in Mbúso."

"So the premier of our great nation has sent one hundred of his cherished Golden Knights to pursue a fugitive who has not even broken a single Búso law?"

"That is true, although not entirely," the knight responded, growing flustered. "It is true that she, the escaped prisoner, has not, or had not, to my knowledge, broken a law in Mbúso, except perhaps for involvement in the abduction of three dignitaries."

"So you are pursuing the fugitive for the purpose of rescuing her hostages?"

"Exactly."

"Except that the hostages may not be hostages, isn't that right?"

"How could you know that?" the knight asked in surprise. "Do you admit they are here?"

"Of course they are here," Galen replied, calmly. "But you failed to answer my question."

"Well, yes, we do not know for certain that the dignitaries are prisoners. It may be that they are willing participants in the plot."

"The plot to rescue an innocent woman from execution?" Galen inquired.

"Not innocent—"

"But you said the prisoner did not break any laws in Mbúso."

"Yes, that is true, *before* the escape. But the escape itself involved two crimes: an unauthorized spellport and—"

"So someone used Spell Magic to rescue an innocent woman from a mob of foreigners who were trying to murder her."

The knight paused, and Hillian smiled at the creative perspective. "Yes," the knight captain said, "perhaps the courts could be convinced to see it that way, except that this 'murder' was authorized by the government of Mbúso."

"So I should welcome you into my home, and betray my guests to you, because you represent a murderous government?" As the knight hesitated, the malini smiled. "A government," he continued, "that is not very popular in this outlawed monastery to begin with."

Head shaking, the knight forged ahead. "Even ignoring the charge of unauthorized spellport, there is undeniable evidence that the fugitive conspired with a known criminal in the attempted murder of an Alabian diplomat."

"Ah, yes," Galen replied, knowingly. "You are referring to Rami Jaser, the Sabarist priest so excited to burn a Giftwitch, yet burned at his own stake."

The knight captain hesitated before adding, "Yes, Dalil Jaser, but we rescued him before he burned to death."

In the viewing room, Eryk shook his head and muttered, "He will return. When you fail to kill an enemy, he always returns."

"But you agreed with her, did you not?" the Mahalist high priest prodded. "Illegal it may be, but you believe she was justified. In fact, you feel there is a poetic justice in the perfect symmetry of it, and you have come to respect this fugitive of yours."

The knight was silent. In the flickering light of the fire, it was difficult to see any facial expressions, but Hillian suspected the priest had struck upon the truth.

"And her savior," Malini Ziraili continued, "this mastermind behind her escape, he very nearly outsmarted you, and his cleverness has won your respect as well." The priest smiled at the knight's openmouthed stare, before concluding, "In fact, a part of you is disappointed you have found them, disappointed you will be forced to bring them before your government to face a 'justice' to which you, yourself, do not completely subscribe."

For a few moments, the two sat in silence. Finally, the knight captain replied, suspicion dripping from the words, "I have spoken to no one of these thoughts, not even my lieutenants. How could you know this?"

Galen smiled and nodded. "Perhaps it is because I know who you are—Ida Wadógo, the first female ever admitted to the knighthood and a tireless advocate for the equal treatment of women—and I have made logical conclusions about your feelings toward the repressed minority. Or perhaps it is because I have been reading your mind."

Then, though nothing was spoken aloud, the knight jumped to her feet.

"Or both!" she exclaimed. "You...you said 'or both' in my head. You are a Mind Mage!"

"Ah, but being a Mind Mage is no longer illegal," the malini noted, "unlike being a Mahalist priest."

The old priest's playful arrogance caused Hillian to wonder what would inspire such confidence. "Why is he unafraid of being arrested for practicing religion?" he whispered. Then, realizing he was whispering, he asked, "Can they hear us?"

"The spell does not prevent it, but they are quite far from us," Adia replied, not whispering but speaking in a low voice.

"As for being arrested," Eryk added, "the captain is unarmed, and her knights wait outside the monastery's impregnable walls and countless traps. You see?" He pointed at Sir Wadógo, who had apparently drawn a similar conclusion and returned to her seat. "She knows he is untouchable."

"Legal or not, I find it extremely irritating," the knight captain confessed, after a short silence, "to have my thoughts, which have always been safely private, suddenly become exposed to the public."

"Not to the public," the malini noted. "Only to me."

"Yes, well, I'm afraid that distinction does not make the adjustment any easier."

"No, no, my child, that is not what is bothering you. You are not the sort of person who has difficulty adjusting to change, having devoted your life, in fact, to the pursuit of it. However, all the changes you have pursued, until now, have been within the limits of the reality you have been taught."

Finding his change of direction intriguing, Hillian stepped closer to the magic window. Knight Captain

Wadógo, too, demonstrated her interest, turning her body to look more closely at the man sitting across from her.

"Not long ago, if I lived on the north side of a lake and you lived on the south side of the very same lake, I would have had only three methods by which I could speak with you: I could travel around the west side of the lake, around the east side of the lake, or through the water of the lake. Everyone in the world understood and accepted these rules.

"But then came Mona Kesler's spellportals, and suddenly there was a fourth way to get from the north side of the lake to the south side...a fourth where there had forever been only three. The rules of the world had been challenged, evaluated, and found to be inadequate. We had been taught these rules by our mothers, our elders, our teachers, and our priests, yet we were forced to accept that they had all been wrong, though only as wrong as their own mothers, elders, teachers, and priests."

Galen shook his head. "But Spell Magic had its own set of rules that could be observed and understood. After hundreds of deaths and disappearances, it became clear that port spells were dangerous without Kesler's brilliantly coordinated network of spellportal platforms. This, and other rules, slowly became part of the teachings. Today, if you ask a young boy how to get from the north side of the lake to the south side, a spellportal is naturally one of the responses you will receive, because he has been reluctantly taught this option by his mother, his elders, his teachers, and his priests.

"But as a Mind Mage, I can speak with you without either of us crossing the lake. Now that it is no longer a crime to practice, Mind Magic is an option that is slowly finding its way into the general teachings. Ah, but if I possessed Gift Magic, I could call forth a winter storm to freeze the lake and walk across it, or I could create a burst of wind powerful enough to carry me *over* it. These are options that fall well outside the rules of reality accepted by the average person."

Finally, he turned and looked at her. In a kind, quiet voice, he said, "When Mona Kesler embraced Spell Magic and introduced the world to spellportation, she was afraid. She was afraid that she would be burned at the stake as a witch. She was afraid that her new industry would bring about some disaster that could not be foreseen."

In the viewing room, both Hillian and Adia glanced at Mona, who shrugged and looked away, shyly.

"But she succeeded," Galen continued. "She saw the Spell Magic option, and she found a way to make the world accept it and add it to the rules. Mona Kesler did more than bring about change *in* the world. She *changed* the world."

"Flatterer," Mona said, smiling.

The high priest of Kila stared at the knight. "You are irritated because you are among the rare visionaries, like my dear friend, Mona, who see the Gift Magic option and know, instinctively, that the world should accept it just as the world has accepted Spell Magic and Mind Magic... that the Gift Mages should no longer be witches, just as the Spell Mages and Mind Mages are no longer witches. But until then, you are compelled to enforce legalized prejudices that do not ring true to you. That, my dear knight, is what irritates you."

As Sir Wadógo dropped her head to ponder the old priest's words, Hillian pondered as well. He had admitted to Adia the possibility that he might be wrong about Gift Magic, which meant he did, as the malini had described, see the Gift Magic option. But could it be true that he already knew the answer and was similarly irritated that his circumstances forced him to follow rules he knew to be invalid?

Before he could formulate an answer, activity resumed in the sitting room. "If I am such a visionary," the knight captain challenged, "then why have I accomplished so little?"

"You have accomplished a great deal more than you think, my child, and you have done so without any support. In Mbúso, and particularly in the Golden Knighthood, you have been striving for change in an environment that is naturally resistant to change. Conversely, Mona was pursuing change in a nation that thrives upon it, and she was supported on the international stage by Hillian Drake and the powerful influence of Vinglandon."

"You see?" Mona teased, nudging her Vingish friend.

"Are you suggesting," Sir Wadógo began, "that I, a Knight of Mbúso, should ally myself with a lord of Vinglandon, my nation's most bitter enemy?"

"If you did so, you would find yourself also allied with Mona and two other powerful forces for change. Imagine the influence that such a united group could wield."

As Wadógo frowned in consideration of the malini's words, the four companions in the viewing room regarded one another, pondering along with the knight. Hillian was the first to voice his thoughts.

"This is ridiculous," he complained in a hushed tone. "We are *not* united."

"We are aligned in everything but religion," Mona responded.

"And what if your religion is being manipulated?" Eryk asked, carefully. "Would you want to know?"

"What are you saying?" Hillian asked, eyeing the master thief with suspicion.

"As a devout Sabarist," the sorceress interjected, "I would feel a responsibility to seek the truth. Do you feel this way as a Jalidin?"

The realization struck simultaneously with the heavy weight of responsibility, and the young nobleman understood that his suspicions were sufficient to change his course. "Yes," he admitted, trusting his instincts and the god who guided them, "I would feel a similar responsibility."

Clenching his eyelids to avoid the three satisfied smiles, Hillian began to consider the ramifications, but the knight captain's response pulled him from his thoughts.

"No, I cannot possibly ally with a lord of Vinglandon or the President of Severlandon without betraying the knighthood," Wadógo declared, after much deliberation.

"Even if your heart is already aligned with them?" the malini prompted.

Shaking her head, Sir Wadógo said, "My primary responsibility is to Mbúso."

"Captain, do you know why Mahalist priests are called banyans?"

Shaking her head, perhaps suspicious at the apparent change in subject, the Golden Knight admitted, "I do not."

Galen smiled and nodded, as if he'd already known the answer. "The banyan tree is known for its unique system of seeds and roots. A banyan seed, even when dropped in the most unlikely location, can grow to form a tree with roots that spread far and wide, emerging from the ground to form new trees, such that an entire forest can form from a single seed." He paused before concluding, "Kila calls his priests to this mission: to spread the seeds of his wisdom, that they may form roots and trees and grow to become a forest of knowledge and understanding."

"I am an atheist, Malini Ziraili. I do not believe you will find me a hospitable environment for your tree of Mahalist wisdom."

"The seed has been planted, my child. It is only a matter of time before it begins to take root."

"Well, you have wasted enough of my time already," Sir Wadógo said, standing. "Where are the fugitives?"

"Perhaps you would like to consider it overnight," Galen suggested.

"There will be no more consideration. Present me with the fugitives, and I will overlook your involvement in illegal religious activities."

Sighing, Galen nodded. "Very well, Captain," he said, glancing briefly at the wall that contained the magic window. "I shall fetch them for you." The old man's energy seemed to have faded, for he labored to rise from his chair.

"Time to go," Eryk announced, and Hillian realized the old priest's sudden sluggishness was deliberate.

*Chapter 4*

# TRUTH

"How do you feel?" the Severlandi president asked, joining Hillian in the stern of the ship.

But Hillian simply continued staring at the receding monastery. It was, as the malini had indicated to the knight captain, an impressive architectural wonder. When viewed across the Bay of Kuúma, the facility seemed immense, comprised of a complex series of small, square buildings wedged into the hills, much like those in Burúji. Unlike the capital city, however, the Mahalist stronghold was surrounded by a massive wall, rising and dipping with the varying elevation that characterized the countryside of Mbúso, and the colorful rose gardens hid not only traps but also underground chambers and secret tunnels that served to amplify both the size and security of the malini's fortress.

"Hillian?" Mona prodded, gaining the young lord's attention with the use of his given name.

"I am overwhelmed," he offered, finally closing his eyes against the salty sting of the Andyric Ocean, which had been angrily pelting his face as if offended at his refusal to find shelter.

"You are not alone," she said.

"Oh, but I am."

"Not true. You are not alone, because I am with you, and I believe Master Rook is with you."

"You both wish to prove Gift Magic is not evil, but I am alone in wishing to prove the opposite."

"You could frame it that way," Mona agreed, "or you could consider it a search for the truth. In that, we are united."

Hillian glanced at her. "As we were being led through the catacomb of corridors and the twisting, spiraling staircases of the monastery, I began to wonder about evidence. And as we rowed that little boat across the gulf to meet this ship, I began to think we might never find any."

"Perhaps not," she countered, "but—"

Cutting through her words, the ship's lookout bellowed, "Pirates!" from the crow's nest, causing a general panic. Very quickly, however, Eryk Val Varen assumed control, convincing the ship's captain to drop anchor and wait for the pursuers without resistance. As the other ship approached, Hillian saw minotaurs for the first time, and he was reminded of the malini's words regarding the rules of reality. Hillian had heard stories of minotaurs but had always believed them to be fictional characters from fantasy stories or fairy tales, like dragons and centaurs, not truths to be integrated with the generally accepted rules of humans, horses, dogs, and sparrows.

With a deafening crack, the lead minotaur landed on the deck of the ship, his black hooves thundering against the wooden planks. Above the hooves, the legs of a bull, covered in rich, black fur, smoothly transitioned to the muscled chest and arms of a man, though the minotaur was easily twice as large and rippling with frightening strength as he steadied himself with a colossal flamberge, a giant sword that twisted and curved in a strange, exotic shape. As the minotaur rose from his landing, stretching his enormous frame to its full height and towering three heads above the tallest human sailor on board, he was followed by six more, three on either side of him but none quite so impressive.

Clearing his throat brought attention to his giant bull's head, black as night with imposing horns nearly twice as long as those of his companions. "I am Lorcan," he growled, his deep voice rumbling like thunder, "and I claim this ship. Let its former captain bring himself forward, that I may end his life with speed and mercy."

"Greetings, Lorcan," Eryk responded, stepping forward.

The minotaur captain was obviously surprised. For a moment, he was unable to find his voice, but finally he responded, "Master Rook, this is your ship?"

"It is today," the master thief replied.

"But it does not fly the Carrion Crow. We could not have known…"

"Do not be concerned, old friend. You could not have—"

Eryk was interrupted by an exuberant cry as another pirate landed on the ship. All faces followed the new arrival as he immediately launched again into the air to perform a forward flip before landing directly in front of Eryk and knocking him to the deck in a violently joyous embrace.

"The Rook, the Rook, the Rook!" the newcomer exclaimed, leaping off the bemused rogue and backflipping to land beside the pirate captain. "By the gods of Otica, Lorcan, it's the damn Rook! I might have bathed!"

As the crazed pirate doubled over, overcome by his own strange laughter, Eryk slowly recovered his feet. "Well met, Gillis," the master rogue said with a smile. "It has been too long, my friend."

Gaining control of his mirth, Gillis clasped Eryk's outstretched arm. "Far too long, Master Rook," he said, followed by more laughter that, to Hillian, sounded oddly similar to the bleating of a goat. As realization struck, the nobleman's eyes widened as he studied what could only be a satyr.

Like the minotaurs, Gillis possessed the arms and torso of a man, but his head, too, was human—complete with a dirty, pointed beard growing from his chin—except for the two short horns that poked through his tangled hair. Also like the minotaurs, Gillis possessed the legs of a beast, but his brown fur stopped short, just below the knees. Hillian marveled at the craftsmanship of the satyr's artificial legs, fashioned from wood laced with a white metal substance, perhaps silver or platinum. They arched backward, in the shape of an archer's bow, bending as the satyr bounced from one leg to the other as he and his pirate brethren spoke to their old friend.

After only moments, Gillis, Lorcan, and the other pirates were gone, their ship receding into the horizon. As the ship's captain tried valiantly to cut through his crew's amazement and confusion and get them back to work, Hillian approached the savior thief. "Master Val Varen, if I may ask, how is it that you are old friends with minotaurs and satyrs?"

Eryk nodded. "In my line of work," he began, "a man finds himself occasionally on the wrong side of the prison bars. One of these occasions involved the dungeon of Chayl, where my crew and I shared the space with fifty or more minotaurs who had been imprisoned, even forced to fight and die in Grolandon's gladiator arenas, simply for being different. So, when my rescue finally arrived, I decided to take the minotaurs with us. And when they informed me that another fifty were imprisoned in Domus Viho, we rescued them as well, including Lorcan and Gillis."

"The pirate captain and the satyr?" Hillian asked.

"Yes, though Lorcan was not a pirate at the time, nor was Gillis," Eryk replied. "Like those we met in Chayl, the minotaurs in the capital city were slaves, bought by the

High King of Grolandon to build the palace at Domus Viho, and after their work was completed, used for His Majesty's entertainment. Lorcan did not become a pirate until I relocated him and the others to the Island of Kiriti."

"What of Gillis?" Mona asked.

"The satyr's story is much more involved," Eryk said.

"Why Kiriti?" Hillian inquired.

"They were in desperate need of a haven, safe from the persecution of human governments, and Kiriti was unclaimed by any of the mainland nations, so it was the obvious choice. Unfortunately, Kiriti has very little in the way of natural resources, so I am afraid it has become a den of piracy."

"The minotaurs bowed to you as they were leaving, like you were their liege lord," the Vingish nobleman observed.

"I rescued them and gave them new purpose, so they treat me with a certain measure of respect. For me, though, they represented the beginning of a new and exciting line of business for my guild."

"Piracy!" Hillian exclaimed. "You are profiting from their piracy!"

"He saves them, Hillian," Mona said, calmly. "He saves minotaurs, fairies, mermaids—"

"And a satyr," Hillian added, faintly.

"Yes, and the Gifted," Eryk continued. "One, in particular, seems to continually require my services." He smirked at Adia, who smiled in return.

"I believe I have done more than enough to pay my debt," the Gift Mage replied, amusement on her face. "How many times has my Gift Magic been useful in your new line of business, Master Rook?"

"Your debt was paid long ago, my friend, until it was recently renewed in Burúji."

They were partners, Hillian realized: Eryk, Adia, Mona, and perhaps even Malini Ziraili. Like a masterful puzzle, the pieces clicked into place, forming a picture Hillian could not have foreseen. His face brightened, the sparkle in his eyes returning.

"Do you see now?" Mona asked, reading the expression on her friend's face. "Lord Drake, allow me to introduce you to my friend, Master Rook."

Eryk's head tilted ever so slightly, one eyebrow arching as he regarded the Severlandi president. By way of explanation, Mona elaborated, "Lord Drake trusted you as Eryk Val Varen, but he has had very little reason to trust you as Master Rook. Now, perhaps if you introduce him to your whole self, he will come to trust both the innkeeper and the rogue, as I do."

Eryk nodded and reached out his hand to his Vingish countryman. "Lord Drake, I am Master Rook. It is a pleasure to make your acquaintance."

"Master Rook," the nobleman responded, the name tasting strange in his mouth. "Honestly, I cannot say it is a pleasure to meet you, but I look forward to learning more about you and your guild." Accepting the handshake but releasing it quickly, he launched directly into the interrogation. "So you are an activist, not a pirate?"

"Well," Eryk replied, "perhaps both." When his lord frowned in suspicion, the master thief clarified, "The piracy trade offers a perimeter defense of the island, involves a fleet of ships for smuggling the persecuted to safer harbors, and generates enough revenue to fund the rescue activity, which, itself, is not a financially profitable line of business."

"Crime as a means to an end is still crime," Hillian replied.

"Legalized prejudice is a crime!" Adia exclaimed. "Church-sponsored murder is a crime!"

"Yes, it is complicated," Mona interjected, with a firmness in her tone that brought an immediate end to the argument. "There is no easy answer," she continued, "which is why we are going to work together to create one."

"For a moment, I thought perhaps Sir Wadógo would be joining us," Adia said.

"Not today, but perhaps she will join us yet," Eryk suggested. "Galen has planted the seed, and I trust it will grow over time."

"Where are we going?" Hillian wondered aloud.

Before anyone could answer, they were startled by a silent arrow that struck the deck only a few paces away. The shaft of the arrow burst open in a cloud of dark smoke. Hillian saw that many more arrows were raining down upon the ship, covering the deck with a heavy, dark cloud. Wondering why the lookout had not alerted the crew, the nobleman glanced to the crow's nest. The final image in the young lord's mind before he succumbed to the insidious fumes was a dead sailor, pinned to the mast with a single arrow.

*Chapter 5*

# POWER

The Lord of Nydia awoke to urgent shaking. Confusion clouded his mind, battling against his feeble attempts to make sense of the chaos swirling about him. Roughly, he was hauled to his feet despite his instinctive reluctance, and the sudden motion inspired his body to violently retch in rebellion. His eyes shifting in and out of focus, Hillian struggled to identify his savior, acknowledging his expectation when Eryk's gloved hand forced the opening of a vial between his lips. The nobleman laughed aloud as it occurred to him that a master thief, though objectionable under normal circumstances, certainly became a welcome companion when a person found himself in need of a drug antidote.

As his vision began to clear and the spinning of his surroundings slowed, Hillian received a sharp slap to the face, dulled only slightly by the black leather gloves.

"What was that for?" asked the nobleman, the shock and irritation in his voice entirely lost upon the rogue, who had already hurried to help the next victim of the narcotic gas.

Hillian glanced about, still lacking in balance and clarity, and slowly digested the situation. As Eryk scurried from one fallen sailor to another, Adia Varani waved her arms in sharp, dramatic motions, directing a symphony of Gift Magic. Her right hand emitted a constant blast of air, which she directed at the deck of the ship, sweeping away the dark narcotic smoke. Her left hand was held aloft, directing the construction of a massive energy shield, wrapping the ship in a tight cocoon. Quickly, however, the sorceress began to cough and choke on the remaining gas, having trapped it inside the energy field. Adjusting her strategy without pause, the young sorceress grasped the air with both hands, twisting and pulling, folding and spreading, until the energy shield became a flat ceiling, halting the barrage of arrows while allowing room for the dark smoke to dissipate. Maintaining the shield with her left hand, she repurposed her right hand, curling it in a fist of instant fire. She hurled fireballs at the unseen assailant for several minutes until she was interrupted by Eryk, who joined her in the center of the deck.

"I cannot reach them if I cannot see them," she declared in frustration, abandoning the fireballs.

"How are they reaching us?" he countered quietly.

"I do not know," she replied, desperation growing in her voice. "Spellcasted arrows?"

Mona, who had quietly joined Hillian amid the chaos, shouted to the ship's captain, "Have you any archers?"

"It matters not," the sorceress cried, exasperated. "I do not know the spells!"

"Could you reach them with Mind Magic?" Eryk asked.

The young woman stared at him, fear leaping to her face, but she nodded.

"She is a Mind Mage as well?" Hillian asked, bewildered.

"All Gift Mages are born with natural ability in Mind Magic and Spell Magic," Mona responded automatically, her eyes fixed upon the young sorceress.

After mere moments, her eyes shut tightly in concentration, Adia screamed and collapsed to the deck, clutching her head in agony.

Kneeling to assist her, Eryk said, "So you found them!"

"It was a trap," she whispered. "They had a skilled Mind Mage waiting for me."

"But they have underestimated you," the master criminal replied, "which gives you the advantage."

The sorceress nodded, rising unsteadily and replacing the energy ceiling, which had disappeared upon her collapse. "Jaser is aboard that vessel, and he directs the Mind Mage...and the Spell Mage, I presume."

"I told you he would return."

"Perhaps not this time," she replied, a wicked grin appearing on her face, reflecting her determination and zeal.

Instead of fireballs or force blasts, Adia hurled lightning, a frightening sight Hillian had not yet witnessed. The blindingly bright streaks leaped from her hands, ripping through the salty air, eager to find their targets but proving as ineffective as their fiery predecessors. Undeterred, the sorceress escalated her efforts, adding fireballs and, eventually, force blasts, until she was hurling all three magical weapons at once, with a lack of results as dramatically intense as the frustration that followed.

Cursing Dalil Jaser and his mercenary mages, Adia adjusted her strategy once more. "Even an invisible ship can be capsized," she cried, calling forth a storm that very quickly matched the ferocity of her rage.

Focused as she was on her efforts, Adia failed to notice that the ship's crew was preparing for another attack on the opposite side. While the ship had been floating aimlessly, without a crew to guide it, a pursuit vessel from Mbúso had caught them from behind, and the captain's shouted orders finally caught Adia's attention.

Without hesitating, the young Gift Mage called forth another storm. With one hand outstretched to the north, toward Jaser's ship, and another outstretched to the south, toward the Búso ship, the depth of Adia's power was apparent as she managed to control two massive thunderstorms at once. The energy crackled through her body, sending short bursts of lightning out of her hands, starting small fires on the deck of the ship, extinguished quickly by the pelting water that fell upon the ship in the energy shield's absence. Eryk implored her to stop, but she could not hear him. He screamed into her ear, told her she would destroy the ship, but with merely a nod in his direction, she blasted him with a fierce gust of wind that sent him sliding across the slippery deck.

With her external conscience neutralized, Adia reached for more power. Her head tilted back, her smile growing wider, the sorceress continued to push her Gift Magic further. Her hair, already as white as milk, grew brighter and more luminescent, until the ship was bathed in what appeared to be the light of a full moon.

In a frightening display, the power of the storms, aligned as they were upon opposite sides of her, began to force the sorceress into the air. Afraid she was losing control, Hillian instinctively dove at Adia's rising body, tackling her to the deck.

When they landed, the explosion was tremendous, destroying the ship and sending the sorceress and the nobleman streaking through the air into the dark nothingness of the Andyric Ocean.

## Chapter 6

# INSPIRATION

From a dark corner table near the door, Hillian Drake nervously observed a tall man enter the Wild Boar Tavern in the center of the city of Chayl. The man looked as wild as the tavern's namesake, tangled red hair covering his head and face. As he strode confidently to the bar, nearly all the patrons acknowledged him with nods or short greetings. He seemed to be well known, even famous, particularly with the females, nearly all of whom wore their ginger locks in plaited braids, exposing their freckled faces in the tradition of Grolandon's common folk.

Three of the women quickly congregated around the man's barstool, and after finishing the last drop of his second ale, he took a long look at each of them before glancing back at the barkeep, whose own red hair was nearly gone from the top of his scalp, though it was as long in the back as his beard.

"Well, who's it goin' to be tonight, eh, boss?" the older man asked jovially, glancing up only briefly before continuing with his work. Hillian smiled as the barkeep confirmed that the man to whom he spoke was master of the tavern.

"Aye, well, this first one here, as you can plainly see, has the most impressive assets..." the tavern master replied. The woman shifted her body to draw attention to the assets of which he spoke. The tavern master continued, "But a fairly uninterestin' style, I'm afraid.

"The second one," he continued, "now she's a bit more creative, but she likes me to be submissive, which don't sound quite right to me tonight." The second woman began to tie the end of a scarf around the man's wrist before he slapped her hands away.

"This third one here, now she ain't known to me, which is tantalizin', I don't have to tell you." He smiled as he locked eyes with the strange woman, one of the few in the establishment whose dark hair and brown skin marked her as a foreigner, before continuing his assessment without glancing away. "There again, the unknown always comes with a risk o' disappointment," he noted, to which the dark woman slowly shook her head, apparently offering her assurance against the stated risk.

"Such a shame, my friend," the barkeep said sarcastically. "Quite a tough decision you be havin' to make."

"Aye, but I think I'll be takin' this here new girl," replied the man, to which she smiled with a sly satisfaction that caused Hillian to wonder how many other men she had seduced in a similar manner. Slowly, the third woman approached the tavern master and placed her hands on his chest, sliding them up to circle around the back of his neck as she reached her lips to his ear.

"Oh, ho!" he cried, amused by her whisper, "this'll be a first! She's married!"

"Forgive me, Master Branch," the barkeep replied in playful sarcasm, "but I can't believe that'd be a first for one such as you!"

"True, true," Branch, the tavern master, said, "but she's tellin' me the husband, well now, he wants to watch!" The barkeep laughed, as did many of the patrons, while the woman led Master Branch by the hand to the corner table.

Hillian steeled himself. His talents in performance and persuasion were well known in the international political community, but the young lord's self-awareness forced him to acknowledge that his effectiveness depended largely on the degree to which he believed in his message. Thus, he was not at all confident in his talents at deception.

When the red-haired tavern master sat, the brown-skinned woman slid onto his lap, distracting the man from focusing on Hillian. Relieved, the Vingish nobleman welcomed his guest to his table.

"Master Branch, I am Lord Frost."

"You can be the Lord o' Winter or the King o' Chayl, himself. It makes no difference to me," Branch replied, his lecherous eyes never leaving the woman. "I been told you like to watch."

"I do," Hillian replied, "and, thankfully, my Lady Frost enjoys herself more thoroughly when she knows I am watching."

"Well, then, let's be gettin' on with the enjoyin'!" the tavern master eagerly suggested, standing so suddenly that the young lady was spilled from his lap and might have fallen to the dirty tavern floor had Branch not grasped her around her waist. He led her down a short hallway behind the bar, with Hillian trailing behind. As they entered a dark back room, the young woman turned and shoved the tavern master backward upon the bed.

"Foster Branch," Hillian announced, closing the door behind him, "Master Rook requires your services."

Several moments passed before Branch found the strength to reply. "Is that so?" he asked, his voice angry but edged with fear, his narrowed eyes glancing back and forth between his two visitors. "Well, Rook can burn in the fires o' Lakis, and the two o' you can burn with him!"

"I'm afraid you have it quite wrong," Hillian replied coolly. "It is your tavern that will burn, as my Lady Frost will demonstrate."

Before the tavern master could retort, Adia revealed her true nature, activating her Gift Magic. Her amber eyes suddenly dark and her hair suddenly a bright white, the sorceress formed a small fireball in her hand and casually tossed it upon the bed. As the pallet ignited, Branch scrambled to the floor. The sorceress and the nobleman waited patiently as the tavern master grasped the flimsy mattress and yanked it from the wooden bed frame. Unconcerned with protecting the flesh on his hands, Branch hurried to protect his tavern, reaching into the flames, flipping and folding the blankets until the fire was extinguished.

Breathing heavily, both from exhaustion and frustration, the tavern master stood and studied the intruders. His face darkened with soot, his arms speckled with fresh burns and old scars, and his eyes burning from smoke and rage, Branch looked at each of them in turn before choosing the nobleman as his focal point.

"Message received," the wild Grolandi man said. Then, demonstrating the knowledge Hillian would have expected from the master of a thieves' guild, he added, "So, this would be the Giftwitch I been hearin' about."

"You would be wise to avoid that word," the young lord advised.

"What should I call her, then?"

"You may call me 'Miss Adia,'" the sorceress interjected.

Appraising her carefully, the master thief nodded. "Miss Adia, then," he muttered before glancing back at Hillian. "And that would make you Lord Drake, not Lord Frost, I'd wager." At the nobleman's nod, Branch snorted. "Both o' you be dead, drowned in the ocean, from what I hear tell."

"We were rescued by a mutual acquaintance," Hillian replied. "A pirate captain who suggested you might be able to help us."

Branch grunted. "So, it were Lorcan the minotaur what sent you to me," he said. "And I suppose he be tellin' you I can break the Rook out o' the Dungeon o' Chayl, is that it?"

"We understand you've rescued him from the very same dungeon once before," Adia said.

"Aye, but what makes the two o' you think I be willin' to risk it again?"

"As Carrion Crow Guildmaster of Chayl, it is your responsibility," Hillian replied. "This is not a request. You will assist us in rescuing Master Rook and President Kesler."

"Aha, the famous beauty o' Mona Kesler," the rogue replied, excitement replacing the irritation in his eyes. He smiled as he added, "I might be gettin' me a kiss out o' this after all!"

Hillian remained silent, choosing to ignore the thief's offensive comment.

Branch pondered for a moment before accepting the mission. "Aye, I believe I could be o' some assistance to you in this here matter, Lord Drake."

"Very good," Hillian said, relieved, though he still did not trust the man.

"So, what be the plan, m'lord?"

"I presume your plan would be more effective than mine," the nobleman suggested, surprised at having been asked.

"True, true." The tavern master chewed his thoughts, grinding them through his mind and his teeth, before saying, "I'll be needin' some time to build a crew."

"Talk to us about this crew."

"For a prison break in Chayl," Branch explained, "six roles be required. A few more might be helpful, but my crew be incomplete without the six."

"*Our* crew," Hillian amended.

"Is it, then?" the master thief asked. Nodding his acceptance, he continued. "Very well, *our* crew starts with a burglar, which would be mine own self, m'lord. However, even a man o' my skill and experience will be needin' two elements to gain entry to the lower level o' Castle Chayl, where the dungeon serves as the king's prison. One o' them elements, a crooked prison guard, is already on my payroll. The other will be needin' to cause a distraction, which will require a skilled charlatan."

"Have you someone in mind for this charlatan?" Adia asked.

"Aye, aye, I got me a few," Branch replied, clearly relishing the role of master planner. "I'll continue, if it please you, Miss Adia."

She nodded, and the plan unfolded further. "Once inside, I be confident we can find the Rook and the president. But then, we'll be needin' an exit strategy. For that, the team would be needin' a long-range archer to make us a zip line from the tallest tower. That makes four."

"You, your prison guard, a charlatan distraction, and an archer," Adia said.

"Aye, and another archer to secure the zip line and protect the landin' location."

"That makes five," Hillian noted, "not six."

"It does, m'lord, but we be needin' us another distraction durin' the exit. Now, this one only needs to be divertin' the guards' attention, not movin' them from their posts, so I be thinkin' maybe a firework display. It be fairly common for the Alchemists Guild to light the night sky while testin' new creations or displayin' their wares to prospective customers. So, then, I be thinkin' our last man could be another charlatan posing as a rich businessman from Domus Viho expandin' into Chayl and wishin' to sample some product for his grand openin' ceremony."

"And that makes six," Hillian concluded. "But you have the two of us."

"Aye, so tell me, Lord Drake, what skills do the two o' you bring to our crew?"

"Well, you have seen that Miss Adia is multitalented."

"True, true," the tavern master agreed. "And you, m'lord?"

"I wish to place both of us at the landing site, Master Branch. I can secure the line, and I believe Miss Adia could replace your expert archer there."

"That she could, I'd wager, and better than most." The tavern master considered, briefly, before offering his summary. "Well, then, we have us the burglar, the prison guard, and the two o' you at the landin' site, leaving us to find two charlatans and a master archer."

"We would like to be involved in the selection," Hillian informed him. "How much time do you require before you are ready?"

Branch thought for a moment, again weighing ideas with his grinding teeth. "If it please your lordship, I be needin' a couple o' hours to assemble me some candidates."

"Very well, Master Branch, we shall await word from you at the Unicorn Palace Inn."

"Do you trust him?" Adia asked as they left the Wild Boar Tavern.

"Of course not," the Vingish nobleman replied, "but, we have little choice."

When they were recalled to the Wild Boar, they found the tavern master waiting for them at the door. "Shall we begin with the first charlatan, m'lord?" he asked.

At the young lord's nod, Branch led them to his office, a room much like the room to which he had previously taken them but set with a desk instead of a bed. One by one, he paraded in a series of charlatans posing as officers of the Golden Knighthood of Mbúso. All of them addressed their judges very formally and conversed with knightly authority, but some were clearly more convincing than others.

During one of the auditions, the door was violently flung open. Two large men entered, wearing the uniforms of the local constabulary, followed by a man attired much more regally. He announced that he was a member of the Royal Guard for His Majesty the High King of Chayl and that the man standing before them was a thief and a master of deception. He barked orders to his subordinates, who roughly apprehended the charlatan and dragged him from the room. The royal guardsman then threatened those remaining in the room, warning them that interference would result in arrest as accomplices. Just prior to exiting, however, he turned, gave a short bow, and then departed.

"Ha!" Branch exclaimed. "I think we have us a winner!"

"I agree," Hillian confirmed. "In fact, that performance was so inspired, I think we should have all four of them!"

"As you say, m'lord," the tavern master agreed. He stood and began arranging a target at the end of the room. As the first archer candidate entered, the nobleman held up his hand.

"This is a small room," he said to Branch. "Is it really very likely that any of your candidates will miss at this range?"

"True, true. Well, now, then, we could go outside, m'lord, but it might attract unwanted—"

"Wait," Adia interrupted. She had been standing in the doorway, looking out into the main room of the tavern. "I have an idea."

Striding out into the crowd, the lithe sorceress leaped onto a table and shouted for attention. "Good men and women of Chayl, please permit me to interrupt your evening. My lord has made a wager with the esteemed proprietor of this establishment, Master Foster Branch, and we would like to test that wager with all of you as witnesses."

Hillian's eyebrows rose as he watched the Gift Mage's performance.

Leaping from the table to the bar, Adia continued her monologue. "Master Branch claims that the city of Chayl is home to the most accomplished archers in the world, but my lord disagreed. Your tavern master wagered, then, that there are bowmen in this very room who possess the skill and precision to perform archery feats complex enough—and impressive enough—to confirm his claim."

After walking casually down the length of the bar, nimbly avoiding plates and mugs, Adia allowed herself to fall into the arms of two men who were most eager to catch her. Turning to one of them, she cooed, "Tell me, good sir, have you a knife to lend me?"

With the man's hunting knife, Adia fastened a napkin to a table before announcing, "If there is an archer in this tavern who can pierce this napkin from the other side of the room with his arrow flying over the rafters while tied to a length of rope, then my good lord will pay Master Branch his wager and concede his claim." All eyes upon her, Adia strode to the other side of the large room, pulled a long coil of rope from a hook on the wall, and asked, "Who would like to begin?"

## Chapter 7

# DELIVERANCE

Silently offering thanks to the Almighty Jalidus for the clouds that conveniently obscured the lights of heaven, Hillian Drake gazed through the thick darkness of Chayl, blowing on his hands in the shadows of the city's Jalidin temple. It was a small church, in comparison to the mighty cathedrals in Domus Viho, Calimygna, and Trigoti that served as the seats of each nation's cardinal, none of which could compare to the Great Cathedral in Porvatis from which Hillian's father, the prime cardinal, directed the entire faith. Still, the temple of Chayl boasted the size and sturdiness of Jalidin architecture, but its walls provided Hillian with little protection from the cold winds of the Andyric coast.

Lost in thought, Hillian flinched at the voice beside him.

"Are you well, Lord Drake?"

Frowning, he glanced at the Gift Mage, who had emerged from the steep stairway of the church's bell tower. "I am both cold and nervous, Miss Adia," he admitted.

"Cold, of course," she replied, squinting, "but why nervous?"

"Unlike you and Master Rook—and even President Kesler, it appears—I am not accustomed to the view from this side of the law."

The Gifted woman chuckled softly, her rare smile providing a small measure of warmth to the anxious nobleman. "Forever the pious Jalidin," she remarked.

"Perhaps not as pious as I could be," Hillian countered, "but I *am* Lord of Nydia, adviser to the King of Vinglandon, and a delegate to the World Council. It is my responsibility to uphold the law, whether in my home duchy of Nydia, elsewhere in Vinglandon, or even in other council nations."

"Even when the law is unjust?"

"As it happens, I have been witness to some of Master Rook's crimes, so I am confident that his incarceration, and the laws upon which it is based, are sufficiently just."

"What of President Kesler?"

"I also happen to know she is guilty of aiding and abetting Master Rook in his unlawful activities, and I have reason to assume she has done so multiple times in the past. Thus, it would seem her imprisonment is just, as well."

Adia shook her head. "Why do you insist upon ignoring the fact that they are guilty only of fighting against injustice, which, by definition, is a just cause?"

Aggravation bleeding into his voice, Hillian retorted, "Miss Adia, I have fought against injustice my whole life, and I have managed to do so without breaking any laws!"

"Until now."

Hillian sighed. "Until now," he acknowledged.

"Even a great visionary may require guidance when he allows himself to be blinded," the sorceress suggested, sadness apparent in her voice.

Hearing both a compliment and an insult, Hillian hesitated before asking, "By what am I blinded? The law?"

"Your faith, Lord Drake...your faith in a church that teaches hate and murder."

With great effort, Hillian resisted the urge to defend Jalidinity. Instead, he attempted to reveal the obvious contradiction in his companion's statement. "If you refer to my religion's policy toward the Gifted, your Church of Sabarism is no different."

"True, but my personal faith is not so blinding that it prevents me from seeing the flaws in my religion."

"And what, exactly, qualifies you to sit in judgment over the ordained dalils of your church?"

"Ordination does not render a priest immune to the fallibility of human nature."

"Are you less fallible, Miss Adia?" Hillian asked, shocked at her hubris.

"Not at all, but my logic and reason are not compromised by my faith or beliefs." Hillian frowned in confusion, so the Gift Mage continued. "I know I am not an evil spawn of hell, Lord Drake, which means I am a creation of Sabar, blessed by him with the Gifts he saw fit to bestow upon me."

"But—"

Refusing to be interrupted, Adia concluded. "Thus, if I come from God, and I am Gifted, then Gift Magic comes from God, which means both of our churches are wrong about it."

Her face bore determination tinged with anxiety, and Hillian realized the sorceress feared his response. It seemed important to her that he acknowledge her statement and perhaps that he agree with her assertions, but his voice faltered, constrained by the indecision in his heart. He could detect no evil in the woman standing defiantly before him, and yet his entire life had been filled with teachings from his priests—indeed, from his own father—that contradicted his instincts.

Before the young lord could begin to navigate such obstacles, however, the whistling of fletchings carried a reminder of his responsibilities. As the signal arrow quietly pierced the grass at the foot of a nearby copse of trees, Hillian and Adia hurried to their posts. The sorceress scrambled up the steps to a favorable vantage point, while the nobleman rushed to the trees.

The second arrow wobbled through the night sky, trailing a heavy rope, before skidding to a stop only a few paces from its predecessor. Hillian hurried to wrap the line around a large trunk, winding it through the lower branches before securing it with several tight knots. Dripping with sweat, his nerves stretched much tighter than the rope, the nobleman waved to Adia, who signaled the others by briefly activating her Gift Magic, her brilliant energy blinking against the dark night.

As fireworks illuminated the darkness to the west, and the rope drew taut and began a subtle pattern of bounce and sway, Hillian marveled at the skills of Foster Branch. Not only had he succeeded in penetrating the castle dungeon and rescuing the prisoners, as demonstrated by the quivering zip line, but his tightly coordinated teams, distributed throughout the city, had each played their parts to perfection to enable the escape, as well. He glanced at Adia, perched atop the bell tower, and prayed he and the sorceress would not prove to be the weakest players in Master Branch's game.

Branch was the first arrival, dropping lightly from the zip line as if he had ridden it hundreds of times. "The lass'll be comin' next," he notified the Vingish lord, "but she'll not be knowin' to drop from the wire, as I did, so you'll be havin' to catch her to prevent that sweet little body from crashin' into that there tree."

No sooner was the warning given than the situation presented itself. Hillian had time to hold his breath before his Severlandi colleague appeared in the darkness, tearing along the zip line at an alarming speed. The young nobleman spread his arms and braced for impact, but his preparations were grossly insufficient, and the force sent them both tumbling into the grass.

With their arms and legs tangled in an awkward mess, Hillian smiled sheepishly and carefully began to rise from his highly inappropriate position atop the Severlandi president.

"Why, Hillian," she whispered, grasping his shirt and preventing his escape, "when I said we were friends, I never meant you should jump on top of me." Her stunning blue eyes smiled, but her perfect lips curled seductively, suggesting a seriousness to the apparent jest.

As the young lord struggled to regain his balance, both physically and otherwise, Eryk landed softly, dropping from the rope almost as quietly as Master Branch had. Smirking at his lord's awkward discomfort, the master rogue quipped, "In prison, she spoke of nothing but you, Lord Drake."

"That is a lie, Master Rook," Mona complained, though her embarrassed smile seemed to imply that his comment carried some hints of truth.

"Well," the nobleman responded, his own embarrassment hidden in the dark, "I am truly relieved to see you both." As he shook hands with his countryman, Hillian was unable to tear his eyes away from Mona Kesler. As fireworks exploded in the sky, casting a glow upon her beautiful face, the young lord's breathing paused, momentarily, upon seeing that she was staring at him, as well.

The beauty of the moment, however, was interrupted by a sharp crack of thunder as the Alchemists Guild demonstrated their mastery over sound as well as light. The horses, led by Master Branch from the stable behind the church, startled angrily, rearing, kicking, and raising a din. Predictably, their neighing and whinnying, particularly in the silence following the firework explosion, brought the attention of castle guards, who began to shout and point at the archer as he zipped down the rope.

Their location revealed, Adia did not hesitate. She clapped her hands together, creating a small explosion and a blinding flash of light much like the fireworks. Her hair flashing into a brilliant white that illuminated the bell tower, she pulled her hands apart with a glowing light stretched between them. With a violent pushing motion, she threw the bar of light toward the oncoming guards. It seemed to grow, both in size and intensity, until it fell upon the stunned guards, pulverizing the leaders before crashing into the bricks and stones of the street, which were shattered into millions of shards that shredded their way through the remaining pursuers.

"May Jalidus have mercy on their souls," Hillian muttered, ashamed of his relief as dozens of men lay dead.

"And may Adia Varani continue to have mercy on ours," Eryk responded as he assisted Branch with the horses.

As the first hints of sunrise began to paint the sky, Master Branch led the small party to the entrance of the

Castlewood Distillery, another of Eryk's many properties, where they quickly dismounted and began their journey to Domus Viho.

## Chapter 8

# INTERVENTION

With the city of Chayl and the early morning sun at their backs, two horses strained to pull the old wagon, burdened as it was with its heavy load. The wagon carried six oversized barrels, each standing on end and insulated with straw from the jarring and bouncing of the road to Domus Viho.

For several hours, the wagon rumbled along the rich, green countryside in relative silence. For several hours, the mares trudged along, occasionally passing through a small village, but generally alone on the flat, dirt road. For several hours, Hillian Drake hid in the darkness, controlling his breathing in a desperate attempt to manage the anxious thundering of his heart.

It was his concentration on silence, in fact, that made it so easy to notice the approach. Long before they arrived, Hillian could hear the sounds of multiple horses behind them, galloping from the direction of Chayl. In only a few short moments, however, they had overtaken the wagon, deftly encircling it and forcing its driver to pull to a halt.

"Halt this wagon!"

"Beggin' your pardon, but on what authority," inquired the old driver, "do you go interferin' with a man o' commerce?"

"I am Lieutenant Síga," responded the rider, presumably the leader, "of the Golden Knighthood of Mbúso."

"Perhaps you missed the signs, Sir Knight, but this here be the nation o' Grolandon, where your Golden Knights have no business bein', much less stoppin' wagons!" the driver retorted.

"We are authorized by the High King of Grolandon to pursue fugitives who have escaped from the Prison of Chayl."

"And I'm supposed to believe that, am I? Well, take a look-see, if you must, for I got me no fugitives...only the fine brews o' the Castlewood Distillery."

In reply, a sword eagerly announced itself with the horrifying sound of steel on sheath. As the wagon driver cried out in alarm, the ringing of the blade quickly transitioned to the dull grating of splitting wood. The shriek lasted only a moment before the man was down from his seat and rummaging through the straw in the back of his wagon.

"What are you doing?" the knight lieutenant demanded.

"Well, what in blazes do you think I be doin'? You put two gapin' holes in my barrel, and I'm just tryin' to stop the leakin'!"

"With tree sap?" the knight asked, suspiciously.

"Aye, it be common practice for haulin' barrels," the Grolandi driver replied, his voice somewhat less frantic, having apparently repaired the damage. "This, here, be mine own recipe, with some sawdust mixed in so it don't be drippin' too much."

"Lieutenant," a familiar voice interjected, "put away your sword and search the remaining barrels in a more traditional manner, if you please."

"As you command, Captain."

Hillian recalled Knight Captain Wadógo from the monastery and wondered how the situation might be different if she had chosen to join them. The thought did little to relieve his anxiety, though, and the young nobleman closed his eyes and forced a reduction in the rate of his breathing. His heart, however, refused to halt its relentless beating, echoing in the tight, dark space, and the devout Jalidin prayed to God that the noise would not be sufficient to reveal his location.

After completing their search and finding nothing but ale, the Búso knights hastened toward Domus Viho. The driver cursed them softly before flicking the reins, signaling to his passengers that the danger had passed. Hillian allowed himself to breathe again, gasping for air in the tiny confines. As the wagon rumbled on, he reflected on Captain Wadógo. Perhaps she was not their enemy, in her heart, as the malini had suggested. Perhaps she intentionally chose to depart before her knights could search the wagon more thoroughly. Had she chosen to observe it over a more prolonged period, she likely would have noticed nothing out of the ordinary. She would have seen the wagon stop in each of the Grolandi villages strewn along the road like pearls on the neck of a noblewoman. She would have observed the old driver stop at a tavern, speak with a barkeep, and obtain a sack of food while red-bearded men unloaded two or three of the barrels and replaced them with similar barrels or crates. Over the course of days, she would have witnessed more of the same unloading and loading in each subsequent village. She would have concluded, most likely, that the driver was a legitimate merchant conducting legitimate business.

However, from a closer vantage point, Captain Wadógo and her knights might have noticed that the last four barrels had never been unloaded. Possibly they would have concluded that these barrels were reserved for Domus Viho, but it may have occurred to one of them that the capital city had an ample supply of its own breweries. One of the knights might have possessed sufficient knowledge of Grolandi ale to know that the Chayl varieties did not command enough interest in Domus Viho to create a market for imports.

If the closer vantage point afforded them visibility into the sacks of food, the Golden Knights would probably have concluded, very quickly, that the rate of consumption far exceeded what would be reasonable to expect from one man of average build. With such evidence, they may have guessed that the driver was feeding his horses with the food, but it may have occurred to someone that there are other ways to conceal fugitives in a wagon.

Perhaps the Almighty Jalidus had, indeed, answered Hillian's prayer, for Captain Wadógo's overly efficient search had left her knights with no such vantage points, and the old wagon driver was free to continue his unlikely trip to Domus Viho. However, shortly after leaving a village, and just as the smell of the Crescent River began to reach Hillian's nose, the driver pulled his horses to a halt.

"What's this now? Why, there's a damn wall 'cross the road, there! Nearly invisible, it is, so I didn't even see it in the sunlight. Oh, but you saw it, didn't you, girls?" the driver said to his horses but certainly to his passengers, as well.

Just as he finished speaking, the familiar whistle of arrows announced the attack. The horses died with terror in their throats and arrowheads in their flesh, while the wagon driver shouted a warning. "Archers in the woods!" he called as he scrambled down from the wagon. As the scent of smoke reached Hillian's nose, the wagon driver coughed, "Poison gas..."

There was nothing more. Escaped or dead, the poor man was no longer talking. Once again, panic began to spread in the nobleman's chest, stemmed only by Eryk's decision to break his own rules and speak.

"We are clearly discovered. Miss Adia, free us from this wagon and erect a protective shield," the master rogue commanded.

Without a word, the Gift Mage responded. In a flash of light, she blasted the false floor of the wagon, sending barrels, crates, and straw into the sky and revealing herself and her companions. As she rose from the wreckage, her brilliant white hair stretched out from her scalp like a lion's mane, framing her face, its beauty more than slightly distorted by the odd combination of angry determination and vengeful eagerness. She quickly complied with Eryk's request to fashion an energy shield but added an offensive element that resulted in several dead archers.

As soon as she relaxed, however, the ground beside her exploded as a bolt of lightning struck only a few paces away. Eryk, who had been scouting the perimeter, was thrown in one direction, while Adia was propelled in the other. Instinctively, Hillian threw himself onto Mona, who remained unconscious on the broken wagon, having already succumbed to the narcotic gas. Shielding her body with his own, the Vingish lord bore the brunt of the blast.

The intensity of the heat was the most shocking to him, enough so that he barely noticed the scream.

Hazarding a glance, Hillian witnessed the sorceress, who had been thrown against the nearly transparent energy wall, writhing in agony just next to the wagon, engulfed in a magical inferno. Ironically frozen by the terrible beauty of the fireball, the nobleman stared as Adia, who had shielded herself from the worst of the flames, gathered her strength to retaliate. As she began to hurl blasts of force and balls of fire, Hillian followed them with his eyes, finally identifying the shape of Ixodis. Casually deflecting Adia's attacks, the Angel of Mercy glowed with the righteous light of heaven, relentlessly punishing the demon Giftwitch with the power of the eternal realm.

But Adia Varani was no demon. The thought sprang, unbidden, into Hillian's mind, and he reacted on instinct. Despite his religious training, despite his devotion to Jalidus, despite his entire upbringing, Hillian found himself leaping from the wagon to defend his companion. The sky had ripped open, pouring rain and lightning upon her, making mud of the dirt road and causing her to slip and lose her footing as she struggled to hold an energy shield with one hand and deliver her magical attacks with the other.

As he raced toward the attacker, dodging the magical blasts, the thought passed through his mind once again: *Adia Varani was no demon.* He was certain it was true, a certainty that led directly to one logical conclusion: the Angel of Mercy was no angel. The entire fabric of angel and demon began to unravel as Hillian's sword jumped from its scabbard. Ixodis was no angel, and Jalidus himself, were he to descend from Himil, would declare the man a fraud and a blasphemer. Furthermore, Hillian knew that by challenging the hypocrisy and fraud of Ixodis, he was doing the work of God.

Filled with righteous rage, Hillian Drake stopped running, drew himself up tall and lordly, raised his sword, and declared, "In the name of Jalidus the Almighty, the god you claim to serve, I command you to surrender and be judged!"

Ixodis froze, perhaps surprised by the insignificant demand, but perhaps affected by the power of the holy name of Jalidus. By the grace of God, the villain's pause gave the sorceress an opportunity to double her attacks, and Ixodis was forced to strengthen his shield and fall back. In fact, Ixodis retreated into the mountain woods without throwing one more fireball, one more force blast, or one more lightning bolt, his energy wall evaporating upon his departure.

It had happened so fast, so furiously, the thoughts crashing into his consciousness, that the young lord simply stood, for a long time, gazing into the woods, his sword still drawn but no longer raised aloft in righteous determination. He was vaguely aware of Adia approaching, burns on her hands and arms. He had some peripheral understanding that Eryk had returned, with a revived Mona. But while these images moved around him, in the gauze and translucence of a dream, he remained frozen, unable to reconcile the conflicts in his heart.

"Surrender and be *judged*?" Eryk asked, incredulous.

"Yes," Adia responded, her voice cracking in pain, "Right after he invoked the name of your god."

"Not *my* god," the master thief corrected. "I am not afflicted with Lord Drake's disease of religious faith."

Whether it was Eryk's mocking tone, or his challenge to Hillian's beliefs, the Vingish nobleman broke from his dreamlike state and interjected. "You should be thankful for my affliction!"

"Why, because it drove away the Angel of Mercy for you?" Eryk taunted.

"Do *not* call him that!" Adia shouted, pointing an electrified finger at the rogue as her hair flashed to white. "He is *not* an angel! His name is Ixodis, and he is a Gift Mage—"

"No, he is not an angel," Hillian interrupted in a steady voice, "but he is stronger than you." As the energy-charged finger whirled on him, the young lord remained calm, clarity lending control to his voice. "He was destroying you, Adia, and I think you understand that my appearance should not have been more than a momentary distraction to him. He could have neutralized me with the flick of his wrist and then returned his focus to you."

"But your distraction allowed me to double my attack," she offered weakly.

"Yes, but we both know you were far outmatched." The sorceress did not respond, and Hillian turned his attention to Eryk. "So if I did not represent a material threat, explain to me why he would have retreated when he had us reeling." The master rogue's eyes narrowed, but he, too, had no response, so Hillian continued. "Beyond the momentary distraction, which was negligible as we have already established, I brought nothing new to the situation other than the name of Jalidus."

Eryk's expression twisted in disbelief, but the faithful nobleman challenged him immediately. "You cannot deny the logic. Your atheist philosophies may prevent you from accepting divine intervention, but with logic supporting it and no evidence to the contrary, you cannot completely dismiss it!"

"Adia?" the frustrated thief pleaded.

Her eyebrows furrowed in thought, the sorceress responded thoughtfully. "In Sabarism, our god, Sabar, has an evil adversary who is characterized as a master of deception. We are taught that Khada the Deceiver, as he is called, is responsible for all the other world religions and that he designed them to attract good people away from the true path by providing them with other paths that appear, at first glance, to be also good."

She paused and turned her attention to Hillian. "So it is in this context that I have always viewed Jalidus: as a fictional persona created by the evil Khada for the sole purpose of deceiving good people...like you."

Before the young lord could truly digest the unexpected compliment, Adia continued, "But I do see the logic. As much as I am reluctant to admit that I was losing to Ixodis, that I was close to being defeated and having my life's goal destroyed, I cannot deny that it is true. And still, he fled. So, I am forced to consider that Sabarists may, in fact, actually be deceived about the nature of Khada's deceptions, and that perhaps the gods of other religions, like your Jalidus, do exist and do have power. Or perhaps we worship the same god—Sabarists and Jalidins and Itamis, and maybe even Mahalists—and Khada has succeeded only in deceiving us into thinking that we do not."

Seeing the stunned reactions of her companions to her philosophical monologue, Adia became uncharacteristically shy. Sensitive to his involvement in embarrassing her, Hillian diverted the attention by asking Mona her thoughts.

"As you know, my country encourages tolerance of all religions, and my administration includes an Interfaith Advisory Board that provides me with various perspectives. In my first term as president, receiving this counsel, I often wondered if each religion may have found and defined but a segment of the truth, the *same* truth, and that the entire picture cannot be seen until one puts the segments together.

"So, while I do not subscribe to a particular faith, I find that I am no longer *without* faith." She looked at

Eryk apologetically, knowing she had tipped the balance against him in the debate.

"But you admitted that he is not an angel," the master rogue recalled, turning to Hillian. "If he is just a man, why would divine intervention be necessary or effective?"

"Because he claims to be an angel, distorting the message of Jalidus for his own ends, just as you suggested to me as we journeyed to Mbúso. That makes him the worst kind of sinner: one who manipulates others into sinful acts by presenting them as the will of God. This is a terrible affront to Jalidus," Hillian explained, "as I imagine it would be to any god." He nodded at Adia. "So, when one of the faithful stands up against the deception, I must believe that Jalidus, Sabar, Kila, or Ayawi would lend the strength of heaven!"

Frustrated, the master rogue shrugged in defeat. "So be it, but surely you will all agree that we need to develop a strong, realistic strategy that does not involve reliance on an imaginary all-powerful being."

Frowning, Hillian said, "Two of the four of us believe in an all-powerful being, and the third acknowledges the possibility of his or her existence, so I am certain we would all appreciate if you would refrain from using words like 'imaginary.'"

Eryk's eyes squinted as he replied in a low voice, "I make no promises."

Always the peacekeeper, Mona interjected. "Master Rook is not wrong, though. We need a strategy."

"Agreed," Hillian replied quickly. "Ixodis seems to be nearly all-powerful himself, and he will certainly be even better prepared for us the next time..." He trailed off as he noticed the expression on Adia's face, but it was Eryk who spoke first.

"They're coming back," he warned, his face bearing a very similar expression of careful listening.

"I can hear their thoughts," the sorceress added, nodding in agreement.

"I can hear their horses," the master rogue replied.

Focusing her attention on the road, Adia smiled wickedly. "No matter," she said. "I will borrow a trick from my enemy." Bringing her burned hands together and slowly pulling them apart, she revealed a brick of energy, reflecting brightly the light that flowed from her palms. With a sudden push, she hurled the brick over the wreckage of the wagon, then repeated the process over and over, quickly building a wall that rose as tall as a small cottage and spanned the width of the dirt road.

When she finished, her breath was ragged and her balance unstable. Hillian began to voice his concern, but Adia dismissed him. "Gift Magic is draining, more so than Spell Magic or Mind Magic, and I am already injured. I am tired, yes, but fine," she insisted.

She was wrong. When Captain Wadógo and her company of knights finally arrived, their golden armor topped with helmets wrapped in black or red turbans, they crashed headlong into Adia's energy barrier, as planned. It was certainly not planned, however, that the barrier would fail to hold them, that the force of their impact would shatter the energy field, or that Adia Varani would feel the shattering as physical pain. As the horses stumbled and several riders fell from their saddles, the Gift Mage screamed and collapsed to the ground.

With their strongest weapon incapacitated, and her scream having completely exposed their location, it appeared that retreat was the only option. "Time to go," Eryk said again, repeating the words he'd uttered when last they retreated from the Golden Knights of Mbúso.

*Chapter 9*

# SANCTUARY

Hastening through the wild brush, with the incline steadily increasing, was a difficult process. Eryk scouted ahead, choosing the best course, though Hillian felt certain that the best course, in the perspective of a criminal experienced in evading the authorities, was far from the easiest course, particularly for a man carrying an unconscious woman. Fortunately, Mona was equally aware of Hillian's burden, so she remained near her friend, pushing back brambles, holding branches, and generally trying to make the journey easier. So, while Eryk's path involved a seemingly endless supply of hazards, the sounds of pursuers grew farther and farther away.

Finally, Mona and Hillian, with the unconscious Adia sagging in his arms, emerged from the heaviest of the wooded area into a more barren landscape, at which point the mountain rose above them at a nearly vertical angle. They found Eryk waiting for them on a shelflike plateau just above their heads.

"There is a cave up here," he said. "It would provide us shelter, and it has a fairly narrow opening that should be easily defensible."

After struggling to safely pass Adia's body up to the shelf, the three companions began to enter the cave. Mona stopped, however, as she noticed another opening.

"That cave there," she observed, "seems much larger."

"That was the first one I noticed, as well," Eryk agreed, "but it would be difficult to defend, so I continued looking."

"Yes, but if there happened to be some evidence of our presence in that cave, it might lead our pursuers to believe we had stopped there and then continued on."

"It would need to be very subtle evidence," the master rogue added, smiling at Mona's eye for strategy, "to avoid being immediately identified as misdirection."

"True," the Severlandi president replied. "What if we—"

"Wait," Hillian interjected, kneeling next to Adia, arranging a roll of cloth under her head, ignoring his own injuries. His left eye was cut and swollen, and his nose had been bleeding, both of which provided dried blood to mix with the smears of mud. The sleeves of his shirt were torn and looked far more brown than white. His tunic was missing, serving as Adia's pillow, which exposed the midsection of his shirt, still white but plastered to his chest with sweat. "I would prefer you both stay here."

"Why?" Eryk challenged.

"I…" Hillian responded, then paused. He shook his head, his mental state reflecting his physical fatigue. Finally, he admitted, "I have no good answer, so I suppose it is instinct. But I feel very strongly that you should stay here with us."

"Hillian," the master rogue responded in a condescending tone, "for all of your strengths, strategy is not—"

"Do not patronize me, Master Rook!" the young lord retorted, employing Eryk's criminal name in aggravation. "We have no Gift Mage to defend us, as we did on the ship, and we have no band of thieves to come to our rescue, as we did in Chayl. Right now, we have only the three of us, and I do not wish to separate!"

The men stared at each other for an uncomfortable moment, but then Mona interjected. "Perhaps that is the wiser course," she suggested.

Eryk glanced at her, then back at his countryman. "Very well," he agreed, to which Hillian sighed in relief. "Then what *should* we do?"

Hillian's sigh nearly transformed into a gasp. He had not expected the question. The leader of their small party, the criminal mastermind, had not only allowed himself to be overruled but had also seemingly deferred his authority. It was just as well, Hillian thought with a nod. He had made his decision, had accepted that Adia was not a demon and that Ixodis was not an angel, and had felt the hand of God guiding him. Perhaps Mona had been right about his potential for greatness, and perhaps it was time for him to assert it.

"I want to go deeper," declared the new leader of the small band of companions, trusting his instincts. "We do not know what may be inside this cave, nor do we know who is still seeking us on the outside, so we need some room to fight and retreat in either direction." Then, looking down at the unconscious sorceress, he added, "And I am optimistic that we will find some water."

"We shall go deeper, then, and I will carry our friend," the master thief responded, scooping up the sleeping sorceress.

"Thank you, Eryk," Hillian responded, his relief and fatigue so overwhelming that he did not register his use of the master thief's given name. Carefully, he and his companions began to walk along the narrow passage, away from the cave opening. The farther they traveled, the darker it became, and the three of them gradually moved closer together. But after Eryk stumbled a second time, nearly dropping his passenger, the nobleman finally stopped.

"I was wrong," he said dejectedly, sitting down on the stone floor. "Our eyes are adjusted, and still we cannot navigate this cave in the dark."

As if on cue, a mysterious voice began chanting:

These caves so dark you cannot see,
they keep us safe and warm and free.
But now, to meet you face-to-face,
let there be light in this dark place!

The cave was suddenly flooded with light. Blinded, the three companions closed their eyes, then blinked and squinted, until finally they could make out a glowing torch. Although seated on the ground, Hillian noticed that the man bearing the torch was looking at him nearly eye-to-eye. The torchbearer was flanked by a dozen men much like him, all with the same short but broad frame, all wearing long brown or black beards, all dressed in armor and helms, and all armed with unusual weapons. Rather than swords, many of them, including the leader, carried huge double-bladed axes, while others held massive hammers or spiked clubs.

Hillian rose to his feet, his hand on his hilt, while Eryk shifted Adia's body to reach for a knife. As Mona began walking backward, the torchbearer spoke.

"Come, travelers, for food, rest, and healing," he commanded in a deep voice that sounded as if it had been hewn from the rock that surrounded them. "Come, and you will not perish this day."

Uncertain if the last comment was intended to be a threat of death through violence or a warning of death through starvation, Hillian was forced to decide quickly. "I am Lord Drake of Nydia. This is President Kesler of Severlandon, and this is—"

"Master Rook," Eryk inserted, choosing to introduce himself with his rogue identity. Hillian quietly wondered what might have motivated Eryk to make that particular choice, but he was afforded little time to ponder.

"I am Dobyn, of Clan Varmingar, loyal servant of Loe, of Clan Avishgar, ruler of the kingdom of Tyr."

"It is a pleasure to make your acquaintance, Dobyn, of Clan Varmingar. But where, may I ask, is the kingdom of Tyr?"

"You are in it, Lord Drake. Our nation is comprised of the caverns and tunnels beneath the Tyrenese and Orbalese mountain ranges."

Glancing first at Eryk, and then at Mona, and finding the same incredulous expression that he certainly bore himself, the Vingish nobleman allowed his surprise to be apparent in his statement. "There is an entire nation of your people living underground, in the mountains?"

"Indeed," their host responded, "though there was a time when Tyr existed above ground, in what you humans have named Ukbawa."

"You are not humans, then?" Hillian inquired, tentatively.

The comment was met with scoffs. Dobyn merely stared, his face expressionless, as he responded, "We are dwarves, but it is a compliment to my family that you were unaware, for we of Clan Varmingar are charged with protecting the secrecy of Tyr."

"So then why reveal yourselves to us?" Eryk asked.

Glancing at the dwarf standing beside him, whose stony face glowered in disapproval, Dobyn nodded. "There are some among us who counseled against it, but I found myself intrigued. It is clear to me that you are being chased, perhaps even hunted, and I believe our king will wish to learn why."

Silence hung in the air as Hillian absorbed the implications. Finally, he asked, "You mentioned food and healing."

"You will all be fed, rested, and healed before you are presented to the king."

"Very well," Hillian decided. "We would be grateful to accompany you."

After a short walk, Dobyn led the humans, along with a handful of his clansmen, to the end of a large tunnel, where an arch had been carved into the stone wall. As the dwarves casually walked through the wall, disappearing, Hillian caught his breath in wonder as he realized that the arch served as a spellportal. Mona's spellportals, connecting every major city of the world, except for Kewu in the isolated mountain nation of Tuskawa, consisted of round platforms that magically transferred all that stood upon them to corresponding platforms in another location. Unlike Severlandon's spellportals, however, which required a Spell Mage to chant a spell for each individual port, the dwarven arch seemed to be permanently activated, and the excitement on Mona's face was a pleasure to behold.

Upon passing through the dwarven portal, Hillian found himself in a large room that was furnished with ornately carved wood furniture, decorated with paintings, and lit by a candle chandelier hanging from the ceiling in the center of the space. A young dwarf, judging by his short and downy beard, stopped in the doorway, startled by the newcomers, before fleeing with heavy footsteps. He returned momentarily with a stretcher and a young female dwarf, similarly bearded. After the two of them helped to gently ease Adia's body onto the stretcher, Dobyn led them all to the infirmary.

After the three conscious humans had received bandages and medicine for their minor injuries, including a salve that immediately reduced the visibility of the Gift Magic finger marks on Hillian's cheek, Dobyn announced that he would be taking them to the baths. At the thought of the three of them stripping down and bathing together, Hillian immediately glanced at Mona. "One of us should remain here with the patient," he declared.

"Lord Drake," Dobyn responded, "I recognize your concern, being in a strange land among potentially hostile people, but you must understand that we could have killed her already, had that been our intention."

Eyebrows raised, the Lord of Nydia responded, "Well, I find your lack of tact somewhat alarming, and I am not entirely convinced that your statement is true, but that is all irrelevant. When she wakes, one of us should be nearby to prevent her from feeling disoriented and threatened by the unfamiliar circumstances. Surely you can respect that."

"Of course. Which of you will be remaining with her, then?"

Hillian nodded at Mona, silently asking her to stay. Whether she understood his reasons or simply trusted his leadership, she volunteered.

"Very well, President Kesler," Dobyn acknowledged. "I shall arrange for a bed to be prepared next to the patient, so you may rest. I will also send some food and drink to you here." Then, turning back to Hillian and Eryk, he continued, "The two of you may follow me."

After bathing and dining, the two men were shown to their quarters. Hillian, however, did not sleep well, waking in fits as his dreams constructed elaborate ways in which his companions were endangered as a direct result of his new and unexpected leadership.

When waking from one such fit, Hillian was startled to find Eryk Val Varen waiting. "What are you doing in my room?" the frustrated nobleman growled.

"I came to get you for breakfast," Eryk offered, amiably.

"Breakfast? We're underground, so how do you even know that it's morning?" Hillian challenged.

"Morning or not, I think you should have some food before you relieve President Kesler."

Sitting up on the bed, Hillian inquired, "Why should I be the one to relieve her, and not you?"

"Well," Eryk replied, grinning, "I have acquired the impression that you would be uncomfortable being nearby when she bathes." Then, with a sly smile, he added, "Although I am not so certain she would be uncomfortable with it at all!"

Stunned at the thought, Hillian was lost in his imagination for several moments before he agreed, "Yes, I might be uncomfortable with that. However..." Distracted by the images in his mind, the nobleman was unable to complete his sentence.

"You are tempted."

Shaking his head like a dog in the rain, vainly attempting to dispel the images from his mind, Hillian objected, "Intrigued, maybe, but not tempted."

"You lie to yourself as much as to me, my lord," the rogue replied, smiling.

"Perhaps," Hillian accepted, nodding, "and perhaps you are right that I should take the opportunity to explore my friendship with Mona."

Pleasantly surprised, Eryk urged his lord. "Friendship or relationship?"

"Well, our current circumstances are not particularly conducive to romance," Hillian added.

"By 'current circumstances,' are you referring to the fact that everyone seems to want us dead, or the fact that we are prisoners of an underground nation of mythical creatures that are not supposed to exist?"

"Do you think we are prisoners rather than guests?" Hillian asked, frowning.

"I do," Eryk replied without hesitation. "If their existence is a secret, they will not allow us to leave."

Hillian nodded. "But it was the only choice to make."

"Of course it was," the rogue responded, "and if they manage to heal Adia, we will be able to escape, whether they wish it or not."

The Vingish nobleman closed his eyes, straining to make sense of the nonsensical scenario. "How did this happen?"

"We were at a severe disadvantage, my lord. As you said, there was no other choice."

"Yes, but I mean the dwarves. How could an entire race of dwarves exist without our knowledge?"

"Most people believe minotaurs do not exist, as well." Hillian nodded as Eryk probed further. "You studied at university...did you learn anything that might explain it?"

"No, in fact, I don't recall any mention of nonhuman races at all," Hillian explained. "I did, however, learn that all of the world's libraries were destroyed in the Great War, nearly two hundred years ago, which means recorded history only goes back that far. I am forced to assume, then, that the nonhuman races were forced into exile prior to the Great War."

"Or during it," Eryk suggested.

"Yes, or during it," the nobleman agreed. Frowning, he noted, "Either way, it is difficult for me to comprehend that our entire race has managed to be so terribly wrong for so many years."

"Or that the dwarven race has managed to stay so perfectly hidden for so many years," the rogue added. "It flies in the face of reason."

Their pondering was interrupted by a knock at the door. When Eryk opened it, the Chief of Clan Varmingar nodded his bearded head. "I apologize for the intrusion, Master Rook, Lord Drake," Dobyn began.

"There is no need for apology," Eryk replied quickly. "Please come in."

Remaining in the doorway, the dwarf explained his presence. "I thought you might be hungry." As both men nodded, he continued, "Would you prefer to eat in your chambers or in the dining hall?"

Sitting on the side of the bed and pulling on his boots, with his back to them, the Vingish nobleman waved his hand to indicate his lack of preference.

"Mister Varmingar, is it morning?" Eryk inquired. Upon hearing the question, Hillian turned around with interest, facing the dwarf framed in the doorway.

"Master Rook," the dwarf replied, "I understand that it is the custom among humans to refer to one another with titles and family names, such as Master Rook or Lord Drake, but the dwarves of Tyr subscribe to different customs. Only our king has a title and, even then, it is used with his given name rather than the family name of his clan."

"So he would be King Loe rather than King Avishgar?" Hillian clarified. "We follow the same practice for royalty, but you are correct that we use family names for all others."

"Interesting," the dwarf replied, nodding. "Well, you may refer to me simply as Dobyn."

"Thank you for the explanation, Dobyn," the nobleman responded. "We will be most pleased to respect the customs of Tyr."

The dwarf nodded to Hillian before returning his attention to Eryk. "And yes, Master Rook, it is, indeed, morning."

"Ha!" the rogue exclaimed.

"I never should have doubted you," Hillian said sarcastically, returning his attention to his boots.

"Dobyn, have you eaten yet this morning?" Eryk asked the dwarf, drawing Hillian's attention once more.

Clearly surprised by the question, the dwarf had no immediate answer. Finally, his eyes squinting slightly in suspicion, he admitted he had not.

"I would like it very much if you would join us for a meal," the thief suggested.

After a very brief moment, Dobyn nodded, so Eryk concluded, "Excellent! And now that Lord Drake has his boots on, let us go to breakfast."

The dining hall was full of dwarves, and the arrival of humans drew a great deal of attention. Many of them paused to stare at the strangers in their midst or to whisper to one another with scowls and expressions of animosity. It was unsettling, even saddening, as it occurred to Hillian that the hostility was probably the same that most of his fellow humans would show toward the dwarves, were they to appear in his home of Porvatis.

While the Vingish nobleman was observing the reactions of the dwarves in the dining hall, his countryman was observing Dobyn's expression. The dwarf was clearly nervous, but resolute, as he led them to a table. Eryk continued to stare at the dwarf until finally breaking the silence with a pointed question.

"Dobyn, why did you agree to dine with us?"

Hillian turned his attention to Dobyn, but the dwarf did not reply. Silence descended once more as plates of food were distributed and the three men began to eat. Finally, after calling for a second round of plates, Dobyn gave his answer.

"Master Rook, since the secrecy was imposed, I believe that I have experienced more encounters with humans than any other dwarf in Tyr. I have fought them, I have killed them, and I have imprisoned them, but I have never had the opportunity to share a meal with them."

Smiling, but receiving no smile in return, the master rogue responded, "Well, I can honestly say we have never had the opportunity to share a meal with a dwarf, so it is a new experience for us all."

"Dobyn," Hillian added, "if you have had more encounters with humans than any other dwarf, perhaps you can answer some of our questions."

Nodding slowly, the dwarf responded. "I presumed that was the purpose of this meal, and I will provide all the answers that are permitted."

Hillian considered the dwarf's use of the word *permitted* but forged ahead with his question. "When you first met us in the cave," he recalled, "you mentioned that dwarves once lived on the surface, among humans."

Dobyn nodded, prompting Hillian to continue. "What caused that to change?"

"The war," Dobyn answered, simply.

"Your nation fled to the caves during the war?" Eryk inquired.

"Certainly not!" the dwarf objected vehemently. "Tyr has *never* fled!"

"Then what drove you underground?" Hillian asked, somewhat confused by the apparent contradiction.

"We were not *driven*; we were..." Dobyn stopped himself midbreath. "The kingdom of Tyr *chose* to migrate to the underground tunnels," the dwarf clarified.

Then, abruptly ending the conversation before the second round of plates even arrived, he stood from the table and escorted the men to the infirmary, where they found Mona keeping watch over a sleeping sorceress. After a short conference with another dwarf, who clearly represented the medical team, Dobyn delivered the update.

"While your companion is healed of all physical wounds, she remains in a deep sleep," he reported. "Our physicians are confident she will wake within two or three days." As the three companions exchanged glances of concern mixed with optimism, the dwarf continued. "Lord Drake, would you or Master Rook care to remain with the patient while I show President Kesler to the baths?"

Eryk quickly volunteered, managing to do so in a casual manner that effectively masked his true motive. If Mona suspected any awkwardness, she gave no hint of it as she left the infirmary with Hillian and Dobyn.

After the bath, her face and hair matching the sparkle of her smile, Mona inquired about the mechanism used to keep the water so warm.

"Mechanism?" the dwarf asked in return, clearly not understanding the question.

"Well, I assume there is some hidden way to warm the water."

Still unsure, Dobyn offered an explanation but with little confidence. "It is spellcasted, if that is what you mean by *mechanism*."

"Yes, of course," Mona said, smiling. "So where do the Spell Mages work, and how does their spell-enhanced water travel to the bath?"

"President Kesler," Dobyn responded, "it is not the water that is spellcasted but rather the basin that contains it."

"But Spell Magic is temporary," the Severlandi politician challenged. "No Spell Mages entered the room while I bathed, yet the water never cooled at all."

Hillian found himself momentarily distracted by the notion of entering the room while Mona Kesler bathed, but his daydream was interrupted by the dwarf's response.

"Ah yes," Dobyn nodded, finally seeing clearly. "Humans and fairies can perform Spell Magic, but only dwarves can make it permanent." Then, almost to himself, as if he were compelled to correct the slightest inaccuracy of his statements, Dobyn added, "Well, dwarves and a very small minority of humans."

"Some humans can perform permanent Spell Magic?" Mona asked, her excitement likely related to the impact that such information would have on the spell-portal industry she'd founded.

"No, not some," Dobyn corrected himself, "only one."

Choosing to explore another topic as Dobyn showed Mona her sleeping chamber, Hillian asked, "This morning, you said you have encountered more humans than any other dwarf."

Dobyn nodded.

"How many have you encountered since the Great War?"

"Including you, seventeen," he answered quickly.

"Seventeen human encounters in the last two hundred years," Hillian said, glancing at Mona. "How many of those seventeen survived the encounter?"

After several moments, in which it almost seemed that Dobyn was in conflict with himself, the dwarf finally spoke, carefully choosing his words. "Lord Drake,

I regret that I must leave you now so I may attend to other pressing business." As he turned to leave, he paused. Looking back at Hillian, he added, "I enjoyed our meal this morning, and I thank you and Master Rook for the opportunity."

"It was truly an honor," Hillian responded, with deep sincerity.

## Chapter 10

# BLESSING

Hillian felt the desperation growing. After four days, there had been no sign of improvement in Adia's condition despite the best efforts of the dwarven physicians and their spell-enhanced medicines. Hillian decided it was time to escalate.

"We need to try something else," he declared.

"Like Mind Magic," Mona suggested.

"I apologize," Dobyn replied, "but we have no Mind Mages here."

"Maybe we go back to the malini," Hillian proposed.

"I'm sure the monastery is under constant surveillance by Golden Knights," Eryk said. "We can't risk implicating the malini any further."

"There may be another way," Dobyn inserted. "I believe the time has come to present you to my king."

Dobyn told his visitors they were required to be freshly cleansed prior to an audience with the king, but Hillian suspected the king himself needed time to prepare. The dwarves bathed Adia as well, and she was carried on a stretcher as the humans were shown into the throne room. On the dais, on a modest throne carved from the stone of the cave, sat a dwarf who bore a distinct resemblance to Dobyn and his clansmen.

The dwarves that accompanied them did not bow, so Hillian suppressed his natural instincts and remained upright while simultaneously attempting to avoid the appearance of disrespect. Not wishing to risk any sign of impropriety, he did not glance at his companions, though he was painfully aware that they watched him, following his lead.

Dobyn led them toward the dais, stepping up to a large, circular platform of cut and polished stones. He clasped his closed fist against his chest and dropped his chin just slightly, and only briefly. Clearly the dwarven equivalent of a bow, the action was already etched in Hillian's memory for his own use.

"My king," Dobyn addressed the monarch, proudly looking him directly in the eye, having raised his chin back to its normal position. "I present to you Lord Drake of Nydia, President Kesler of Severlandon, and Master Rook." He stepped back, clearly finished, surprising Hillian in his abruptness.

Stepping forward, Hillian mirrored Dobyn's salute, eliciting a raised eyebrow and smile from the king. His companions repeated the salute, amusing the king even further.

"Welcome, welcome," he said, laughing. "I am Loe, of Clan Avishgar, King of Tyr, and I am pleased to meet you." His jovial demeanor immediately eased the tension in the throne room, relaxing the humans and dwarves alike. "Tell me, Lord Drake, who is your third companion?"

Following the king's gaze, Hillian looked at the woman lying peacefully on the stretcher, held aloft by four dwarves who seemed to have the strength to hold her for eternity. "This is Miss Adia Varani," he responded. Looking at the king again, Hillian quickly continued. "King Loe, I want to thank you for your generous hospitality. Your people rescued us from the caves above and provided us with rest and nourishment, and your physicians have done an excellent job in healing our wounds." His head dropping involuntarily, Hillian's voice caught in his throat as he choked, "Unfortunately, Miss Adia's injuries are more than physical, and I am afraid she is beyond reach."

"I apologize, Lord Drake, for allowing you to be misled, but you are wrong on multiple counts." Hillian frowned in confusion as the king continued. "First of all, the dwarves of Tyr do not permit the presence of humans out of hospitality but out of survival. Our nation has survived, and even thrived, since the Purge because we..."

He stopped, his eyes squinting in distrust. All three of the humans had reacted to his latest words, and he clearly felt compelled to address it. "Are you uncomfortable with that term, *purge*?" he inquired. "What word have you given to it, then? Perhaps something that avoids the implication of human guilt?" he asked, his voice tinged with anger.

Without hesitating, Hillian responded. "King Loe, we have no word for it, and we can only guess the terrible tragedy to which it refers."

"Then guess," King Loe commanded.

"I must assume that your nation uses the term *purge* to refer to the events that led to the migration of dwarves from the surface of Crozada to the caves beneath the mountains," the Lord of Nydia explained. The king's expression did not change, so Hillian forged ahead. "But, you have my word, until Dobyn surprised us in the cave, none of us knew of the existence of dwarves."

King Loe exchanged a look with Dobyn before returning his glare to Lord Drake. "Go on," he commanded again, though his voice softened, if only slightly.

"On the surface, the average educated adult considers dwarves to be nothing more than characters of legend or myth, along with fairies, dragons, and goblins."

A grumbling arose from the dwarves assembled, including the king. "I trust," he growled, "that your next comment will explain why we should not be insulted to be compared to goblins."

"Goblins exist, as well?" Hillian asked, surprised, though immediately realizing that he should not be. The dwarven monarch scowled in response, and the Vingish lord shook his head. "King Loe, I apologize if I have offended, but please understand that I have lived my entire life under the assumption that humans were the only race on Keb, with no reason to believe otherwise."

"Until now."

"Actually, those assumptions first began to erode when our ship was boarded by minotaur pirates, only weeks ago. At that point, I learned that Master Rook had been operating a smuggling operation for several years, rescuing minotaurs and fairies from persecution."

"*This* Master Rook?" the king asked, motioning to Eryk.

"Indeed," Hillian replied. "But it was not until meeting your dwarves that I began to see a pattern. In fact, he and I discussed this topic shortly after arriving in Tyr, and we marveled at how unlikely it seems that the entire human population could be so wrong, so misguided, and so unaware for so long."

The dwarven king stared at his human guests for a long time. Finally, he looked at Eryk and asked, "What this man says about you…is it all true?"

Eryk nodded, but the king was persistent. "Tell me yourself," he commanded.

Without hesitation, Eryk responded. "When I first began to accumulate some amount of wealth, I began spending a small percentage on rescuing those less fortunate, such as commoners mistreated by their noble masters, immigrants persecuted for their ethnicity or religion, or women abused by their fathers or husbands. I developed a network of like-minded contacts and allies around the world, including Lord Drake in my home of Vinglandon, President Kesler in Severlandon, and Malini Ziraili in Mbúso.

"As my allies worked to strengthen the laws to protect these unfortunates, I found that many of my rescues began to involve nonhumans. Over the years, I have rescued three hundred and twenty-nine minotaurs and one satyr from prison or persecution, and I have established a safe haven for them on the island of Kiriti. I have rescued six hundred and…well, fairies are difficult to count, actually, but definitely more than six hundred fairies, assisting their migration to the relative security of their ancestral home in the Janni Wood and, when that was no longer safe, establishing a secret haven for them on the outskirts of Calimygna. I have also rescued seventy-eight merpeople, relocating them to the outlying caves and grottoes off the coast of Severlandon."

He paused for a breath but delivered the final blow before anyone could prepare. "In all, I have rescued over one thousand men, women, and children who were threatened and persecuted simply for being not-exactly-human."

As the assembly digested the gravity and scope of Eryk's statements, his face grew dark. "And I have rescued over twelve thousand humans."

Mona gasped, and Hillian's eyes grew ever wider. Dobyn's head tilted in awe, but King Loe's guarded expression showed no change.

"Two or three thousand were being persecuted for their ethnicity, their gender, or their class, but well over ten thousand for their religion."

Then, as if it forced its way out of his mouth despite his best efforts to keep it buried, the final number was revealed. "And one for her Gift Magic."

As the audience gasped and whispered, Eryk frowned in confusion. The dwarven king, however, smiled at his guest's discomfort.

"You had not intended to share so much with me," he stated, with no hint of question in his voice.

Slowly, Eryk shook his head, agreeing that his intentions had failed him.

"The platform on which you stand is enchanted with a powerful truth spell." His smile was the embodiment of a cat playing with a mouse. Turning his attention to Mona, the king added, "Now let us hear your truth, President of Severlandon."

"King Loe, my first encounter with a minotaur or satyr was on that same ship, and my first encounter with a dwarf was in the caves above. As for rescuing, I live in a nation that is known for religious freedom and equal rights for all sexes and colors, but I have personally witnessed the same persecutions of which Master Rook speaks. In my country, the truth has long been hidden behind a veil of tolerance, so I have thrown my support, politically and financially, behind all efforts, both legal and illegal, to fight the shadows of prejudice. I assisted Master Rook in arranging the fairy communities just outside my nation's capital as well as the merfolk haven off our northern shore." She trailed off, searching her memory for more information, when her eyes drifted to the stretcher. "Oh," she exclaimed, "and I worked with Master Rook in the rescue of Adia Varani!"

His eyebrows furrowed, King Loe glanced at the stretcher, then at Hillian, and then at Eryk. "And why did she need rescuing?" he inquired, returning his attention to Severlandi president.

Immediately, Mona recognized her mistake. She glanced at her companions, her eyes begging forgiveness.

"Because she is the Gift Mage I mentioned," Eryk announced. His comment had the desired effect, diffusing Mona's panic, but had the undesirable side effect of transferring that panic to the dwarves.

As the four dwarves abandoned their patient, leaving the spellcasted stretcher to float above the truth platform, King Loe stood from his throne and shouted at Dobyn, "You have brought a Giftwitch in our midst!" He was shaking, though it was unclear whether it was fear or anger that caused his condition. "I will have your head for it!"

"You hypocrite!" Hillian cried, his anger ignited with a ferocity sufficient to stop the king from continuing his tirade. "Your entire nation has been exiled by prejudice, and yet you allow your own prejudice to condemn this dwarf to death?"

In the awkward silence that fell upon the platform, King Loe again sat upon his throne. He stared at Hillian as he inquired, "What would you have me do, Lord Drake? With your Giftwitch companion, it is clear that the four of you represent a significant threat to the kingdom of Tyr."

"And why is it clear? You have no idea how powerful she is or what her intentions are to your nation, because she has been asleep the whole time we have been here!"

"And if she wakes? How can you expect me to accept that risk to my people?"

"But there is no risk!" Hillian was agitated, frustrated, and with the tone of his voice and the animation of his features and mannerisms, he walked a fine line between passionate and disrespectful. "You just listened to the three of us telling you, while standing on your spell-casted platform of truth, about how we are united in our fight for equality, for the end to prejudice, for inclusion of all people. In fact, you have more reason to trust us than to distrust us!"

Again, silence descended on the throne room as the dwarven king considered the words that had been hurled at him by his human visitor. "I want to trust you, Lord Drake of Nydia. I do. I want to believe in cousin Dobyn's theories that not all humans are threats to our safety and security and that we could live peacefully among them once more. But I cannot allow your companion to remain here, in her current state, as I have no way to assess the risks that might be encountered upon her waking."

Hillian began to respond but stopped as the king held up his finger, a gesture the human leader interpreted as optimistic. "However, you requested this audience," King Loe reminded, "because our best efforts, in both physical medicine and Spell Magic, have failed to revive her. So, it appears that it is time for you to depart from our nation and continue upon your journey, and you will do so with my blessing."

As soon as the king's last word left his bearded lips, his subjects breathed a collective gasp. Nodding, King Loe recognized their surprise. "Yes, for the first time since the Purge, I will send humans out of Tyr with both their lives and their memories."

As his countrymen whispered and stared, Dobyn leaped upon the platform, saluting his king.

"Dobyn, of Clan Varmingar," the king addressed him. "You are not free from my wrath just yet, cousin. You would be wise to take care in what you ask of me."

"King Loe," Dobyn responded, standing proudly, "I request that you permit me to accompany them."

"To the surface? Among the humans?" the king asked, incredulous.

"To the end of their journey, wherever that might be," Dobyn clarified.

"Your request would involve great risk, Dobyn. Your life would be at risk. Our nation's security would be at risk. I do not think—"

"My king," Dobyn interrupted, speaking quickly, "I implore you to think not of the risks in doing so but rather to ponder the risks of *not* doing so. You take a significant risk in trusting these humans to return to the surface with knowledge of our existence, but I could act as a supervisor of that trust. If your trust is betrayed, I could take action to mitigate the risk to our nation.

"Furthermore," he continued, pausing only momentarily for a short breath, "you wish to trust these humans because you have been nearly convinced of their good intentions, but you have no evidence to convince you of their effectiveness. You may believe they will continue to pursue their mission to bring an end to discrimination and persecution, but you have no influence on the outcome. Were I to join them in their efforts, I could lend dwarven assistance to their mission to better ensure its success, all the while ensuring the goals and needs of Tyr are adequately represented."

After a short silence, during which the dwarven king's expression remained stoic, Dobyn offered one last argument. "As Chief of Clan Varmingar, it is my responsibility to protect the security of Tyr from the human threat. To fulfill that responsibility, I *must* accompany them."

Shaking his head, the King of Tyr grudgingly assented. "Very well, Dobyn, of Clan Varmingar, I hereby grant your request to travel to the surface with the human,

Lord Drake of Nydia." Turning to Hillian, the dwarf king continued, "And you, Lord Drake, are hereby free to leave Tyr with your life, your memories, and your companions. This offer is extended to you on the condition that you assent to the companionship of *my* representative, Dobyn, of Clan Varmingar."

"King Loe," Hillian addressed the dwarven monarch, without hesitation, "I thank you for your blessings, and we would be honored to have the company of your representative, Dobyn, of Clan Varmingar."

"Very good. I suggest you travel to the Forest of Ard Shaab, where you will find the elves who possess the skills in Mind Magic that your companion will require." Oblivious to the shock and surprise exhibited by the humans upon discovering they would be leaving one mythical race only to visit another, King Loe turned his attention back to Dobyn. "Outfit yourself quickly, cousin, for I wish you to be on your way within the hour."

## Chapter 11

# HEALING

The sun was setting into the Kaoric Ocean in the west, still high enough in the sky to paint the clouds orange and color the horizon with purple and pink, but low enough to cast a shadow between the Forest of Ard Shaab and the westernmost edge of the Tyrenese Mountains, from which the strange group emerged. Four travelers walked from the cave's mouth, carefully picking their way down a rocky hill until they reached the grassy plains of Akhdiria, lush and green, supporting wildlife of all kinds. Birds soared overhead as deer and bison munched on the long grass, receding as the Vingish nobleman and his companions approached.

With his left hand, the Lord of Nydia grasped the stretcher that bore Adia Varani, while his right hand rested on the hilt of his sword. To his left, Dobyn held his handle in place, resting it upon his shoulder, while Mona and Eryk walked behind them carrying the rear handles.

"You seem nervous, Lord Drake," the dwarf observed. Hillian merely nodded, his eyes looking in every direction except toward his new companion, scanning the beautiful countryside for Gifted villains, bigoted dalils, and stubborn knights. "I was under the impression," Dobyn continued, "from our conversations, that it would be palatable…" He trailed off with a sigh.

"What?" Hillian asked, in an irritated tone that matched his frown.

Shaking his head, Dobyn replied in a low voice, "I did not wish my presence to cause you anxiety."

Hillian stopped, suddenly, causing each of the others to stop as well. "Dobyn," he said, his tone significantly softer, "words cannot describe the joy and honor I feel at being able to offer you a place at our table, and if your presence has caused me any anxiety, it is only because it has made me more acutely aware of the absence of others. We were saved, both our lives and our mission, by minotaurs from the island of Kiriti. I want to give them a seat at our table, too, along with the elves and the merfolk."

"That would be a big table," Eryk observed, dryly.

"Well, then, you are fortunate to have me," Dobyn replied, "for, I assure you, dwarven carpenters make the best tables."

As Eryk and Mona laughed softly, Hillian smiled at the humor in the dwarf's eyes and allowed himself to relax, if only somewhat.

As the light from the sun was nearly extinguished, Mona broke the silence. "Hillian," she said, twisting his gut with her informal address, "I want to compliment you on your handling of the dwarven king."

Glancing behind him, Hillian nervously voiced his appreciation. "Thank you, Mona."

"You are most welcome," she replied, her famous smile matching the beauty of the sunset. "Do you not agree, Master Rook?" she added.

"He did well," Eryk acknowledged, almost grudgingly, "though it was Dobyn's monologue that rings in my memory."

As the dwarf grunted a sound that may have been thanks, Hillian's fears were realized as he noticed the approach of horses from the south. "Master Rook, do you see those horses?" the nobleman asked.

Looking south toward the Akhdirian capital of Waiid, the rogue replied, "Yes, perhaps twelve of them."

"Do you think they will reach the woods before us?"

Squinting, Eryk estimated the speed at which the horses galloped, measured against the speed at which the four companions could travel on foot, and replied, "Yes, even if we run."

"Then we will face them here. We are outnumbered, so we would do well to have a plan."

In the few short moments leading up to the horsemen's arrival, Hillian's mind spun through the scenarios. The plan was simple, lacking the time for much else, but the Vingish lord was not entirely confident it would be effective.

As the horses pulled to a halt, Eryk immediately began to play his part, deftly taunting the lead pursuer upon recognition. "Why, Lord Drake, it is none other than your old friend, Dalil Jaser! Now, I heard a nasty rumor that you perished, Rami, burned at the stake in a delicious twist of irony."

Jaser's face, covered in burn scars, became red with rage, and his one eye squinted menacingly, the other hiding behind a dark patch of leather. As Jaser spoke, Hillian shuddered at the severity of damage the dalil must have suffered if even spell-enhanced medicines could not save the man's eye.

"The knights of Mbúso found me before I perished," the dalil said through gritted teeth.

"Yes, we are all thrilled to see that!" Eryk replied. "And look, Lord Drake, he has bought some friends." The master thief placed special emphasis on the word *bought*, clearly distinguishing it from *brought*, which may have been equally appropriate but not nearly as biting.

Sighing, Jaser spoke with an air of importance, tinged with hatred. "Mister Rook," he said, placing his own emphasis on *Mister*, which he intentionally used instead of the more respectful *Master*, "we—"

"Dalil Jaser," Eryk interrupted, smiling, "you, of all people, should know that I am a master of my trade, for I look around and see you surrounded by second-rate bottom-feeders, dredged from the muck of Trigoti's back alleys, while all the highly skilled rogues remain loyal to me."

"You miserable cur," the priest responded to the goading, enraged. "You, you maggot, you dung of maggots, I will bury your severed limbs in the muck of Trigoti!"

"My, what strong language from a holy man!" Mona contributed in a mocking tone as Eryk's lips curled in a smirk.

"Dalil, they are going to attack," warned the woman on the horse to Jaser's right.

"And I cannot read the small one," added the woman to his left, surprised concern written on her brow.

"There are only four of them, and they are holding a stretcher!" Jaser ranted in response. "If they think—"

Releasing his handle, Eryk moved with the swiftness only a master thief could possess, launching two throwing knives in one fluid motion. As the blades bore into the throats of the Mind Mages, Eryk was already flinging more blades at the archers who were hastening to notch their bows.

The spellcasted stretcher floated exactly where it had been left as Dobyn let go of his handle to roll two small balls into the grass at the horses' feet. Just as three Spell Mages began their incantations, the dwarf chanted his own quick spell:

Child's toy,
explode! Destroy!

The balls obeyed the dwarf's command, decimating the Spell Mages and several of the others nearby. Before the dust settled, Dobyn's battle-axe and Hillian's sword had finished the rest. As Eryk traveled from victim to victim, cutting throats, Hillian turned to find Rami Jaser pinned beneath the mangled corpse of a dead horse.

Hillian moved slowly, pointing the tip of his blade at Jaser's throat. He shook his head, but he could not find words. The dalil just closed his eyes, tightly, awaiting his death, but the blow did not come.

"Finish him," Eryk commanded, facing him from amid the carnage, blood dripping from his hands.

"I cannot," Hillian replied, sighing as he lowered his sword.

"Last time, we did not finish him," Eryk responded, "and he returned. When you fail to kill an enemy, he always returns."

Mustering all the lordly authority he could manage, Hillian looked the master rogue directly in the eye. "We are not going to murder him."

"Then he will return."

"So be it," Hillian accepted, firmly, wiping his blade upon his breeches before returning it to its sheath.

"These twelve are not returning," Dobyn observed, wiping his battle-ax on the grass.

Incredulous, Mona asked, "Twelve dead, and the three of you without a scratch?"

"Dobyn's bombs did most of the work," Hillian noted.

"Aye, but not before Master Rook eliminated the threat of a Mind Magic attack," Dobyn pointed out.

"But it was Hillian's plan that made it work," Eryk said, turning to the nobleman with his compliment. "Well done, my lord."

Hillian smiled with pride as Mona nudged him. "Well done, my lord," she teased with her incredible smile.

As he led them into the Forest of Ard Shaab, searching for a path, the Vingish nobleman considered the path he had already traveled. At the beginning of his journey, Hillian had been a hostage, forced to participate against his will. In a few short weeks, he had become a leader among leaders, directing a criminal mastermind, a head of state, and a clan chief over one hundred years old.

Soon, the forest itself began to consume the Vingish lord's thoughts. The grassy plains had been rich and teeming with life, but the forest was overwhelming. There were trees, of course, of several varieties, and they seemed to share the space peacefully, without competition or crowding. There was a myriad of beautiful flowers and interesting plants decorating the forest floor with spectacular colors and patterns.

Perhaps most surprising was the wildlife. Of course, there were small woodland creatures, scrambling around the trunks of trees and diving behind bushes.

Unexpectedly, however, Hillian found the forest floor to be filled with gazelle, deer, and antelope. The deer skittered away as the companions approached, but the other horned animals were unafraid, occasionally following them with curiosity, and Hillian was almost certain that one or two of them, in the distance, had borne riders.

The roof of the woods, in addition to its floor, was equally unexpected. The branches were filled with birds of all kinds, adding their plumage to the colorful tapestry of the forest while filling their guests' ears with the sweetest, most harmonic singing any of them had ever experienced. As the companions weaved around the trees, failing in their desperate attempts to find a path, they disturbed the environment, sending the birds into the air, with golden butterflies, delicate white moths, and rainbow dragonflies joining together in a carefully choreographed routine that took Hillian's breath away.

"This is said to be a *haunted* forest, is it not?" the nobleman asked, confounded.

"It is, yet I would not describe it as frightening," Mona responded, sharing his confusion.

"Humans believe the forest to be haunted only because the elves wish them to think so," Dobyn clarified.

"But men have gone mad from one night in Ard Shaab," Eryk noted, dubiously.

"Mind Magic, combined with superstition, has kept the elven secret for two hundred years," the dwarf explained.

They continued traveling through the woods, finally encountering the River Madin. Lacking any countering influence and surrendering to his natural inclination, Hillian led his companions along the riverbank, following it downstream, deeper and deeper into the forest.

Eventually, they reached the end of the riverbank and found themselves standing at the top of a rocky hill. The river snaked its way down the incline, rushing around the rocks in dangerous rapids that seethed and foamed, collectively furious at not being steep enough to be a waterfall. At the base of the rapids, the water grudgingly surrendered to the quiet calm of Tantahir Lake, which sparkled with an eerie luminescence as it stretched out in all directions.

Eryk whistled, noting that the lake was larger than the expanse of forest through which they had already traveled, and yet it was still surrounded by more of Ard Shaab's mysterious trees. From their vantage point atop the hill, Hillian could see that the far side of the lake funneled violently into the Iigra River, which rushed northward until its rapids were dissipated by the River Nina branching off toward the west.

"There," Dobyn said, pointing to the eastern shore of the lake. After straining his eyes, Hillian confirmed the presence of two figures, standing near the water.

*Welcome, humans, and please welcome your dwarf companion.*

Seeing the shared reaction in the faces around him, Dobyn understood. "What are they saying?" he asked.

"They welcome us," Hillian answered. Then, frowning, he asked, "Can you not hear them?"

"Dwarves are naturally resistant to Mind Magic," Dobyn replied with an irritation that seemed to imply this was common knowledge.

"Well, of course," Eryk inserted, sarcastically. "What *do* they teach in that university of yours?" he teased, smirking at his lord.

Hillian smiled, shaking his head. "Now we just have to find a way down this hill," he observed.

*You will find a reasonable path just inside the trees.*

"Thank you," Hillian responded aloud. He said to Dobyn, "Just inside the trees."

After venturing back into the woods, the companions did, indeed, find a more hospitable path down the slope. As they approached the foot of the hill, with the edge of the trees only steps ahead, Hillian found himself conflicted. Excitement coursed through him as he thought of meeting elves, the mysterious, ethereal, mythical creatures. It occurred to him, however, that he would very likely have felt the same if he had been given the opportunity to anticipate his introductions to minotaurs and dwarves.

Still, excitement was not his only emotion of anticipation. He had led his companions into imprisonment by the dwarves, nearly costing them their lives, yet he had managed to lead them out safely. That experience had instilled him with some amount of confidence, and he felt that a dwarven companion lent additional credibility to the story he would be delivering to the elves, but he could not avoid a sense of fear and trepidation.

"Fear not, Lord Drake." The voice was deep but exceptionally smooth. As the companions emerged from the trees, they could see it belonged to the tall, muscular male elf awaiting them at the water's edge. His skin was powder white, with a hint of evergreen fading in and out across his bare arms, legs, and face. His long hair, the complement of his skin in its deep green, peppered with white, was pulled back behind his pointed ears.

His emerald eyes locked with Hillian's as he said, "We have read your minds, and you have already been judged." He smiled, perhaps as a friendly gesture, but equally in response to Hillian's surprised expression. "We receive you as friends, not as enemies or prisoners, which is why you have not experienced the hauntings of Ard Shaab."

"So you have been secretly invading the privacy of our thoughts while we come to you for aid?" Eryk asked with an unexpected ferocity.

"Master Val Varen," the second elf began. The moment her voice touched his ears, Hillian's grip softened on the stretcher handle, and his muscles relaxed. Her voice was like honey, covering him in a film of sweet, golden paradise. He watched her lips move, soft lips with two perfect peaks and an amazingly symmetrical curvature, but he could not digest her words, distracted as he was by her exquisite features. Her skin sparkled like white diamonds, accented by shimmers of robin's-egg blue. Her eyes, a perfect match to her lavender lips, glittered like amethysts, exploding with spirit. Her hair, an even lighter shade than the eggshell blue, was sprinkled with white like soft clouds in a clear sky, framing her beautiful face with the perfect complement to her skin tone. She was different from anything he had ever seen, and she was breathtaking.

And then she was blushing.

"Master Val Varen," the male elf said, "your thoughts are like whispers, inevitably more audible when the feelings behind them are more..." He paused. "Impassioned."

Ashamed, Hillian wondered what thoughts his companion must have communicated to make his own thoughts comparatively irrelevant and unnoticeable. Glancing at Eryk, the Vingish lord smiled as he witnessed the master rogue staring at the ground in humiliation.

"My friends, I present to you Ora Fen," the male elf said, pausing to allow his female companion a short curtsy, "representing the elves of Dath'Duine. I am Warrick Heimdall, representative of the Ke'Andara nation and Lord of the Tantahir Portal Protectorate—"

"*Protectorate?*" Hillian interrupted.

"What sort of portal?" Mona asked simultaneously.

"Lord Drake, Dobyn of Tyr, Master Val Varen, and President Kesler," the elven lord continued, "as I said, we receive you as friends. The monarchs of our two nations wish to offer you assistance for your ailing friend and guidance for your journey. Come with us through the portal."

Hillian nodded, adding, "Lead the way."

Lord Heimdall nodded, and then he and the beautiful Ora Fen turned and walked toward the water. They continued walking, the surface of the lake rising to their waists, then their chests, then their necks, and then they were gone.

Hillian began to follow, but the stretcher did not budge. He looked at Dobyn first.

"I do not swim," the dwarf explained.

"It is a magical portal," Hillian responded. "It does not appear to require swimming or getting wet at all. Let us go halfway and then evaluate."

So, they did, and Hillian's assessment was correct. While they could feel the coldness of the water upon their hands, no moisture was left behind when they withdrew them. Eryk wished to see if they could breathe underwater, so he dropped down to his knees, ducking his head below the surface. Like the elves, he vanished.

"Apparently, submersion equals transportation," Mona observed.

"Right," Hillian added. He lifted Adia from the stretcher and held her in his arms. He adjusted her body until her head was even with his, then looked at his remaining companions.

"Dobyn—" he began but was interrupted by Eryk's head popping back up from the water.

"So, as soon as you are fully underwater, you get transported," he announced.

Mona smiled and winked at Hillian, but the amusement could not penetrate his trepidation. "Push the stretcher under," he ordered. Dobyn and Mona did so, and it vanished as expected. "Eryk, Dobyn, please go under, retrieve the stretcher, and wait for us."

When they were gone, Hillian looked at Mona, felt compelled to say something, but failed to find the words.

As the nobleman stood frozen and mute, the beautiful politician waded close to him, verbalizing her encouragement. "Do not underestimate yourself, Hillian." As she spoke his name, she placed her soft hand on his cheek. "Miss Adia is in good hands." Lightly stroking his face, she added, "We all are."

With a smile, Mona dove gracefully into the water, leaving Hillian alone with his scattered thoughts and the sleeping sorceress. Slowly, the Lord of Nydia turned and walked farther into the lake, carefully holding Adia's face against his own. When the water had reached their necks, he suddenly crouched, dropping them both below the surface.

He was relieved to find that he could, in fact, breathe underwater and that Adia was breathing easily as well. And while he felt a nauseating tug on his stomach, he attributed it to the fear and stress of an unfamiliar and unpredictable situation. After waiting for several minutes, his crouched legs began to ache, and he surrendered. Stretching his legs, he raised his head, and Adia's, out of the water.

Quickly, he realized the magic portal had functioned properly, without his knowledge. His three companions waited for him with the stretcher, farther inland due to Dobyn's limited stature. Behind them, on the grass beyond the muddy bank of the lake, stood their elven guides, Ora and Warrick, but they were surrounded by hundreds more. From a distance, the elves all looked very similar, but Hillian quickly realized they reflected the elven hosts, with pale, white skin bearing subtle hints of either green or blue, and matching green or blue hair. It seemed that both the nations of Dath'Duine and Ke'Andara had gathered to welcome the strange visitors.

After Hillian eased Adia's body back onto the stretcher, he took his place at the handle. As the four companions carried their friend closer to the shore, Dobyn pointed out that many of the elves held short bows with arrows notched. "They welcome us as friends, yet they are prepared to engage us in battle, if necessary," he declared in a low voice.

"It will not be necessary," Hillian responded, partially to reassure his dwarven companion but also to ease the fears of any elves that may be listening to the conversation with Mind Magic.

Without words, Warrick and Ora led the companions through the crowd, heading around the shore of the lake, which Hillian decided was certainly a pond, perhaps fed by a natural spring, for it was much smaller than the lake on the Ard Shaab side of the portal and there was no river on any side of it. Instead, it seemed to be surrounded by an enormous palace, with columns, balustrades, and ornate carvings. Statues leaned out from the windows, and ivy clung to the white stone surface, making intricate patterns all around the structure.

After a short walk, throughout which they were followed by a large portion of the crowd, they reached a massive, white stone staircase that led to the palace entrance. Inside, the richness and luxury bore a resemblance to the Royal Palace in Porvatis, but their guides walked swiftly, and Hillian had very little time to admire the décor. Soon they had arrived at the throne room.

"Your Majesties," Warrick Heimdall announced with a bow and a flourish, a stark contrast to the curt salute used in Tyr. "May I present to you our visitors from Crozada? Lying on the platform is Adia Varani, the Giftwitch who requires our assistance. Her companions are Hillian Drake, Lord of Nydia and representative of Vinglandon; Dobyn, Chief of Clan Varmingar and representative of Tyr; Mona Kesler, President of Severlandon; and Eryk Val Varen, Master Innkeeper, also known as Rook, Grand Master of the Carrion Crow Thieves Guild."

Hillian glanced at Eryk upon the mention of the latter's dual identities, but the rogue merely shrugged and quipped, "They read minds."

"Visitors, both human and dwarven, I present to you the monarchs of the elven nations. King Uli, ruler of the blue elves of Dath'Duine," Warrick announced. Uli's hair was long, pulled back in a knot quite like Warrick's, but the king's hair was dark blue, nearly black.

"And monarch of the green Andari elves," Warrick continued, motioning to the elegant female elf seated on the throne next to King Uli, "Safeda, Queen of Ke'Andara." Clearly much older than the monarch of Dath'Duine, Safeda's hair was far more white than green. When she spoke, however, she seemed entirely ageless.

"Welcome, humans. Welcome, dwarf," the queen announced in a pleasant tone. "I am truly honored to have you as guests in my home." She smiled and seemed completely genuine. "I wish to reassure you of your safety and of your freedom to leave whenever you wish, though I do hope you choose to remain with us for some time. We hope you will give our physicians and mages the opportunity to heal your companion of her mental wounds and allow her to rejoin you, and we all have a great many questions for her and for each of you. However," she paused, glancing at the king by her side, "I want to make it very clear that you are not required to entertain or answer our questions, and we have both pledged that we will not extract any information from you against your will. Instead, we wish to provide an open and willing exchange, as we understand you have many questions for us.

"To put you further at ease," she continued, "and to provide you a service we trust you will find valuable, Ora Fen, one of your guides through the portal, will serve as your trainer. She will teach you how to erect mental defenses, both passive and active, that will protect your mind from those who wish to use Mind Magic against you."

Suddenly, Dobyn jumped and gasped.

King Uli laughed.

"Did you…?" asked Queen Safeda, accusingly.

"I did not extract anything from his mind, Safeda. I heard him think the training would not be necessary for a dwarf, and I thought it my responsibility to advise him of his error." The queen frowned, to which Uli responded, "I merely sent a message and made sure he heard it."

Eryk smirked, chuckling. "It would appear that the dwarves' *natural resistance* is not so resistant after all."

"Perhaps from some," King Uli clarified, "but not from me, and not from Ixodis."

"You know of Ixodis?" Hillian asked quickly.

King Uli simply stared, his amused smile fading into a frown, but Queen Safeda answered for him.

"We do. In fact—"

"Queen Safeda," the king interrupted, without bothering to look at her. "We agreed we would not forcibly extract from these humans the information we desire, but we have most certainly *not* agreed to freely share our information with them. We have offered them quite enough."

Hillian had no interest in sparking an argument, so he interjected. "If I may…," he began but waited until the monarchs' eyes were on him. "Only days ago, we stood before King Loe, of the dwarven kingdom of Tyr, on the verge of losing our heads. And yet, we found common ground, a point at which our lives were worth more to him than our deaths."

Turning his attention to the Dathin monarch, Hillian continued, "There are no fools here, King Uli. We do not ask for your trust, and you can be sure you do not have ours. It is a simple matter of economics, of costs and benefits. We do not expect that you will share your information with us—or your hospitality, your physicians, your Mind Magic trainers—until and unless you believe the benefits outweigh the costs. We ask only that you allow us the opportunity to convince you."

The elven king smiled. "Thank you, Lord Drake," he said, "for your simple and logical perspective. I, personally, appreciate your approach, but I am afraid your description of benefit and cost has forced me to rethink our position on your Mind Magic training and the healing of your Giftwitch companion. I trust you will excuse us, as we will require some time for discussion."

"Your Majesty," Hillian replied, "if your discussion is expected to determine how much the elven nations are willing to give and what will be required from the five of us in return, I do not know how you could have that discussion without our involvement."

Angrily leaning forward in his throne, the blue elven monarch retorted, "I am King of Dath'Duine, and I do not tolerate such impertinence, not from my Dathin elves, not from the Andari elves, and certainly not from a *human*!"

"King Uli," Queen Safeda said, her voice stern but still relatively pleasant, "we agreed to have an open exchange."

"No, Safeda, *you* decided that, but I never agreed!"

"Or disagreed," the queen reminded him.

"You are the only ones who can help her!" Mona suddenly blurted. "What leverage could we possibly have?"

"She is right, of course," Hillian agreed, nodding at his Severlandi companion. Turning back to King Uli, he suggested, "Open discussion, use your leverage, and if the results are still unfavorable to the elven nations—"

"Then we ask you to leave," Safeda finished, nodding.

Hillian just stared at Uli. "Or you could always just kill us."

Maybe it was the way he said it, or maybe it was how he had locked eyes with the Dathin king, but something about Hillian's comment prevented anyone else from speaking, so the words hung in the air, waiting.

Still staring at the human, King Uli finally responded. "Very well," he said, "but I want everyone else out.

The two of us, the four of you, and the Giftwitch in the hospital under heavy sedation."

"No sedation, no separation. The five of us, the two of you, and as many others as you wish."

"Sedation but no separation, and the dwarf must be unarmed."

"She is already unconscious. If you insist on sedating her when her health is already in question, I am certain the four of us will be far too distracted with worry to be of any value to you whatsoever."

King Uli had no response. Finally, it was Queen Safeda who spoke.

"Lord Drake, just as the act of sedating her would cause you to be distracted, the failure to sedate her would cause King Uli to be distracted. We must find a suitable alternative to address both concerns."

"Then read my mind."

There was shock from both sides, but Hillian was undeterred.

"The truth is that you could do it without my permission. And if we threaten your nations, you *will* do it, despite your commitments to the contrary. This whole negotiation, the economics of benefit and cost, all this can be resolved in mere moments if you just read my mind."

After a moment, in which it seemed the monarchs were discussing Hillian's proposal mentally with one another, Queen Safeda nodded.

"Very well, Lord Drake. We will be entering in tandem, so you may wish to brace yourself."

## Chapter 12

# CALLING

"Good morning!" Eryk shouted, clapping his hands eagerly. "Did you hear the news? Miss Adia has awakened!"

Groaning, Hillian covered his head with a pillow. "I was there, you imbecile," he grumbled, through the feathers and fabric.

"Oh, yes, of course, a thousand pardons, my lord!" Eryk responded in an extremely loud, exaggerated mock apology. "Was last evening's celebration too much for my lord? Did that elven wine give my lord a headache?"

Hillian just groaned again.

"Interesting. And would you say this headache is worse than the one you were left with after the elven monarchs invaded your mind four, or was it five, days ago?"

Groaning once again, Hillian said, "No, that was worse."

"Well, then this is *not* the worse headache you have ever had!" Eryk clapped again as he shouted, "Outstanding news!"

"I hate you."

"Do you?"

"Yes," Hillian responded, casting off the pillow and rising to one elbow, "you and your insane wine tolerance."

"Innkeepers drink a lot."

Hillian nodded, frowning, and rose from the bed as an awkward silence fell between the two men. Hillian shuffled toward the basin with his fingertips pressing on his temples. After washing and dressing, he joined Eryk at the window.

For several moments, they stood gazing at the throngs of elves moving about in the forest and village below. Finally, Hillian sighed.

Eryk raised his eyebrows in question.

"At the risk of whining even more," the Vingish lord began, still rubbing his temples, "it just does not seem fair."

"What, the wine tolerance of an innkeeper, or two entire nations of elves packed into one small forest?"

"All of that, and more. Your wine tolerance is truly unfair, but at least that has been true ever since I've known you, so I have come to accept it. However, your duality as both innkeeper and master criminal...that is new information and has been difficult enough for me to digest by itself, but it is even more unfair when contrasted with your noble and selfless rescue activities, which leads us to the third item, which, as you said, involves the larger nation of Dathin elves being exiled from its home on Crozada and forced to share this small space with the Andari nation on the continent of Otica."

Perhaps wishing to guide the conversation to the least awkward topic, Eryk asked, "Were you aware, with your university education, that Otica even existed...that Crozada was not the only continent on Keb?"

"No, in fact, the vaunted educators of the University of Porvatis somehow omitted that information from the curriculum," Hillian responded in frustration. "Although, based on the conversation last evening, it is apparently common knowledge in Tyr."

Eyes squinting, Eryk suggested, "You told me all the libraries of Crozada were destroyed in the Great War. If we can assume the dwarven libraries did not escape this destruction, then we must assume that much of the Tyrian knowledge of history is passed down by word of mouth. The dwarves are aware of Otica and of other races, yet the humans are aware of neither."

Hillian shook his head. "Pathetic."

Eryk's head shook as well, as he corrected his lord. "No, not pathetic," he insisted. "Intentional."

"Intentional? Are you suggesting that there is some worldwide conspiracy—"

"Continent-wide," Eryk interjected.

"Fine, yes, so there is a continent-wide conspiracy to prevent the human population of Crozada from learning about the existence of other races or other continents?"

"We already know there is a conspiracy to prevent the human population of Crozada from learning that Gift Magic talents are no more evil than musical or athletic talents."

"That is not a conspiracy. That is one man."

"If it is only Ixodis, then explain to me why Jalidinity and Sabarism, rival religions, believe in the exact same Angel of Mercy. Are you suggesting Ixodis is in control of the world religions?"

Hillian sighed. "My father is in control of Jalidinity, and I'm fairly certain he is not being influenced by an evil Gift Mage."

Staring through the glass, Eryk posed a question. "Are you familiar with the history of Vinglandon's invasion of Grolandon?"

"I believe my father referred to it as *settling*, rather than *invasion*, but yes, I am familiar."

"Did your father tell you how the knights of Vinglandon executed the mystics of the ancient One Spirit religion as well as anyone who dared speak out against the Almighty Jalidus?"

Frowning, Hillian answered honestly, "He did not, but I did learn of that at university. The knights are said to have tolerated the killings, but the Jalidin monks in the Order of the Dawn are said to have carried them out."

"Your position on Giftwitch burnings, the reason you condone it, is based upon the idea of religious freedom, correct?" When the nobleman nodded, Eryk continued, "So was it evil for Vingish knights and Jalidin monks to murder hundreds in Grolandon for the express purpose of *eliminating* their religious freedom?"

"Yes, which is why the King of Vinglandon facilitated the unification and, subsequently, the independence, of Grolandon."

"But the mystics were already dead, and the One Spirit faith with them, so the unified nation of Grolandon was established as a Jalidin state with no religious freedom at all, much like Vinglandon."

"Well, yes, but…"

"So, by eliminating the mystics, an act you have already acknowledged as evil, the influence of Jalidinity was greatly expanded."

Hillian was unable to respond.

"Could it be that the elimination of the Gifted is both similarly evil and similarly necessary for the continuation of Jalidin power? Is it possible your father may have justified it as such?"

Straining against Eryk's logic, Hillian relied upon the comfort of doctrine. "Perhaps if he were merely a man, but as the prime cardinal, my father is the living instrument of Jalidus."

"As was the prime cardinal who directed the Order of the Dawn to murder the Grolandi mystics, an act you agreed was evil. Does that suggest Jalidus is capable of mistakes?"

"Certainly not!" Hillian cried in outrage.

"Well, then, the only alternative is that his living instruments are capable of misinterpreting his guidance. Is that what you are suggesting?"

Hillian was silent, searching his mind and heart for answers. After many moments, during which he watched his companion fight the urge to smirk triumphantly, the nobleman finally relented. "Until now, it was very clear in my mind that my father, as the anointed high priest of Jalidus, spoke and acted with heavenly guidance. But during this journey, I have concluded that Adia Varani, the only Giftwitch I have ever personally encountered, is not, in fact, an evil demon."

"Praise Jalidus!" Eryk exclaimed, his sarcasm doing little to hide his genuine excitement.

Undeterred, Hillian proceeded. "Yes, and I have also discovered that both my father and my university have failed to educate me about the existence of nonhuman races or of another continent." Hillian shook his head and raised his hands in a sign of defeat. "Truthfully, I do not know. I feel that Jalidus came to our aid in Grolandon and helped me to drive away Ixodis…"

Eryk scoffed and rolled his eyes. "You are contradicting yourself. If the Gifted are not demons, then why would Jalidus get involved?"

"Well, maybe because *Ixodis* is evil, Eryk. Not Gifted evil, or demon evil, but just human evil."

"There is no good and evil, Hillian. That is a myth, artificially manufactured by religions to control the masses and support their own agendas."

"And here, again, is the contrast. The atheist thief with no moral compass—"

"Oh, very nice. Now we see it all coming out."

Hillian continued as though Eryk hadn't spoken, "No regard for the law and no sensitivity to the abstract concepts of right and wrong."

"Says the noble lord who is aiding and abetting international fugitives."

"No, I will *not* permit you to turn this around on me. This is about you and your mixed-up, twisted, criminal messiah complex that makes no sense at all!"

Eryk's neck tightened, but his voice was controlled, even quiet. "Do you know what a criminal is?" he asked. "I am a criminal because I fought back against a broken society. The Vingish model of royals, nobles, and peasants, with all its injustices…that was broken, Hillian, and you felt it just as much as I did. And we both fought back against it."

"Please do not expect me to believe you started stealing and killing to fight back against a broken society."

"Why not? That is precisely the reason anyone steals or kills. If society is designed to leave you shivering in the cold and starving, you are forced to make a choice.

You can accept your fate and let society put you to death, or you can fight back and take what society should have given you to begin with."

Hillian's eyes narrowed as he said, "And once you gathered enough money and enough power to escape the death sentence society had assigned to you, why not stop fighting?"

"I did. I left the thieves guild, moved away from my home of Trigoti, and created a new life in Porvatis. I bought an inn and made myself into an honest tradesman."

"An honest tradesman," Hillian repeated, raising his eyebrows in suspicion.

"Yes, for a time. But my guests, my employees, and my neighbors...they were all still suffering from society's injustices. But I...well, I knew how to beat the death sentence. I knew how to fight back and win, and I wanted to show them."

"So you took more honest folk and turned them into criminals?"

Eryk sighed. "Perhaps. I hate the way you use that word, but yes, essentially, you're right. Most of them were already breaking one law or another, though ineffectively, but I organized them, and it saved their lives. I built a new society, where people did not have to quietly slip away into the dark night of death."

"But when you started working with me," Hillian said, "we were changing society the right way, improving circumstances for women, prisoners, commoners, and immigrants through the right channels, in accordance with the law."

"Well, after a man has a palace-class inn in every major city in the world, he earns the right to mix with nobles and change society the right way. But if I only had one small tavern-class property on the low end of Porvatis, would you have been interested in my input?"

Hillian frowned.

"No, of course not," Eryk answered for him. "The right way was not available to me in the early days, but I had my own way. And then, as I built it up and expanded, it came to the point where I could offer a better life to people without involving them in the compromises. I could pay my staff enough to give them a life they could not have dreamed of, and I could pay my barkeeps enough to earn their loyalty and honesty. My way, the only way I had, began to grow away from the thievery and more toward the honest work."

"So the wrong way, the less-than-legal way—is that over now?"

Sighing again, Eryk shook his head. "No. Thank you for not saying *criminal*, but no, the less-than-legal side stopped for a time, but then something happened. Perhaps it was my ego, my 'messiah complex,' as you say, or perhaps it was a sense of vengeance, of ultimate victory over the society that had tried to break me."

Hillian was confused, but Eryk, staring out into the woods of Ke'Andara, rolled on. "A nobleman had died, with no heir, leaving a western duchy of Vinglandon without a lord. There were two nobles with equal claim to the land, and the king was forced to select between them. The younger of the two had married a commoner, so his status was tarnished, and it became clear the king was going to select the other. So, I had the older one assassinated."

Hillian was shocked, without words.

"The king had no choice then and awarded the land and the title to the younger noble, despite his marriage to a commoner. Very quickly, the new lord made his duchy a better place for commoners, which is exactly what I had hoped."

"So you committed murder but for the greater good of society."

"Yes, and it worked. I tried it again, in one of the smaller city-states of Grolandon, and it worked again. I used my network of spies and burglars to collect information about political appointments, heirs, and elections all over the world, and I slowly began to guide the outcomes—"

"Through assassination."

"And election tampering, blackmail, various methods. For example, in Severlandon, during their border disputes with Akhdiria, I arranged for a presidential candidate to fall out of favor by spreading rumors that he was particularly fond of Akhdirian whores, resulting in the election of the first female head of state in history."

"*You* are responsible for Mona Kesler's election as President of Severlandon?" Hillian asked, not entirely certain whether to be disgusted or impressed.

"And the world is better for it, as I trust you would agree."

Hillian was silent, thoughtful, before finally observing, "Now I understand why you jump to conclusions involving worldwide conspiracies."

"Perhaps I am jumping to conclusions, but consider the fact that Kila Maháli, the one religion on this continent that does *not* consider Gift Magic evil, exists in a nation where religion is as illegal as Gift Magic. So, everyone is covered: the religious, the atheists, and the pacifists."

"If there is a conspiracy against the Gifted," Hillian allowed, "one must assume Ixodis is involved."

"I agree. And if there is a conspiracy against the non-human races, seemingly having originated at the same time as the conspiracy against the Gifted…"

"You believe the two are related."

"I do."

"And that Ixodis is involved in both."

"Indeed."

Hillian paused to contemplate. While the journey had truly been thrust upon him, he had accepted that a quest for truth was a worthy endeavor, one of which Jalidus himself would approve. Initially, however, the truth he sought involved only the nature of the Gifted, but the path was twisted, winding in and out of mountains and magical forests, leading to an entirely new question of truth.

"What happened in that war?" he asked aloud.

"Only one of us would know," Eryk replied.

"The dwarf," Hillian realized. "Of course."

"He was there," Eryk reminded.

Without another word, Hillian turned from the window and strode from the room. When they arrived at the elven hospital, a luxurious place of healing and recuperation that bore very little resemblance to the functional minimalism of the infirmary in Tyr, they heard laughter in Adia's room.

Hillian smiled as he and Eryk entered, the cheerfulness of the room infecting him. The elves had hosted quite a celebration the previous evening after Adia Varani had finally awakened, and while the abundance of wine had affected the Vingish lord in a somewhat negative way, the general mood among his companions was extremely positive.

*Greetings, Hillian!* the Gift Mage exclaimed in his mind, using the nobleman's given name.

"Why use Mind Magic when I am standing right here?" he inquired, audibly, to her inaudible greeting.

"Ora says I need to practice," she replied. "She has been a very patient teacher."

The female elf greeted the men as she rose from her chair next to Adia's bed. "Lord Drake, Master Val Varen."

"Hello, Ora," Hillian replied. Eryk, however, was unable to respond, smiling awkwardly at the Dathin Mind Mage.

Suppressing a smile at Eryk's discomfort, Hillian fought against his own nerves as he was greeted by his Severlandi companion. "Good morning, Hillian," the beautiful president said, her radiant smile eclipsing the elven beauty beside her. Like Adia, Mona had begun using his given name more often, but it had an entirely different effect when spoken by Mona's lips, and Hillian's stomach twisted in anxious confusion.

Just before the silence became awkward, Dobyn offered his own greeting. "Hillian, Eryk," he said, quietly reminding them of his presence.

Jolted from his trance, even forgetting to return Mona's greeting, Hillian turned his attention to the dwarf. "Dobyn," he began, "we need a moment of your time. Would you walk with us?"

"Lord Drake," Ora interjected before the dwarf could reply, "I caution you to guard your thoughts."

"I beg your pardon?"

"I apologize, but the line of questions you wish to pursue is not a safe topic in this environment."

Eryk frowned. "You read our thoughts?" the rogue accused.

"I am afraid they were strong enough to hear without any effort," Ora replied, "and it is likely that others have heard them as well."

"What is dangerous about our thoughts?" Hillian asked.

"I apologize, Lord Drake, but I am not comfortable discussing it," she admitted.

"Ora," Adia said, "could you create a bubble of protection, as you have been teaching me...but large enough to include all of us?"

The elf frowned, her expression clearly demonstrating her fear. "Of course," she answered, "but if I maintain it longer than would be expected for a Mind Magic training session..."

"Then what?" Adia pushed.

"There are some who would become suspicious."

"Then let us be brief," Adia said. "Are we protected?"

"Yes."

"Hillian?"

Nodding, the nobleman turned to his dwarven companion. "Dobyn, I apologize if this is asking more than you wish to disclose, but it is imperative that we understand the role of Ixodis in the Purge that King Loe mentioned."

"Quickly, Dobyn," Mona urged.

Shaking his head, the dwarf made his decision. "Very well. If I am to contribute to your success, perhaps you need to know the full truth. Ixodis was one of several Giftwitches who led a human army to wage war against Dath'Duine. He offered to betray them on the condition that all magic disappeared from Keb."

"What?" Adia exclaimed, alarmed and confused.

"Ixodis would betray his brethren and put an end to the bloodshed, but only if all traces of magic were eradicated."

Hillian reeled. Eryk's theory had been substantiated, but the conspiracy was proving to be far more offensive than he had expected.

"Ixodis, himself, would take responsibility for destroying all current and future Giftwitches, but all magical races would be required to hide from human eyes, forever."

The words hung in the silence that followed, like smoke on the humid air of Trigoti Bay.

"How could that possibly be successful?" Mona asked.

"King Loe expressed the same doubt and was convinced that it would last only long enough to eliminate the threat, but he was wrong. We all were." The dwarf looked at Ora, including her in his reference.

Nodding, the elf agreed. "Queen Safeda felt the same, as I understand it, as did King Uli the First. But Ixodis had found a way to mix the forbidden spells of necromancy with Gift Magic, absorbing the power of his victims, making him practically omnipotent. King Uli's attempt to confront him resulted in thousands of deaths among the Dathin elves, including the king—"

"Leaving his son, the current King Uli, as monarch of a broken and frightened nation," Hillian concluded, "which explains his reluctance to assist us."

As both elf and dwarf nodded, Eryk explored a different topic. "What of the other races? Did the minotaurs, fairies, and merpeople agree to this bargain?"

"Most of the fairies fled, but the minotaurs are not a naturally magical race, so they thought themselves exempt, and the merfolk simply could not be troubled," Dobyn replied, somberly shaking his head. "Ixodis hunted them all until there were few remaining."

"Further convincing the elves and dwarves to remain silent," Mona surmised.

Again, the dwarf and elf merely nodded, words clearly unnecessary.

Perhaps the weight of the moment distracted him, or perhaps his survival instincts overrode his anxiety. In any case, Eryk looked directly at Ora and spoke to her directly. "But, Ora, you are Dathin, are you not? A subject of King Uli? Why do you not share his reluctance to aid us?"

Glancing briefly at the floor, Ora raised her beautiful lavender eyes to the master rogue. "Master Val Varen, the war took place two hundred years ago, and I am yet six years shy of one hundred. I have lived my entire life in Ke'Andara or in the forest colony, both of which are mixed. So, while I may be Dathin, I am a subject of Queen Safeda as much as King Uli." After glancing away shyly, she added, "And it appears I am more aligned with my queen, and with you, than with my king."

"So are we in danger here?" Mona asked. "Does King Uli consider us a threat?"

The Dathin female's eyes widened. "Yes," she answered, simply. "As soon as I release the protective shield, King Uli will read your minds, and I am fairly certain he will seek to eliminate the threat you pose to his nation's safety."

"And then he will eliminate you," Eryk noted.

The look she gave him was filled with both acknowledgment and fear.

"Come with us," Hillian suggested. When Ora's expression shifted to excitement tinged with indecision, the nobleman pressed further. "Queen Safeda wishes us to succeed. That much is clear, for why else would she exert her influence on King Uli to heal a Gift Mage?" As the elf's indecision began to waver, Hillian delivered his final pitch. "Just as Dobyn represents the dwarven nation, you can represent both elven nations in helping to ensure our success."

He had her. She nodded, faintly, but that was enough. Switching his attention to Adia, he asked, "Can you travel?" She, too, nodded, and the nobleman shifted to his friend, who he was slowly beginning to trust once more. "Eryk, we need an exit."

They moved quickly but, exposed in the full daylight, were easily followed. Eryk quietly dispatched the two Dathin elves that trailed them from the hospital, attracting no attention, but it did not take long for surprised gazes to become nervous whispers. Hillian began to see a pattern form, hazy like a picture in the clouds, but clear enough, nonetheless. The youth of both nations watched with indifference, and even subtle approval, while the older elves were far more delineated by ethnic cultural identity. The elder green elves of Ke'Andara simply turned away, as if seeing nothing of consequence, while the older blue elves of Dath'Duine felt compelled to interfere. After the fifth Dathin elder lay dead in their wake, Hillian requested a change in tactics.

"Eryk," he implored, as they rushed along the winding path through the trees, "we are attempting an escape, not a war."

"Of course," the master rogue replied, sarcasm dripping like the sweat that fell from his face, "when they raise their bows and loose their arrows, we could simply dance around them."

"Adia, are you strong enough to erect a defensive shield?" Hillian asked.

"I am so sorry, Hillian," the sorceress replied, her face pained in guilt. "I should have done so already." Suddenly, a dome of glowing translucence surrounded the small party, traveling with them as they hurried toward the portal.

Hillian shot a meaningful glance at Eryk, who simply shrugged. "I stand corrected," he conceded.

"Ora, could you do the same with Mind Magic?" Mona suggested, inspired by the hovering shield.

"My protection has been in force since it was requested of me in the hospital," the Dathin elf replied.

Then, smiling shyly, she added, "Though it is not quite so splendid!"

"It more than serves," Eryk mumbled, glancing only momentarily at the elven beauty before joining Hillian in continuing the march.

As they drew nearer to the portal, the attacking Dathins multiplied, but their arrows had no effect. At the edge of the water, however, they were met by one Andari elf surrounded by a substantial host of Dathin warriors. All of them, perhaps warned by Mind Magic, brandished swords rather than bows.

Signaling his companions to halt, Hillian assessed the situation, staring for several moments at Lord Warrick Heimdall, the green elf leader. Ignoring protocol and custom, he failed to even address the elf by name, instead stating the fact he felt was most relevant. "You realize," he began, "that we have a Gift Mage among us who could kill all of you with merely a gesture."

"Indeed," replied the elven leader, "but she would be required to drop her shield to do so, and my archers and Mind Mages would be free to end this."

"This is nothing, Hillian. I can shield us while also attacking," the Gift Mage said.

The Vingish nobleman considered for but a moment before shaking his head. "No, you are not yet fully recovered, and I want no more casualties. Let us simply continue walking. If we do not engage, we cannot be stopped."

As they resumed their forward motion, slowly and deliberately moving toward the water's edge, the Andari elf uttered a war cry in the ancient elven tongue, rushing the glowing dome with sword raised, followed by many of his warriors. The attack suffered dramatic ineffectiveness, but Ora was clearly affected.

"Why, Warrick?" she asked, pain apparent in her voice. "You are Andari, not Dathin! Why do you oppose us?"

Warrick Heimdall glared at the Dathin female. "*Us?*" he seethed. "You are Dathin, Ora, so how can you join with a Giftwitch? You know the history…what you are doing is both treason and insanity!"

"Oh, Warrick, you are blinded by history and clinging to the insanity of the past!"

"I am clinging to my duty! I am Lord of the Tantahir Portal Protectorate, entrusted to protect the security of *both* nations."

"I, too, am of both nations," Ora replied calmly, "and I see the difference between *security* and *imprisonment.*"

Her comment induced a surprising effect. Unable to reply, Warrick lowered his sword and was slowly followed by his Dathin warriors. As Hillian and his companions continued forward, the elves parted, abandoning their fruitless attempt to interfere.

When they emerged on the Crozada side of the portal, on the eastern edge of Tantahir Lake, Dobyn was the first to speak. "Where are we going?" he asked.

Hillian immediately fixed his attention on the President of Severlandon. "Mona, would we have protection in Severlandon?"

She smiled. "My Lord Drake," she said, her use of the possessive inspiring a sly smirk and raised eyebrow from Eryk, "surely you know you needn't even ask."

"And yet I must."

"You shall all be protected in Severlandon," the Severlandi beauty replied, smiling as she transfixed the nobleman with her stunning blue eyes.

"Well, then," Eryk said after several moments, "to get to Severlandon, we'll have to cross the lake."

"Or the river," Ora suggested. "A rope bridge hangs at the narrowest point, just after the branch to the River Nina, perhaps three hours downriver."

With a great deal of effort, Hillian forced his eyes away from Mona's bright blues, reluctantly returning to the business of the moment. "Very good, but let us stay close together so that we all remain protected by both Mind Magic and Gift Magic."

As Ora led them around the edge of the sparkling Tantahir oval, Hillian was struck by the beauty of the water rushing out of the large body of water, combining and collaborating to transform from the stillness of a lake to the powerful current of a river. The light danced along the ripples, glinting and sparkling, much like Mona's eyes.

Hillian's trance did not go unnoticed. "What thoughts are so distracting to you, my Lord Drake?"

Eryk teased the nobleman, repeating Mona's possessive reference.

The Lord of Nydia glanced at Mona, then glanced quickly away in embarrassment. "I was thinking about your conspiracy theory, which is now confirmed," he lied.

Smirking, Eryk gracefully accepted the half-truth, allowing his lord to redirect the conversation. "The total eradication of magic, but for the sake of humankind," Eryk tasted the words as they left his lips. "It is not completely unthinkable."

"Much like assassinating a nobleman for the sake of Vinglandon," Hillian added, drawing curious looks from Dobyn and Mona.

"Perhaps, though the nobleman being assassinated was a vile disgrace to humanity, whereas the Gifted infants being massacred are innocents with no history of wrongdoing."

"Neither are particularly palatable to me," Hillian clarified. "But apparently more than palatable to King Uli."

Shaking his head, Eryk sighed. "Patriotism and religion are the two greatest barriers to reason."

It was a strange and entirely foreign feeling, but Hillian found himself agreeing with the master rogue's sentiments. Chuckling at himself, the nobleman admitted, "Perhaps you were right when you characterized faith as an affliction, and perhaps it applies to patriotism as much as religion."

Eryk stopped walking, the suddenness of which caused Dobyn to stumble into him from behind. Apologizing to the dwarf and quickly resuming his forward progress, Eryk marveled at Hillian's growth. "That is a profound statement, my lord, and a significant departure from the position you passionately defended in Burúji, only a handful of weeks ago."

Nodding, the nobleman agreed. "It appears that those weeks have exposed me to the antidote of truth," the nobleman replied, "but we are now pursued by an entire nation of elves who remain afflicted."

"We will succeed, regardless of their affliction," Eryk insisted.

"Perhaps, but what will they do when we succeed? Will they support us?" Turning suddenly to Dobyn, Hillian asked, "Will King Loe?"

Confused by the vagueness of the question, the dwarf requested clarification. "What, exactly, would you be asking him to support?"

"The changes, Dobyn!" Hillian responded, his exuberant thoughts outstripping his words. "We will need dramatic changes to create a world in which all nations and peoples can live together in peace."

"*All* peoples?" Adia asked from her position at the back of the line. "Even the Gifted?"

Hillian stopped and turned to the sorceress. "Yes," he said, his voice a ponderous mixture of triumph and surrender, "even the Gifted."

She stared at him, but just as Hillian began to wonder about her response, she launched at him, toppling the nobleman into the mud in an unreserved embrace of joy and relief.

As his companions enjoyed a moment of mirth, Hillian pondered the journey Jalidus had set before him. On the Cliffs of Kuúma, he had accepted his moral responsibility to seek the truth about the Gifted and, on the road to Domus Viho, he'd found it. Adia was not evil, which meant the Gifted were not demons but simply humans born with magical talents, choosing their paths just as all humans were forced to do.

Then, when she was injured and helpless, Hillian had accepted the responsibility to lead his companions to safety but, imprisoned by the dwarven king, he had learned of the Purge. Faced with a possible conspiracy of widespread murder and persecution, the devout Jalidin was forced to consider that his responsibility had changed. Among the elves in Ke'Andara, Hillian had received more clarity with the confirmation that Ixodis was the true villain and, on the bank of the Iigra River, deep in the Forest of Ard Shaab, Hillian had finally found his purpose. He would lead his friends and allies in stopping Ixodis and repairing the damage the sorcerer had wrought.

His contemplation was pierced by Eryk's urgent cry. "No!" the master thief shouted, pain bleeding from his voice, but then Adia screamed, collapsing upon Hillian, clutching her head. Ora's scream, a splash, and a sharp pain in Hillian's leg were followed by Dobyn exclaiming, "I don't swim!" Pain mixed with confusion, Hillian searched for meaning, finding the sky filled with arrows, just as Mona tumbled past him, carrying a protesting dwarf into the river. Praying for strength, Hillian gripped Adia's trembling body and rolled into the water, kicking off into the current. As he screamed at the pain in his leg, the cold water filled his mouth, and then his lungs.

## Chapter 13

# GUILT

It was the pain that woke him, or perhaps the cold. Both, he realized, for the shivering served to aggravate the poorly dressed wound on his leg, and the infection caused a fever that resulted in the shivering. Hillian smiled, appreciating the symmetry of his troubles, and forced himself to rise from a bed of wet leaves that had failed, quite miserably, to shield him from the night.

Struggling to his knees, he raised his eyes to heaven. "Lord Jalidus, God of Mercy, I pray to you," Hillian mumbled, his lips swollen and blue. "Please, Lord, forgive me for my weakness and grant me the strength to atone for my sins and failures." His head dropped, as his face cracked in agony. "And Lord," he begged, his bloodshot eyes filling with tears, "please grant strength to Mona and Eryk, to Adia—please, Lord, let her be alive—and to

Ora and Dobyn. Guide them to safety, Lord, and guide me to them."

Finding his crude staff, Hillian hauled himself to his feet, resolute to ignore his pain, his hunger, and his guilt. One impossible step after another, he marched for hours. He knew his Mind Magic defenses, as insufficient as they had been to begin with, given what little training he had managed to receive from Ora, had faded along with the strength of his body. Were he found and attacked, either physically or mentally, he would be lost.

"No," he said to himself, his voice low and husky with fever and fatigue, "think not on such things. They have not found you, not yet," he encouraged himself, "and you are protected by the strength of God." That might actually be true, he thought, if his intentions were, in fact, worthy of support from the Almighty.

Shaking his head, he attempted to dispel his doubts once more. "Stop it," he commanded, mustering what traces remained of his lordly voice. "Ixodis is evil, or at the very least misguided, turning his God-given Gifts into weapons of the devil. Jalidus has guided me to these people and these circumstances, because it is his will that I stop this abomination and protect his children."

As if in answer, the light of the sun broke over the horizon, casting a beautiful pink and purple glow to the sky, magically reflected by the sparkling river such that the world seemed warmer, gentler, and more welcoming.

Hillian eagerly accepted the response to his prayer, rare as it was, and quietly thanked his god.

As he turned in a circle, however, marveling at how the dawn illuminated the forest, the nobleman spied the shapes approaching from the south and was forced to accept the painful truth that heavenly gifts are customarily intertwined with trials for the faithful. Hillian did his best to strengthen his Mind Magic defenses as he scurried into the brush, swinging his staff behind him in a halfhearted attempt to obscure his passage through the leaves. Perhaps he was not trying. Perhaps he did not truly wish to escape, for he suspected King Uli's soldiers would capture him rather than murder him where he lay, and there was a strong attraction to the food and medicine that would likely accompany his imprisonment. Still, his faith insisted that his material needs were insignificant when compared to the holy quest to which he had been assigned, so he once again closed his eyes and prayed for strength.

"Pathetic." The voice was familiar, but it was the scoff that crystallized Hillian's recognition.

"He has other qualities, Eryk," Mona defended, as the nobleman's spirits soared.

Hillian laughed. "Thank you, Lord!" he whispered, his body relaxing for the first time in days.

"What, now I'm *your* lord?" Eryk replied. "What sort of mushrooms have you been eating?"

"No," Hillian responded, "I was thanking Jalidus."

"Oh, of course, by all means, thank him. I was the one who insisted we come back for you—"

"That is *not* true!" Mona disagreed.

"And I was the one who found you, though with your paltry skills, Mona probably could have tracked you by herself. She certainly wouldn't have needed heavenly assistance; that much is certain!"

"Say what you will, Eryk. I asked Jalidus to guide me to you, and here you are!"

"Well, you didn't find us, actually. *We* found *you*, so it seems you have it wrong, once again."

"Would it be so bad to have a god on our side?" Mona asked playfully.

"No, indeed—it would be a *blessing*," Eryk retorted, stressing the word with a healthy dose of sarcasm as he reached to help his lord out of the leaves and bushes. "You look horrible," he noted, once Hillian stood upright.

"He looks wonderful," Mona declared, placing her hands on the sides of Hillian's face. She paused, long enough for him to see the wetness around the rims of her magical eyes. When she kissed him, he did not respond. He was frozen, stunned by the dramatic swing of emotion and circumstance, such that he remained motionless when she withdrew, smiling gently.

"I pulled you out of the river, and all I got was a thank-you," Eryk joked, "and here he is, cowering in the dirt, and he gets a kiss?"

"Life's not fair, is it?" Mona replied, patting Eryk's shoulder. Taking Hillian's hand, she began walking downriver. "Come, my Lord Drake, let us be off."

Hillian followed, obediently, only vaguely aware of the staff Eryk placed in his hand. After several labored steps, Hillian finally found his voice.

"Have you seen the others?" he asked.

"We have taken rooms in the village, just a short walk from the forest," Mona replied. "Dobyn is there, tending to Ora."

"Ora was apparently the key target in the elven attack," Eryk added.

"Logical," Hillian noted.

"Of course, but she took an arrow in the back before I got her into the river. She was near dead by the time I found Mona and the dwarf."

Hillian nodded, processing the information, before asking, "And what of Adia?"

Eryk sighed. "I saw her, but I was unable to catch her," he explained. "She had surrounded herself in an energy shield, which served as a vessel of sorts, making her float on the surface of the water. She passed by too quickly." Glancing at his lord, the master rogue added, "I am sorry, Hillian."

"We will find her," Mona insisted, squeezing Hillian's hand, but her optimism felt hollow to the Vingish lord. He frowned, the pain in his leg amplified by the guilt in his heart. Adia had been in his arms, and he had lost her. If she was gone, the responsibility was his alone.

When the three companions finally emerged from the Forest of Ard Shaab, Hillian's spirits rose as he beheld the vast expanse of the Kaoric Ocean. The light of the sun reflected off the waves, bringing hope to the shores of Severlandon. Relief washed over him, like ocean waves upon the shore, and his body, weakened beyond measure by injury, fatigue, and hunger, responded. The nobleman collapsed.

When he awakened, Hillian Drake felt both wonderful and horrible. His wound was healed, he knew immediately, and he was invigorated by a dreamless sleep. Still, in the very moment of his waking, his thoughts were invaded by terrible guilt. Adia was gone, and she had been lost while in his care. The Vingish lord's throat constricted, and he struggled to draw a breath. His heart thundered in his chest, its deafening sound serving to further escalate his panic.

Without warning, his face was assaulted by a cupful of water. Stunned, the nobleman's hands instinctively leaped to defense, covering his eyes and wiping the dripping fluid away. Safe to open once more, Hillian's eyes found their assailant.

"Dobyn!" he cried. "What are you doing?"

"Apologies," the dwarf responded, his voice as emotionless as his face, "but I simply cannot permit you to surrender to your demons."

The Lord of Nydia regarded the serious eyes peering at him from the face of a bearded mountain cliff. The dwarf's nostrils were exceedingly large for such a small man, Hillian noticed, and evoked memories of the caves Eryk had found when they'd been fleeing the Búso knights in Grolandon. Like rats in a country cottage, the ridiculous thoughts quickly multiplied, spilling from his mouth in a mad giggle as Hillian wondered if his own face resembled his home of Nydia as much as Dobyn's resembled the caverns of Tyr.

Having exhausted his supply of water, apparently, the Chief of Clan Varmingar resorted to the next available weapon. The small wooden cup was not heavy, but the force of its impact on Hillian's chest inspired the desired effect. The swarm of giggling rodents was dispersed, leaving the nobleman's mind relatively clear.

Without a word, Hillian rose, nodded to Dobyn, and walked deliberately out the door. Followed by the dwarf, Hillian paused outside of the room, marveling at the improvement in his leg. "Thank you, Dobyn. You have truly worked a miracle on my injury."

The praise inspired a rare smile in the forest of the dwarf's face. "I have a great deal of experience using Spell Magic on battle wounds."

"In the Great War?" the Vingish lord inquired.

"I was too young to fight in the war," he replied, "but our skirmishes with the goblins are never-ending."

Hillian nodded, trying to imagine a life in which an entire nation was forced to constantly battle enemies simply to retain the right to be confined to underground tunnels. As he shook his head in disbelief, he spied the master thief arriving at the top of the stairs.

"Greetings, Eryk," Hillian called.

"All better, then?" the master thief asked. He seemed confused, his frown and distracted eyes incongruent with his jovial voice.

"Well, I was overcome by panic and guilt, which I believe may have been an unexpected result of the medication," Hillian declared, wondering at the trouble that must be brewing in Eryk's mind, "but I was cured when Dobyn threw a cupful of water in my face."

Eryk raised an eyebrow at Dobyn, who refused to look at either of his human companions. "It was necessary," the dwarf said, flatly.

Eryk nodded, but the expected smirk did not appear. As an awkward silence began to descend, Hillian sought to prevent it from alighting. "Where are the ladies?" he asked.

"Come," Eryk replied, without a glance, turning to lead them to a second room.

When they arrived, all was not well. Though Ora was nearly fully recovered from her life-threatening wound and greeted the nobleman with a gentle smile, Mona eagerly rose to embrace him, whispering concern into his ear. "We are not welcome here," she told him.

Hillian nodded, trusting her instincts, which made sense of Eryk's strange behavior. Immediately, he broached the topic with the master thief. "Eryk, is there something wrong? Are we in danger?"

"No, of course not, other than the mad sorcerer, the Sabarist priest, the stubborn knights, and the angry blue elves that all wish to kill us," Eryk responded, his sarcasm seeming forced and somehow artificial. "No trouble at all."

Both aggravated and concerned, Hillian clarified, "I mean here, in this tavern. Are you certain we are among friends?"

Shaking his head, dark thoughts in his eyes, Eryk replied, "Calm yourself, Hillian. We are safe here."

Unconvinced, the Severlandi politician shook her head, prompting the nobleman to press further. "It does not feel safe," he asserted.

Uncharacteristically, Eryk's voice rose as he replied, "I am telling you, this is *my* inn, these are *my* people, and we are *safe* here!"

The intensity of the master thief's reply served to further convince the Vingish lord that all was not, in fact, well, but it was clear that Eryk would not be forthcoming. It was the same each night, as they traveled from town to village, sleeping in Master Rook's taverns and inns. Hillian should have found comfort among the throng of loyal Carrion Crows. He should have been calm and relaxed within the boundaries of the famously tolerant Severlandon. However, Hillian could not help but notice the distinct absence of tolerance in Eryk's properties and elsewhere. As they progressed along the Severlandi coastline, the Vingish lord felt that he and his companions were more frequently expected, as if news of their coming preceded them. They were increasingly met by frantic women rushing to protect their children and suspicious men brandishing fishing spears or butcher's knives as if they might need to use them as weapons.

In one of the larger towns, they were approached by the local constabulary as they were dining. Eight uniformed men approached the table, and one of them, whose uniform seemed to indicate a higher rank, spoke to Dobyn and Ora.

"I apologize for interrupting your meal, but you'll need to come with us," he said in an uncompromising tone.

"And why would that be?" Hillian inquired.

"These two match the descriptions given at the scene of a crime two nights ago," the constable replied.

"And one night ago," added another constable.

"And this morning," the leader replied, nodding.

"So all the crimes are being blamed on elves and dwarves?" Hillian inferred.

"Look," the lead constable said, his voice growing more forceful, "I don't know what game you're playing at, but pretending to be fairy-tale creatures is not the best way to avoid getting caught."

"Lord Drake, I am afraid that justice may be elusive in this community," Ora suggested softly.

Nodding, Hillian looked at Mona, wondering if she could leverage her presidential authority, but was distracted by Eryk, who was glancing about the dining room. Several of the patrons were leaving, perhaps to avoid being caught amid trouble, but the nobleman was nearly certain that some of them were following unspoken orders. When his eyes finally fell upon Eryk again, Hillian received a nod of encouragement.

"We wish to make no trouble, Constable," Hillian said, turning to the leader. "We would be happy to accompany you."

The constable nodded. "Your cooperation is appreciated, but we are only interested in these two," he said, motioning to Dobyn and Ora. "The three of you may accompany us, if you surrender your sword to me until your friends are safely in custody."

The dwarf and the elf were shackled, wrists behind their backs, and led by four constables into the night, followed by the remaining four, who served as armed escorts for Hillian, Eryk, and Mona. As they approached the next tavern, two men tumbled out of the bright entrance, engaged in a drunken fight. As the constables halted, the two in the rear dropped to the dirt, followed quickly by the next two. Before the four leaders realized they were under attack, they, too, fell to the ground, Eryk's throwing knives in their backs.

The brawlers, no longer exhibiting any signs of drunkenness, nodded to Eryk, who greeted each of them with a unique handshake Hillian had witnessed several times in the past. "Horses await you around the corner, Master Rook," one of them announced. As the other searched for keys among the fallen constables, Hillian concluded that the handshake was a signal of Eryk's Carrion Crow Thieves Guild rather than the Innkeepers Guild, as he had always assumed.

When the elf and dwarf had been freed from their shackles and Hillian had retrieved his sword, Eryk led his companions to the stables behind the tavern, where he was met by a dark-skinned boy holding a bloody knife. "The stable master was reluctant to cooperate, Master Rook," the young man reported. "I was forced to convince him." The convincing had been fatal, clearly, based upon the pool of blood at the stable entrance.

"Why is that?" Hillian asked, his curiosity overpowering his haste.

Glancing at the Vingish lord before returning his gaze to his master, the young thief replied, "He was unwilling to aid an elf and a dwarf."

"This is not my Severlandon," Mona muttered, her voice deeply troubled.

Before Hillian could conjure the appropriate words of consolation, the young guildsman's eyes widened. "I forgot," he said, "Master Rook, I have a message for you." The young man reached into his tunic, produced a folded piece of parchment, and handed it to his grandmaster.

Carefully unfolding the note, Eryk scanned its contents. Smiling, he lifted his eyes to his countryman. "Adia lives," he told Hillian in a soft voice filled with hope, though tinged with doubt.

"Thank you, Jalidus," Hillian prayed aloud.

"Perhaps we do have a god on our side," Mona suggested, only partially in jest.

"Where is she?" asked Dobyn, returning the group to the reality at hand.

As his companions all looked expectantly at Eryk, the master thief scanned the remainder of the message. "Where did you get this?" he asked.

Looking up from his work, the young thief, who had begun spreading straw upon the bloody pool at the stable entrance, replied quickly, "Mistress Helena gave it to me, Master, just after you left the tavern, and ordered me to bring it to you here."

"What is your name, boy?" Eryk inquired.

"Dassef, Master."

"And your parents?"

"Heather and Salac, killed in the border disputes," the young man replied with a mixture of sadness and pride.

"An Akhdirian father and a Severlandi mother?" Eryk asked. The boy nodded.

Mona shook her head in grief as Eryk patted the young man's shoulder. "Dassef," he said, his voice filled with encouragement, "you have done me a great service today." The boy smiled, light returning to his young eyes. "Tell Mistress Helena what happened here and tell her Master Rook wishes you to have *avarden loi*."

The boy repeated the strange phrase, frowning in confusion.

"Just tell her," the grandmaster commanded with a smile. "Go now, Dassef."

The dark-skinned boy smiled, nodded to his master, and obeyed. When he had run beyond range of hearing, Eryk acknowledged his companions' questioning looks.

"It means 'award of loyalty,'" he explained. "He will be given his choice of trade, both at the tavern and in the guild."

"Are you truly awarding him for loyalty," Ora asked gently, in her soft voice, "or out of pity?"

The master rogue frowned at the elven woman. In his element, with people rushing to do his bidding, Eryk's confidence apparently exceeded his nervousness, as he had no trouble addressing the beautiful elf maid directly. "The boy was certainly resourceful and quick to make the right decision," he said. After a pause, he added, "But I suppose it doesn't take a Mind Mage to see that I pity him, more for being the victim of prejudice than simply for being an orphan."

"Severlandon has improved since the border disputes," Mona insisted, her brilliant blue eyes clouded with guilt. "Akhdirians are no longer persecuted simply for the color of their skin."

"Perhaps not," the master thief agreed. "And in your capital city of Calimygna," he added, "Akhdirians and other foreigners are probably not even harassed. But out here, in the villages and towns, I suspect poor Dassef is treated with suspicion and disdain, much like we have seen directed at Ora and Dobyn."

A single tear dropped from Mona's eye, collecting in the curve on the side of her small, delicate nose. As she wiped the moisture with her hands, Mona's face hardened with determination and resolve. "I will fix this when I return—I swear it!"

Nodding, Hillian agreed. "Yes, we will be making *many* changes when we return," he declared.

## Chapter 14

# PIETY

Having determined that Eryk's taverns and inns did not provide the safety and security for which they had hoped, the companions unanimously agreed to spend the night under the stars. As they huddled around a small campfire in a lightly wooded area, well away from the coastal road, Hillian broached the topic that had been nagging at the edges of his mind since their encounter with the constables.

"You knew we were not safe," the nobleman accused the master thief, without any hint of a question in his voice.

Eryk was silent for a moment before nodding, somberly accepting guilt. "Ever since the first village outside the forest, my innkeepers have been warning me that our nonhuman guests are not welcomed by the locals," he admitted, "but I was sure my status would protect us."

"It did not."

"No, it did not," the master rogue acknowledged.

"And yet," Ora interjected, "we are not sleeping in a Severlandi jail tonight."

"Right," Mona agreed, "and our rescue was a direct result of your status."

"Perhaps," Eryk said, nodding, "but I cannot trust that we will be as fortunate next time."

"So what now?" Dobyn asked, looking at Hillian.

Hillian shook his head, succumbing to the sadness and guilt that filled his heart. "Our purpose was to save Adia, and I have lost her."

"Our purpose has become bigger than the Gifted," Mona observed.

"It has always been bigger than the Gifted," Eryk said.

"And Adia lives," Ora added.

Grateful for the reminder, Hillian turned to Eryk. "What does the message say?"

Retrieving the letter from his pocket, the innkeeper read the contents. "The package you have lost has been found. Proceed on your original course, and it shall be delivered to you along the way."

"Is that all?" Hillian asked, the pitch of his voice rising in despair. "That could mean anything!"

"There is no other package that has been lost, my lord," Eryk replied with a calm confidence that failed to infect the nobleman.

"But you cannot be certain!" Hillian replied, the rate of his breathing steadily increasing.

"Have faith, Hillian," Mona offered, placing her hand into his, squeezing in reassurance. "Jalidus is with you."

Staring into her beautiful blue eyes, Hillian remembered his prayer. The grace of the Almighty Jalidus had reunited him with her, and with Eryk, Dobyn, and Ora. Perhaps the message, in its ambiguity, in its uncertainty, was another answer to his prayers. Perhaps Jalidus had a plan for Adia, and for him.

"I need to pray," Hillian whispered.

"I will pray with you," Mona offered, a significant gesture from a self-proclaimed agnostic.

Her warmth washed over him like the summer winds of Haggle Bay, sweeping away the indecision and self-doubt that screamed and clawed to retain their hold upon his confidence. Unable to smile, Hillian nodded before returning his eyes, bright with conviction, to Eryk.

"I need a Jalidin church," Hillian announced.

"That would not be wise—" the master rogue began.

"Eryk, listen to me," the Vingish lord said, his tone somewhere between commanding and pleading. "You trusted me in Tyr, you trusted me in Akhdiria, and you trusted me in Ke'Andara. I need you to trust me now."

Frowning, the master thief pondered, his eyes squinting as he regarded his Vingish countryman. Hillian felt invaded by the scrutiny but forced his eyes to remain hard and unyielding. Finally, a dull pain spreading along his clenched jaw, the stubborn nobleman was rewarded with a nod.

"Very well, then," Eryk said, his voice clearly convey-ing his disapproval, "and I presume you wish to go now, when the ungodly hour would raise suspicion among the priests, rather than wait for morning, when you could easily blend in with other worshippers."

Hillian glanced at Mona, but she could not make the choice for him. He closed his eyes but found nothing to aid him in the quiet recesses of his mind. Despite the lack of advice or logic, Hillian knew the answer, trusting that his instincts were guided by the grace of God.

"Tonight," he declared. "Right now."

"Of course," Eryk replied with a wry smile that clearly communicated his bitter amusement.

After riding steadily, if not hurriedly, for several hours, the companions arrived at the outskirts of a quiet town. In the light of Keb's dual moons, bright Numinos aggressively rising to chase gentle Lumos from the night sky, the spire of a Jalidin temple was easily visible, reach-ing for Himil from the center of the small community. Hillian sighed in relief at the absence of walls or city gates, silently thanking the Almighty for providing such a warm welcome.

At Hillian's insistence, Eryk remained behind, mak-ing camp with Dobyn and Ora, while Mona accom-panied the Vingish lord in his mission of piety. After passing a handful of sleeping cottages, the two travel-ers were stopped at the guardhouse on the edge of the proper city entrance.

"Good evening to you both," one guard called, pleasantly.

"Good evening to you," Hillian returned.

"Welcome to Buscade. What brings you to our fair city this night?"

"My wife and I travel to the capital to attend her brother's funeral. Tonight, her grief has forced us to seek a place of prayer."

Frowning, the guard demonstrated his suspicion. "I should warn you," he said, "the churches of Buscade do not provide food or shelter to those wishing to avoid the costs of an inn."

"We do intend to avoid the inns, as you surmise," Hillian responded, "but we are camped with some other travelers upon that ridge." Briefly motioning toward Eryk's campfire, he returned his attention to the guard. "Rest assured, we enter the city only for prayer."

They rode slowly, with no conversation, passing scores of sleepy homes, several dark shops, and the occasional bright tavern or brothel, before finally meeting resistance with only two buildings separating the travelers from the large oaken doors of the church. In their path stood three men with the clear intention of blocking their progress, soon joined by several more. As they pulled their mounts to a halt, Mona glanced at Hillian, fear barely concealed behind the determination in her eyes.

As the men advanced, Hillian made a quick decision, leaping from his mount. "Thank Jalidus!" he cried, improvising. It was easy to identify the leader, and Hillian strode confidently to him, hand outstretched in greeting. "We are so relieved to see you," he lied, rather impressively. "There are *thieves* in these streets!"

The lead rogue, obviously stunned by the unexpected behavior, stopped advancing and reluctantly accepted the nobleman's outstretched hand. When Hillian adjusted his fingers in a desperate attempt to recreate Eryk's secret handshake, the thief's eyes grew wide in surprise. Pressing his advantage, the nobleman added, "I'm sure my master would be greatly in your debt were you and your friends to escort us safely to the temple."

Moving slowly, as if spellbound, the lead thief nodded and pointed at the church, merely steps away. His companions frowned in confusion as Hillian effused gratitude.

"Thank you, my friend! And look at that, we were nearly there and could never have found it without your assistance." Having never released the handshake, Hillian grasped the thief's arm with his other hand, pulling the man closer. With a sly smile, he whispered, "Our master will be ever so grateful."

The thief nodded again, frozen in the surreal awkwardness. As he watched the nobleman return to his horse, the rogue stepped carefully to the side, followed by his men.

As the massive oaken doors gave way, a young ordinal, a member of the lowest order in the Jalidin priesthood, met them at the entrance to the temple. As the young priest nodded and stepped aside, they were greeted by the gadrinal, a priest of the second order and likely the chief cleric of Buscade.

"Good evening, weary travelers," the elder priest intoned, smiling. "May this house of Jalidus…" He paused as he regarded Mona, his eyes flickering recognition, before completing his welcome. "May this house of Jalidus provide you comfort and grace."

As they proceeded to the sanctuary, Mona whispered, "He recognized me," concern apparent in her quiet voice.

"That seems unlikely," Hillian challenged, unwilling to acknowledge the truth he had witnessed with his own eyes. "Are you certain?"

"Before he was elevated to gadrinal, he served Cardinal Cauda in the capital."

Lord Drake nodded, his frown deepening. If the gadrinal had served under Cardinal Cauda, the Jalidin high priest of Severlandon who sat on President Kesler's Interfaith Advisory Board, then it was, indeed, quite possible that Mona had been recognized. As he knelt at the altar, Hillian wondered what the gadrinal might do with such knowledge and what risk it might pose. Mona squeezed his shoulder as she knelt, placing herself a respectful distance from her friend.

Hillian closed his eyes and prayed. "Lord Jalidus," he mumbled, his voice nearly inaudible, "please grant your humble servant strength and, above all, wisdom." His eyes clenched as the passion of his request overwhelmed the pious Jalidin. "Help me, Lord. If our purpose truly be your will, I implore you, provide me with guidance and direction. Allow me to be your instrument, to perform your work in this world."

It was simply too short. They had traveled much of the night to make his prayer possible, had lied to the prison guards, had narrowly avoided an altercation with a band of thieves, and yet Hillian found he was unable to conjure any more words, thoughts, or emotions.

Slowly, reluctantly, the Vingish nobleman admitted that his prayer had come to an end. He opened his weary eyes, only to find the tranquility of the temple replaced by a flurry of activity. As young ordinals filled the balcony, jostling one another for the best view, city guards poured into the temple, instantly blocking every possible exit. Hillian rose from his knees and stepped closer to Mona, who, already standing, wore a stoic expression. They waited together as they were approached by a cluster of soldiers.

"What is the meaning of this?" Hillian asked, stepping forward.

Sliding past the Vingish lord, the captain addressed the woman at his side. "Mona Kesler?" he asked.

Her tight nod was barely noticeable, but it was sufficient and the guard sighed, clearly dreading the task at hand. "Madam President, I am terribly sorry, but it is my duty to arrest you for treason…"

"Treason?" Hillian cried in shock. "She has been out of the country for weeks. How could she have committed any treasonous acts?"

The guard captain waited patiently until Hillian was finished. Then, his focus remaining on Mona, he continued, "Pending the outcome of your trial in international court for conspiracy to undermine the World Council."

"What? Conspiracy?" Hillian shouted, but his outburst was interrupted by the patient captain's steady voice.

"Lord Hillian Drake, is it?" the old soldier inquired, to which Hillian nodded. "You are also named in the international conspiracy charge, and I have been asked to take you into custody for extradition to Vinglandon."

Shaking in his outrage, Hillian opened his mouth to deliver a dissertation on politics and persecution when his arm was roughly squeezed.

"Be still, Lord Drake," Mona commanded in a steady voice, the tone of which left no room for discussion. "The laws of Severlandon will provide us opportunity to defend ourselves, but now is not the time."

Hillian understood what his friend asked of him, but recent events had challenged his faith in the Severlandi legal system. He was, however, being arrested in a sacred chapel, directly after pleading to his god for guidance. God had answered his prayers before, the pious Jalidin reminded himself, and perhaps he could have faith that another answer had been delivered.

## Chapter 15

# GRACE

As they were led from the temple, Hillian felt he was touched by the grace of Jalidus, resulting in a crisp awareness of his surroundings. Most of the guards, it was clear, were reluctant to be arresting their president, suggesting that Mona Kesler's popularity remained strong despite the accusations against her. Conversely, the Jalidin priests appeared to relish the event, especially the gadrinal, who hovered, nodding in satisfaction, on the threshold of the temple.

In his native Vinglandon, the priesthood supported the nation's government, but perhaps only because the government supported the national church. In Severlandon, where freedom of religion significantly diluted the power of the priesthood, Hillian wondered if the government was regarded as an enemy of the church, at least to some extent. As he pondered the notion further, Hillian recalled that Mona was the first president to establish the Interfaith Advisory Board, a collection of thought leaders from all religions, and even including atheist and agnostic philosophers from the world of academia. Prior to her administration, only Cardinal Cauda and his predecessors had advised the presidents, giving the Church of Jalidinity preferential status, though unofficial. So perhaps, Hillian concluded, President Kesler, specifically, was regarded as an enemy of the Jalidin church for eliminating the perception of a national religion, thereby further eroding the power of Jalidinity in Severlandon.

It was ever more apparent, however, that she was not an enemy to the city guards. Shortly after leaving the church, the captain was assaulted with questions and suggestions from his men, all of them suggesting that the small jail of Buscade was no place for the President of Severlandon. The old soldier argued that all the nation's jails contained accommodations that were more than satisfactory, even in smaller towns like Buscade. Two guards quickly countered, almost in unison, that the jails (and the guardhouses, others added, and the constable stations) enjoyed such a reputation only because of the value President Kesler placed on law enforcement and civil service, further demonstrating the fact that their prisoner deserved special treatment.

Hillian nearly smiled at the exchange as he glanced at Mona, but his amusement was quickly smothered by the betrayal that sat upon her brow, dragging her beautiful face toward the ground and, for the first time in the nobleman's memory, extinguishing the ever-present vibrance in her eyes. Guilt swept into his heart and mind, replacing all other thoughts with the singular desire to find some manner by which to console her. In fact, the urge to protect her, to comfort her, to brighten her, was so strong that Hillian caught his breath in surprise.

The Vingish nobleman wondered when his feelings for Mona had begun to change. He was attracted to her, certainly, but that had always been the case and was far from unique, for Mona Kesler was widely regarded as one of the most beautiful women in the world. A certain chemistry existed between them, but that, too, had always been true, demonstrated by their highly successful political collaborations.

Perhaps it was the nature of the chemistry that had changed, subtly shifting from professional to personal. "Deeply personal," he acknowledged aloud, his muttering drawing a glance from Mona. She raised her eyebrows in query. Hillian smiled, a small gesture meant to reassure her, and was rewarded with the hint of a smile from the beautiful Severlandi president. As she looked away, Hillian's smile widened. Jalidus provided challenges of adversity, he mused, but for those who remain hopeful, who remain faithful, how rich the rewards!

The guardsmen eventually won over their captain, each contributing a small sum of coin to lodge their president in the finest inn in the city of Buscade. When she was informed of the decision, her face remained expressionless. Tight-lipped, she responded, "Lord Drake stays with me," the only five words heard from her lips since the temple. Mona Kesler had never been known for conforming to social norms or observing the traditional definitions of appropriateness, and sharing a room with a foreign dignitary of the opposite sex was apparently no exception. She stared at them, her eyes cold, ignoring the sneers she must have expected to accompany such a demand. They did not refuse her, of course, and Hillian was left to wonder if he would be invited to share the bed.

As they were shown to their room, the Vingish nobleman continued to watch his friend, but Mona immediately retired to the bed, with no suggestion of invitation. It was a manor-class inn, not as impressive as Eryk's palace-class Unicorn Inns, but certainly more comfortable than the jail would have been, and Hillian was quite content with the chaise longue and the ample supply of pillows and blankets.

Comfortable, but not at peace, the Lord of Nydia found himself unable to sleep, his mind distracted by several topics, each competing for his scattered attention. His concern for Mona, and his feelings toward her, held the leading position for much of the night, only occasionally losing ground to his feelings of responsibility and failure regarding Adia Varani and the Gifted. Laced through both topics, and an underlying theme for his sleepless night, was the question of his mission and, more specifically, his worthiness for it.

In the Forest of Ard Shaab, Hillian had concluded that he had been charged with the monumental task to stop the blasphemy of Ixodis and to guide the world in righting the wrongs of the sorcerer's evil legacy. Yet, despite his certainty that such a responsibility had been assigned by the Lord Jalidus, Hillian could not prevent waves of doubt from eroding his conviction. The loss of Adia represented a significant blow to his confidence, and yet he had forced himself to remain optimistic that they would be reunited, but how would their reunion be possible if he and Mona were incarcerated in a Severlandi prison? How would he be able to influence the world and achieve the holy mission to which he had been assigned?

Hillian prayed for peace many times until finally realizing that such a selfish prayer was little different from praying for riches. He wished for peace so he could sleep, so he could temporarily put an end to his mental and spiritual conflicts. Neither peace nor the resulting slumber, he acknowledged, brought glory or service to God. Instead, Hillian repeated his prayer from the temple, begging Jalidus for wisdom, understanding, and grace.

As sunlight seeped in through the curtained window, alighting upon the Vingish nobleman, so, too, did the hand of God. Hillian woke with an epiphany that served to energize him with faith, not only in Jalidus but also in his holy mission, his purpose, and his calling. It would not be necessary to find Adia Varani, for she would find him, he was certain, and the entire world would bear witness.

He rose suddenly, throwing open the curtains and basking in the glow of the morning sun. How strange it was, he mused, to be filled with such clarity after struggling so long in the dark, murky shadows of internal conflict. How wonderful it was to be graced with such certainty after so many nights of indecision!

"Too bright," groaned a voice behind him. Wheeling around, he spied Mona stirring in the bed, covering her eyes with a blanket, and he discovered that his newfound clarity extended to her, as well.

"Good morning, Mona," he said, approaching the side of the bed.

"Tell me, Hillian," she began, speaking from within her blanketed cocoon, "what exactly is good about this day? We are still under arrest, are we not, and heading to Calimygna to be tried as criminals?"

She squinted as he gently pulled back the blanket so he could see her face. He softly stroked her cheek with his hand. "It is a good morning, Mona Kesler," he insisted, placing a tender kiss on her forehead and then, to her surprise, on her lips. "Trust me."

His face lingered, merely a breath away from hers, and she suddenly reached up and pulled him in, kissing him passionately, gripping the back of his neck. When she released him, she smiled. "You had better know what you're talking about, Hillian Drake," she warned him, "because I am not in the mood for disappointment."

"Was that kiss disappointing?" he asked, a sly smile on his lips as a confident glint sparkled in his eye.

"Well, now, that was not the sort of response I would expect from you!" Mona teased, visibly impressed.

"You failed to answer the question," he reminded her.

She laughed. "Indeed, it was not," Mona confirmed.

"Well, that kiss was inspired by Jalidus himself, so take it as a sign from the Almighty that your day will not be disappointing."

"Really? That kiss came from God?"

Hillian chuckled. "What's wrong, Mona, you've never had a holy kiss before?"

Smiling, she relented. "Very well, because of the holy kiss, which was far from disappointing, I shall enter this day with faith and trust." Then Mona graced him with a seductive smile, adding, "Please understand that I may require similar encouragement, later in the day, to maintain my optimism!"

～≫

After a hasty breakfast, the guard captain was eager to depart. "We can make the capital by nightfall," he pointed out, "but we must be on our way." He hurried his prisoners and his men to the door, where their horses were waiting.

"Captain, may I have just a moment inside before we depart?" Hillian inquired, ignoring the quizzical expression on Mona's face. "I wish to thank the innkeeper for an excellent experience, particularly given the fact that I do not expect to enjoy similar accommodations once we reach Calimygna."

The old soldier agreed but sent one of his guardsmen inside to supervise. Hillian approached the barkeep, politely interrupting the large woman's conversation with a patron. "Excuse me, but I wish to speak with the master of this inn."

"Master Rune is busy," was the brusque reply.

"Eryk Val Varen owns this inn, does he not?" the nobleman asked, intending to capture the barkeep's attention. The ploy was successful, and the woman nodded, fixing her squinted eyes on the rude man addressing her. "I am Hillian Drake, Lord of Nydia, the Vingish duchy in which Master Val Varen resides. I plan to deliver to him a full report of my experience at this inn, and I am in a terrible rush, so it would be ever so helpful if you could fetch Master Rune immediately." He smiled, knowing that his use of Eryk's name had sufficiently frightened the woman, who nodded and rushed away, returning with a middle-aged, well-dressed man with a fake smile.

"Edwin Rune, Master Innkeeper," he introduced himself, holding out his hand.

"Hillian Drake, Lord of Nydia," the nobleman replied, extending his hand and adjusting his fingers into the secret sign of the Eryk's thieves' guild.

Master Rune's false smile melted as he glanced at the handshake before returning his eyes, only slightly widened in surprise, to Hillian's. The nobleman waited, smiling, until the innkeeper returned the secret shake, acknowledging his status as a Carrion Crow.

"Master Val Varen is a close personal friend," Hillian declared, finally releasing the innkeeper's hand. "He was to meet us here later today, but since we are departing early, I wonder if you would give him a message on my behalf."

"It would be my pleasure, Lord Drake," the innkeeper replied, nervously. "What shall I tell him?"

"If you have an opportunity, please explain to him that President Kesler and I are being escorted to Calimygna to stand trial for protecting a Giftwitch." Master Rune's eyebrows rose, but Hillian continued, adding, "As it is an armed escort, and I do not wish to endanger Master Val Varen, it would be extremely unwise for him to attempt to reach us along the way, though I do hope he will visit us in the capital."

Apparently, the message did not reach its intended recipient, or perhaps it was misunderstood, for they encountered a group of bandits blocking the road just after midday. Hillian knew, without any evidence, that the men were Carrion Crows, and he immediately began to scan the area for Eryk.

"Move aside," the guard captain called out. "We have no gold, only prisoners."

"It is your prisoners we desire," the brigand leader replied, his men raising crossbows. "Surrender them, and you may go on your way."

"Captain," Hillian spoke quickly, "allow me to talk with him. I give you my word I will return, and there will be no trouble."

"And if you do not return, or if there is trouble," the captain replied, after only a momentary hesitation, "I am afraid I cannot vouch for the safety of the president." It was a threat, and perhaps the only leverage available to the old soldier, but the words rang empty. He was a good man, an honorable man, and Hillian strongly suspected he would die protecting Mona rather than hurt her.

The Vingish nobleman spurred his horse, riding ahead of the armed escort toward the crossbow-bearing bandits. Pulling his steed to a halt, he spoke plainly. "Tell your master that we do not wish to be rescued, and we will not go with you if you persist." The leader squinted, but it was not he who replied.

*Hillian, what are you doing?* Ora asked in his head.

*Tell Eryk we do not wish to be rescued,* Hillian replied, silently. *Tell him to have his men disperse.*

*He wishes to know if you have a plan,* she informed him after a short pause.

*Try to reach Adia and rendezvous at the capital*, he commanded. *Be ready to act, but make no further attempts at rescue until and unless I call for it.*

There was no response for several moments, but his answer came when the bandit leader nodded and turned his horse, leading his men away from the road. When he returned to the guards, the old captain asked him the obvious question.

"How did you do that?"

"I told him that we would fight alongside you and your men and that we were willing to die. He asked me why he should care, and I asked if his employer would pay the bounty if we were dead. Apparently, the answer was no."

"Why?" Mona inquired, confused.

He looked at her, smiled, and said, "Because I trust in the laws of Severlandon, I trust these men, and I trust Jalidus."

The confusion and concern melted from her face. "And I trust you," she whispered.

## Chapter 16

# REVELATION

With no further delays, they reached the capital city just after dusk. After shaking hands and bidding them good luck, the guardsmen of Buscade turned them over to the custody of the jailers of Calimygna. Like their Buscadian counterparts, the guards at the capital bore a deep and abiding respect for President Kesler, perhaps even more acute, agreeing immediately to her request that she and Hillian share a cell and voluntarily providing food, wine, pillows, additional blankets, and various other comforts.

After the guards reluctantly abandoned them to their quiet, underground cell, Mona finally confronted the nobleman standing beside her. "We are in a dungeon now, Hillian," she noted, whirling to face him. "I do trust you, but would you please favor me with an explanation? Why is this better than being rescued?"

Hillian smiled. Mona's eyes were so bright, so luminous, the Vingish lord was convinced he would be able to see them even without the dim light of the torches flickering through the bars of the cell. Wanting nothing more than to provide for her the same measure of comfort that her eyes provided for him, the nobleman launched into his explanation with exuberance. "Because this way, there will be a trial. And because you are president, the trial will become a spectacle, so the proceedings will be carried throughout not only your nation of Severlandon but the world as well."

"This is your plan?" she asked. "This is the vision Jalidus sent to you?"

"Revealed to me," Hillian corrected her.

"Oh, so you're a prophet then, receiving holy revelations from the Almighty?"

Hillian was certain that her sarcasm was driven by fear, and perhaps panic, rather than by actual disrespect, so he attempted to calm his friend. "Perhaps I'm not explaining it very well," he acknowledged, "but you said you trust me." His hands found her cheeks, and he cradled her face gently. "Trust me now," he urged. "I finally know, without a doubt, that I am on the right path."

Mona sighed. She fell against his chest, her indomitable strength exhausted. "Very well, my Lord Drake, I will trust you, but it may be time for another holy kiss."

He was sure she was smiling, and his fingers traced across her cheek to her lips, confirming his suspicion. Her lips were so soft, so perfect. He slowly brought his own lips to hers but held her face as she attempted to press against him. The kiss was like a feather, skimming, brushing the surface, scintillating the nerves, and yet teasing with the promise of more. Her hands rubbed his chest for two, three, maybe five breaths before grabbing handfuls of his shirt and yanking him closer. She devoured his mouth, her passion overwhelming the poor man, causing him to lose his balance. As Hillian stumbled backward, Mona followed, crashing on top of him. Releasing his lips, she sat upright, straddling his hips, and ripped his shirt open.

"Mona," he protested.

"Oh, do be quiet, Hillian," she ordered, enforcing her command by attacking him with another passionate kiss.

For perhaps the first time since leaving Porvatis, Hillian enjoyed a peaceful sleep. He woke in a dark dungeon cell that smelled of urine and feces, yet his spirit soared. Snuggled against him was the most beautiful, most amazing woman on Keb, who had given herself to him, body and soul, with absolute faith and trust. That, alone, would be enough to raise any man's spirits, but Hillian was also uplifted by his sacred mission—his revelation, as Mona had named it—and he was more confident than ever that he would bring success and glory to Jalidus.

Further demonstrating the favored status in which they held their president, the jailers allowed Mona—and Hillian, as well, upon her request—to bathe and dress before appearing in court. Refreshed and inspired, Hillian unveiled his plan. "I believe I am supposed to represent you in court," he told her.

"Will you be representing *me* or representing the mission revealed to you by Jalidus?"

She raised a legitimate question. Hillian was convinced the idea of defending Mona in court was a true revelation, provided to him by the grace of God. However, if his motivation for representing her was driven not by a desire to ensure her acquittal, but by a desire to use the trial to influence public opinion, perhaps he was betraying her.

"I believe I am uniquely qualified to represent both," he concluded. "After all the work we've done together on international policies, I've studied the laws of your nation as much as any Severlandi barrister."

Mona nodded, slowly, before adding, "And you are an accomplished public speaker with a gift for persuasion."

"And I can address your case and my God-given mission at the same time."

She stepped close to him, placing her hands on his chest. "Just promise me you will not lose sight of the former in your efforts to address the latter."

The courtroom was full to overflowing, bringing a smile to Hillian's face. Mona's face was neutral, expressionless, but he felt certain that the mix of emotions affecting her would naturally include anxiety and embarrassment. Hillian was nervous as well, certainly, having been afforded neither time nor resources for preparation, but his heart was bursting with confidence, emboldened by his faith.

As Hillian seated himself beside Mona, the judge addressed him. "Lord Drake, this hearing does not concern you. Please choose a seat in the general population."

"With all due respect, Your Honor," the nobleman replied, "this hearing does concern me, for I am serving as the defendant's legal counsel."

The old judge frowned. Leaning forward, he fixed his beady eyes on Mona. "Miss Kesler—"

The Vingish lord was quick to interrupt, standing to address the judge. "Unless she has been impeached, Your Honor, in direct violation of the constitution you are sworn to uphold, she remains *President* Kesler."

A murmur rose in the courtroom as the judge shifted his gaze to Hillian. "You are a subject of the Vingish crown, not a citizen of Severlandon," he noted, bitterly. "What knowledge do you possess regarding our constitution?"

Hillian smiled in satisfaction. "I know that it specifically forbids the impeachment of a president in his or her absence," he declared.

His small eyes squinting, the judge nodded, acknowledging his defeat. He would not surrender, however, throwing another challenge at the foreigner standing before him. "True, but it also requires legal counsel to be provided by a barrister with credentials from a Severlandi institution."

"I am aware of that requirement, Your Honor, but also of the exception provided for cases involving international law, for which foreign legal credentials are permitted."

"Which you possess, I assume."

"In Vinglandon, all highborn lords are permitted to practice law, as are all graduates of Porvatis University. I am both, making me doubly credentialed."

Though it seemed impossible, the old judge managed to squint his eyes even further. After a long pause, he finally nodded. "Very well, Lord Drake, this court accepts you as President Kesler's legal counsel. She is charged with four counts of aiding and abetting the escape of a prisoner from police custody, one count of escape from police custody, and one count of treason for undermining the World Council." Finished reading the charges, the old judge looked up from his parchment, returning his squinted eyes to Hillian. "How does the defendant plead?"

"Not guilty, Your Honor."

"Very well. The court shall set a trial date one month hence." The old man raised his gavel, but Hillian interjected before the down stroke could be made.

"Your Honor, the defense moves that President Kesler be immediately released from incarceration with no bond and no restrictions."

"Objection!" the prosecutor exclaimed. "On what grounds?"

After glancing at the prosecuting barrister, the judge looked back at the foreigner, his bushy white eyebrows raised expectantly.

"On the grounds that she has already spent two nights in police custody," the Vingish nobleman replied, calmly, "in direct violation of the constitutional provision protecting the office of the president from imprisonment."

"Objection!" the prosecutor shouted again. "Vice President Emory was sworn in as president, so the nonimprisonment clause no longer applies to the defendant."

Hillian frowned. "Your Honor, Mona Kesler has not been legally impeached, so if it is true that Bryce Emory has been formally named president, such an act can only be viewed as an illegal attempt to usurp the office and overthrow the government. *That*, Your Honor, is treason, and it would be the responsibility of this court to issue warrants for the arrests of all involved, including Vice President Emory—" Hillian's frown transformed into a wicked smile as he continued, "—none of whom would be protected by the nonimprisonment clause."

Immediately, the prosecuting barrister requested a private discussion in the judge's chambers, for which Hillian was required to be present. When they emerged, the judge declared that the prosecution had dropped all charges against the defendant except for the charge of undermining the World Council, which would be based solely on the outcome of the international tribunal.

Mona was astounded. "How did that happen?" she asked, surprised and elated.

"The prosecutor declared Emory's elevation temporary, based on your incarceration in Chayl," the Vingish nobleman explained. "I challenged that such a claim would only make sense if the vice president claimed to be unaware of your release, which would invalidate all charges of escape or facilitating escape. The prosecutor agreed but pointed out that it would not invalidate the charge of undermining the World Council, so that is where we stand."

Mona threw her arms around Hillian, hugging him vigorously. "You are a brilliant, brilliant man!" she declared.

His smile creeping back to his lips, the Lord of Nydia quipped, "Thou shalt never doubt me again."

In response, she kissed him, a tender yet passionate kiss that electrified his entire body.

"And what of the charges against you?" she asked.

"I received no resistance when I encouraged them to release me from detention and remand me to the custody of the president."

When she smiled, her eyes glittering like diamonds in firelight, Hillian found himself wondering exactly when the light had returned to her face.

Though Mona begged him to stay with her at the president's manor, the Vingish lord counseled against it. "Rumors swirl," he informed her, though he was confident she already knew and simply did not care. "I have freed you to return to your office, and I urge you to focus your mind on your nation. Leave your case to me. I must find Eryk and the others and plan our next step."

He took a carriage to the capital city's Unicorn Palace Inn, where he hoped to make contact with its owner. Upon arriving, Hillian found that he was expected.

"Welcome, Lord Drake," greeted the innkeeper, a young man with light hair and a fuzzy mustache. "We have prepared a room for you with a hot bath and a change of clothes." While Hillian bathed, a meal was served by an attractive young woman who curtsied and said "m'lord" whenever she entered and exited his room. While such displays were customary in his home of Vinglandon, where nobility still commanded respect among the common folk, Hillian found it odd and out of place in Severlandon. Finally, as she poured his wine and cleared away his plates, he put to her the question.

"Brella, is it?" he asked.

"Aye, m'lord," she replied with another curtsy.

"Have you been in Calimygna long, Brella?"

"Nay, m'lord, I only just arrived this one mornin' past, from the Unicorn Palace Inn at Porvatis."

Hillian nodded, beginning to understand. "Where you served Master Val Varen," he guessed.

"Aye, m'lord. The master were kind enough to give me charge o' his personal quarters. I been his faithful servant for nigh on five years now."

Of course. Eryk had summoned a trusted servant from home to be his eyes and ears, and perhaps to carry messages to and from the inn and wherever the master rogue was hiding. "Brella, if I were to write a letter to Master Val Varen, do you suppose you could see that he receives it?"

"Oh, letters be unwise for secrets, m'lord, but I been asked to bring you to see the master as soon as you be ready for it."

In the cellar beneath the kitchen, among barrels of potatoes and onions, racks of salted venison, and casks of ale and wine, Brella led her guest to a wall of shelves filled with bottles of oils and spices. She scanned the labels until she found one bearing a crude drawing of a chess piece. A rook, Hillian realized with amusement, though not the bird of the same name that served as the symbol of Eryk's Carrion Crow Thieves Guild. It was clever enough to be overlooked by the Severlandi authorities, were they ever inclined to search the inn, but simple enough for an unlettered commoner like Brella.

The serving girl lifted the spice bottle and felt beneath it for a moment before pulling away a small square of wood, leaving a hole in the shelf into which she thrust a key. When she turned it, the wall behind the shelves groaned and creaked. After replacing the square and the bottle, she pushed the wall open, admitting the two of them into a dark tunnel.

After closing the wall behind them, she took his hand, whispering, "M'lord, if it please you." Hillian chuckled softly. In the royal court of Porvatis, it would have been disgraceful for the unmarried Lord of Nydia to be caught holding hands with a noblewoman, much less a common serving wench, but in the darkness of the tunnel, he found the gesture most welcome. More than once, he stumbled into her, feeling the soft curves of her young body, and thanked Jalidus she could not see him blush.

It was not a long walk, but Hillian's eyes had become accustomed to the dark by the time they reached the tunnel's end, where he released the girl's hand and wiped his sweaty palm on his breeches. He watched as she felt along the wall for a lever, which she pulled, opening another secret door much like the one in the Unicorn's cellar.

As they passed through a very similar storage room, Brella explained, "The tunnel has taken us 'cross the stone road, m'lord, and down a bit to the Rat's Nest Tavern."

"Where I should find Master Val Varen, I presume."

"Aye, m'lord, but on this here side o' the road, you be better off callin' him Master Rook."

He followed her up the narrow steps, through the kitchen, a much dirtier place than its counterpart across the road, and into the common room. The Pegasus Room, the common area in every Unicorn Palace Inn, was regarded as one of the finest dining establishments in the world. The Rat's Nest common area, in contrast, was true to its name, filled with the nastiest smells, sounds, and people Hillian had ever encountered, and more than a few actual rats scurrying across the dirt floor. It made the Wild Boar Tavern in Chayl, where he and Adia had met with Foster Branch, seem like a manor-class inn, and Hillian was eager to follow Brella up the stairs and away from the scampering rodents, brawling guests, and greedy glances.

The memory of Chayl brought Adia into the forefront of his mind, succeeding in distracting him, if only temporarily, from the serving girl's seductive curves and the consequent memories of his night with Mona.

In a small, cramped room, Eryk sat on the floor with Dobyn and Ora. "Thank you, my dear," the master thief said, greeting Brella with a devilish grin. "As always, I would be lost without you."

She returned his smile and bent to kiss him lightly upon the cheek. "The master is too kind," she replied, her voice singing in delight. As she took her leave, Hillian's companions greeted him.

"It is good to see you," the elf maid said, smiling as softly as she spoke.

"Aye," the dwarf grunted with a nod.

"Welcome, my lord," Eryk declared. "Come, sit, and let us hear of your adventure!"

"And your plan," Dobyn added, characteristically focused on the next steps rather than tales of adventure.

Hillian breathed deeply, taking a moment to reorient himself. His was the command in this strange crew, a fact that remained odd and surreal to the unlikely leader. He reminded himself, however, that it was his vision, and his holy revelation, that must guide them and set their direction, so it fell to him to lead them. "Ora, are we protected by a Mind Magic shield?" he began. When she nodded, he asked her a second question. "Have you found Adia?"

"Yes, I have conversed with her through Mind Magic," replied the elf maid, to Hillian's enormous relief.

"She was rescued by merfolk," Eryk explained, "and my guildsmen have her hidden on the outskirts of the city."

"Merfolk..." Hillian repeated, remembering Eryk's admissions to the dwarven king. "Would these be the same merfolk you rescued and relocated to the grottoes off the coast of Severlandon?"

"I assume so," the thief responded. "It was a thriving community when last I visited."

"Eryk, I require a bit of information, and I trust that your network of spies will be able to gather it." The master rogue nodded, waiting expectantly for the specifics. "President Kesler and I are to be tried by the World Council's International Tribunal."

"This much I have already gathered," the master rogue said, a note of irritation in his voice.

"Yes, well, now I need you to discover details. When will this trial take place, and where? Will she and I be permitted to vote and, if not, who will be replacing us on the tribunal? What are the specific charges, and what evidence is available against us? Get me anything and everything about these trials."

Turning his attention back to the beautiful Mind Mage, Hillian described the first part of his plan. "Ora, as soon as we know the time and location of the trial, I want you to reach out to Queen Safeda. Tell her that elves, dwarves, minotaurs, and the Gifted will be revealed to the human world at this trial and we want her support. Ask her to send as many elves as she can."

Eyes wide with surprise, and perhaps fear, Ora nodded, but then frowned. "What shall I say if she refuses?"

The nobleman shook his head. "This is happening with or without the elves. If she and King Uli wish to sacrifice their places on Crozada to the dwarves and minotaurs, so be it."

Dobyn huffed. "An ambitious plan, but what if you are refused by the dwarves and minotaurs, as well?"

Hillian smiled at the stony face of his Tyrian companion. "If we receive support from any of the exiled races, I shall be pleasantly surprised, but it is the invitation that matters." The dwarf's bushy eyebrows bent in a frown of confusion, compelling the Vingish lord to explain further. "Tell me, Dobyn, if you had made it your life's goal to hide the existence of magic from the world, and you learned of a gathering of magical races, what would you do?"

A grin carved itself into Dobyn's face. "I would stop it," he said.

"Yes, and I'm confident Ixodis will feel the same," Hillian said, turning back to Ora, "if you can ensure that he hears your communication. Send similar messages to King Loe of Tyr and Lorcan, leader among the minotaurs of Kiriti...to the malini, Galen Ziraili, at the Great Monastery of Kila on the Cliffs of Kuúma and to Sir Ida Wadógo of the Búso Knighthood...to the merfolk and fairy folk and—"

His list of recipients was interrupted by Brella, who startled them all as she threw open the door in haste. "M'lord!" she shouted to Eryk, breathlessly, but he cut her off with a wave of his hand.

"Brella, my dear, I am not a lord. I am a commoner, just as you are."

"Apologies, Master Rook," she corrected herself, "but someone has tried to murder the president!"

# Chapter 17

# CORRUPTION

Panic and guilt struck, simultaneously, ruthless in their assault upon the Vingish nobleman. His throat constricted, but it mattered little as his lungs had ceased to function. The room began to spin and sway, and nausea gripped him fiercely.

Before the vomit reached his mouth, Ora's soothing voice slipped through the chaos in his mind. "Fear not, Hillian! Eryk has matters well in hand."

Hillian glanced nervously at the master thief, who smiled reassuringly. "Relax, my friend. Let us hear the rest of Brella's report."

The nobleman struggled to control his trepidation as he turned his attention to the serving girl, who spoke to Eryk. "The assassin has been captured, Master Rook, as you planned, and awaits you in the stable.

"So you planned this?" Hillian cried, enraged. "You used Mona as *bait?*"

"She was never in danger, I assure you."

Hillian was not reassured. "And did she know that, or did you keep your plan from her as well?"

Eryk just stared at his lord, allowing the silence to hang in the room until the point of awkwardness. It was an effective tactic, as Hillian's heartbeats slowly returned to a steadier cadence. "She couldn't know," he determined, answering his own question, "just as I couldn't know, because our thoughts were not protected by Ora's Mind Magic shield."

Eryk continued to stare, waiting for his lord to arrive at the obvious conclusions. Hillian did not disappoint. "So now we interrogate the prisoner, while Mona remains at her manor so she does not lead our enemies to us."

A small smile appeared on Eryk's calm face. "Very good, Hillian," he said. "We'll make a Carrion Crow of you yet! I understand you have already mastered our secret handshake."

Hillian allowed himself to laugh. "Do not jest about such things," he said, smiling, as he rose from the floor of the small room. "Let us proceed to the stable then."

The prisoner was dressed in a white robe, cinched by a woven belt of purple hemp. He was bald and barefoot, the image of a flaming sword branded into the side of his neck.

"You are a Brother of the Morning," Hillian declared in recognition.

The man did not respond, but the elf and the dwarf looked at him expectantly.

"He belongs to the Order of the Dawn," Hillian explained, "a secret brotherhood of militant monks within the Jalidin priesthood, dedicated to cleansing the world of threats to the church. My father has denounced them, but even he has been unable to eliminate them entirely."

"Your father is…" Dobyn inquired.

"The prime cardinal," Eryk responded, "high priest in the Church of Jalidinity."

"Why murder the president?" Hillian asked, his voice as hard as a blacksmith's anvil.

"To carry out the will of Jalidus," the monk replied.

"Are you a prophet?" Hillian asked, with almost no condescension.

The man hesitated but finally shook his head.

"That *is* disappointing," Eryk quipped. "I was *so* hoping to meet a prophet today."

"Well," Hillian replied, ignoring the sarcastic thief, "if you are not a prophet, how can you claim to know the will of Jalidus?"

"The order is guided by the luminary," the non-prophet replied in righteous indignation.

"What is the luminary?" Dobyn asked.

"Cauda," Hillian replied. "He was a cardinal, a priest in the highest order of the clergy, until my father discovered him as the leader of the Order of the Dawn and excommunicated him."

"He leads us still," the monk declared in defiance. "He will not permit his holy purpose to be extinguished by the prime cardinal's momentary weakness."

"Why would you tell us this?" Ora asked.

"We are servants of Jalidus, protected by his grace. We have naught to fear from the godless."

"Where do we find this Cauda?" Eryk asked.

"Cardinal Cauda would likely be praying with his congregation at the cathedral," the nonprophet replied.

"He is no longer a cardinal and no longer has a congregation," the Vingish nobleman insisted.

"Oh, but he is, and he does," the monk replied, his voice brimming with superiority. "He was reinstated yesterday morning."

"The morning after the two of you were arrested," Dobyn pointed out.

"Impossible!" Hillian cried. "Only the prime cardinal could have reinstated him, and my father would never—"

"And yet he did," interrupted the bald Brother of the Morning. "Praise Jalidus!"

They left the prisoner in the stable, and Hillian tried not to think about the poor man's fate. Fortunately, the nobleman's thoughts were consumed by another topic, though it was equally unpleasant. If his father had, indeed, reinstated Cardinal Cauda, knowing the man's involvement in the Order of the Dawn, the implications were staggering, and Hillian was forced to reevaluate the remaining remnants of his limited worldview.

Overwhelmed, he found he could not tolerate the confines of Eryk's small room at the Rat's Nest Tavern. To escape his claustrophobia, he required fresh air, so the master thief led the four of them to the roof.

"It doesn't prove anything," Eryk offered.

"Perhaps not, but it suggests a great many things," Hillian replied, looking out over the dirtier, less prosperous streets of Calimygna. Severlandon's capital was one of the richest cities in the world, but even without a class system separating the highborn nobles from the lowborn peasants, it was clear to see that the wealth was no more evenly distributed than it was in Vinglandon.

"What does it suggest?" Eryk asked.

Hillian broke from his distracted musings and focused on his old friend's question. "Well, Ora confirmed that our would-be assassin told us the truth about Cauda's reinstatement."

"The truth so far as he knows it," Eryk clarified.

"Right, and what he knows for certain is that Cauda has been restored to his former post as Jalidin high priest of Severlandon, giving him and his Order of the Dawn control over all the church's resources in this country."

Eryk nodded but said nothing, allowing Hillian to continue.

"And if Cauda returns to his former seat on the president's Interfaith Advisory Board, he and his order will have access to political resources as well, and Mona's life will be at great risk."

"I can protect her in her home but not in the Capitol," Eryk admitted.

Hillian nodded somberly, his mind methodically processing the information and working its way back to the original question. "My father is certainly capable of drawing these same conclusions," he stated, "and yet he reinstated Cauda nonetheless."

"You assume."

"Yes I do, and I'm confident in the accuracy of that assumption, given that the high cardinal is the only person in the Church of Jalidinity with the authority to reverse an excommunication or to appoint cardinals."

"Which suggests?" Eryk prompted.

Hillian sighed. "Which suggests that my father, the prime cardinal, the high priest of the International Church of Jalidinity, secretly supports the Order of the Dawn."

"Which suggests?" Eryk asked again.

Hillian frowned. There was more? He closed his eyes and forced his thoughts to push beyond his personal context. "That my father is corrupt?"

"Which suggests?"

"Argh!" Hillian cried in frustration. "You are beginning to irritate me with that question!"

"Come now, my lord! Does it not occur to you that the Order of the Dawn and the Angel of Mercy are both tools of Jalidinity, used to expand the influence and power of the church? Who would reap more benefit from their activities but the high priest?"

The nobleman froze in shock. It had not occurred to him, but the idea was impossible to ignore. "Are you suggesting that my father is not only in league with these villains but that he directs them, as well?"

"I do not suggest it," Eryk clarified. "The evidence suggests it."

Staggered and stunned, Hillian required time to think. Stepping away from Eryk and the others, he stood on the edge of the roof, gazing south toward his home-land, consumed by feelings of betrayal and loneliness. Eryk tried to console him, as did Ora, and even Dobyn made a valiant attempt, but none of them could possibly understand the depth of his loss. In the underground kingdom of Tyr, when Eryk had suggested that a conspir-acy against the Gifted and the nonhuman races might be supported by the Jalidin Church, Hillian had not wanted to believe. When both the elf and the dwarf had validated the conspiracy, Hillian had remained reluctant to accept the church's involvement. When the priests in Buscade eagerly assisted in his and Mona's arrest, Hillian had convinced himself it was a misunderstanding. Even when the monk from the Order of the Dawn revealed Cardinal Cauda's reinstatement, suggesting his father's corruption, Hillian had remained blind, choosing to be-lieve Ixodis was the true enemy.

But Eryk was right. He had been right all along. Despite all instincts and justifications to the contrary, Hillian was forced to accept that his father, the spiritual guide to his king and anointed shepherd of his god, was as criminal as Eryk, as misguided as Cauda, and as sinister as Ixodis. The more he pondered, the more it all aligned.

Hydronimus Drake had married Hillian's lady mother to gain the influence of her title, which assisted in his ascension through the ranks of the powerful Jalidin priesthood, a fact that should have been apparent when he excommunicated her for declaring freedom of religion in her duchy of Nydia. Shortly after the king had refused to strip her of land and title, she'd been assassinated by a Brother of the Morning. Upon her death, Hydronimus began to dismantle the Order of the Dawn and arranged for Hillian to receive various appointments in the capital, keeping the young Lord of Nydia under his father's close supervision in the royal palace. After these appointments led to Hillian's assignment to the World Council, and his latest collaboration with Mona Kesler would have outlawed witch burnings throughout Crozada, Hydronimus had appealed to his son's devout faith. Witch burnings should be permitted because of religious freedom, he'd convinced his son, despite having ostracized and murdered his own wife for supporting the very same concept.

Hillian fell to his knees as the truth assaulted him. *His father had murdered his mother!*

The nausea overpowered him, and Hillian retched uncontrollably. The heaving continued, mercilessly ravaging his body until tears ran down his cheeks from the pain in his abdomen, his chest, his everywhere. Hillian collapsed into a pool of his own filth, lying on the rooftop, overcome with despair.

"Oh, Hillian!"

Lost as he was, drifting in a dark haze of hopelessness, the Vingish lord immediately recognized the voice, but his throat was raw and burning, and he could not find his voice. She cradled his head in her lap, with no regard for the vomit in which she knelt, as hushed voices spoke in the background.

"She threatened to expose you, Master Rook," Brella whispered. "Your men refused to bring her to you, so she demanded to be brought to his lordship, so I brung her here through the tunnel. I beg your forgiveness, Master."

"It's all right," Eryk replied. "You did well. Now run and see if you can find a wash basin and some clean clothes for them both."

"Yes, Master Rook."

"And Brella, see that the clothes are simple, such as might be worn by you and your brother."

Hillian slept, at peace in Mona's arms, his troubles expunged from his body along with his dinner. When he awoke, he was aware of his other companions standing at a respectful distance, but his eyes were locked on Mona's angelic face. "You were supposed to stay at your manor," he croaked.

"Hillian Drake," she exclaimed, choking on her words as her eyes filled with moisture, "you are an insufferable fool!"

She did not leave his side, helping him to the room and assisting him as he washed and dressed. Her touch was tender, and his heart filled with joy, his spirit with hope.

Hillian marveled at the degree to which her affection, her concern, her very presence seemed to change everything. His strength returned, amplified, and he held her hand as he looked over his patient comrades. Ora Fen, the elegant and beautiful elf maid, returned his gaze with optimism. Dobyn, of Clan Varmingar, displayed nothing in his expression but dwarven determination. And Eryk Val Varen, the hardened Master Rook, sported not his characteristic smirk but a genuine smile. "Are you amused?" Hillian asked his friend, briefly wondering when he had begun to think of Eryk as a friend once more.

"I am relieved," was the response.

"Were you worried?"

"Perhaps. It is good to have you back, my lord."

Hillian returned the smile. "You asked Brella to find us simple clothes because you know we must travel," Hillian said, not as a question, but as a statement of fact. When Eryk nodded, the Vingish lord continued, looking at each of his companions in turn. "First, we reunite with Adia, and then we are going to talk to Cauda."

"So, you believe your father is behind both the Order of the Dawn and the Angel of Mercy?" Mona asked as they walked through the slums of Calimygna, guided by the powerful light of Numinos, the brighter of Keb's two moons.

"I do, as much as I wish it were not so," Hillian replied somberly.

"But surely not the Purge," she asserted, "for your father was not alive two hundred years ago."

"True, Ixodis bears that responsibility alone, but creating the myth of the Angel of Mercy to justify that monster's ongoing atrocities…that may very well be my father's doing."

"And you have come to this conclusion by evaluating your father's pattern, from his treatment of your mother to his manipulation of you, but you have no actual evidence."

Hillian fought against the anger that rose in his chest. Mona's hand still clasped his own, a reminder that she cared for him and believed in him, and her line of questioning should not be construed as anything but legitimate support. "Cauda will provide the evidence, and if he does not, we will confront my father next."

They trudged through the mud, doing their best to avoid beggar children, starving dogs, and piles of waste, both human and otherwise, until they reached what could only be described as a hovel, though even that seemed overly kind. The thatched roof was in such poor condition that Hillian felt it might fall upon them as they entered, and the interior smelled of death and dung. Rodents and insects scurried from their feet as they followed Eryk to a filthy table, one of only four in the entire establishment, which boasted no bar, no other patrons, and no staff. An eternity passed before an enormous woman thundered in through the same door, carrying a crude wooden bucket that sloshed yellow liquid to the floor with each slow, wobbling step.

"Well, if it ain't the damn master o' the damn house," she said, her angry voice nearly as deep as the dwarf's. Her blond hair was long and dirty, matted to her equally dirty skin. Her clothes, barely more than rags, indicated her poverty, but her blue-gray eyes were filled with fire and spirit as she growled at Eryk, "You here to take more o' my damn money, Master Dirty Bird?"

"We're here to pay you for some damn mead, you hateful old hag!" Eryk shouted, feigning hostility, but when a smirk followed his insult and was returned by the barkeep, Hillian realized it was all just a game.

"Eryk, you li'l bastard, come here and give Mama Bear a damn hug!"

As the arrogant rogue stood to greet her, she slammed the bucket on the table and enveloped him, her giant arms wrapping him up like a sausage in a biscuit. When she finally released him, she lumbered across the room to a cabinet, leaving Eryk gasping for breath. "What the devil brings Master High and Mighty out to the Piss and

Moan?" She shuffled back to her guests and tossed down five wooden cups, sending them spinning and skittering across the table.

"The Piss and Moan? Is that what you're calling it now?" Eryk asked, dipping his cup into the bucket. Dobyn was the first to follow suit, but Hillian waited to judge the dwarf's reaction when the cloudy yellow substance hit his tongue.

"Eh, well, it's a damn sight better'n what you called her."

"And what was that?" Mona asked, amused.

"Master Too Damn Big for His Britches named this place The Shield o' the City.'" Her guffaws were so rich they nearly ruptured the feeble walls. Still laughing, she added, "Can you believe that, missy? The Damn Shield o' the Damn City, he names her." The large woman nearly choked on her riotous laughter, brown spittle flying from her mouth.

"Mama, we're here to meet a friend," Eryk said after patiently waiting for the barkeep's laughter to subside, at least to some degree.

"Dammit, boy, you know you ain't got no friends out here 'cept me!" The laughter erupted from her once again, and she doubled over, rolls of flesh bouncing and jiggling.

"Eryk, is this woman your mother?" Ora asked, eager curiosity filling her lavender eyes.

Eryk chuckled. "I'm afraid not, though she would likely make a better mother than mine ever did. No, she's just Mama Bear. She's everyone's mother, and for as long as I can remember, she's been right here, serving up that sweet maternal abuse of hers right alongside her sweet honey mead."

"The mead is exceptional," Dobyn noted, dipping his cup for a second serving. Hillian decided to give it a try, and his first sip made the dwarf's comment seem entirely insufficient. The texture was perfect, smooth and light, and its rich sweetness seemed to fill his mouth with happiness. It was too good, too much better than any mead he had ever tasted, so he was instantly inclined to believe Mama Bear when she offered an explanation.

"Well, now, it'd damn well better be, darlin', or else them bee fairies out there ain't worth a damn thing!"

"*Bee fairies?*" Hillian asked, unable to conceal his confusion.

"Fairies made this mead?" Dobyn exclaimed, spitting a mouthful upon the floor, unable to hide his distaste.

"Yeah, a bunch o' damn bee fairies, brought here by the good Master Beekeeper, who loves to spend his money on the damn colony but can't spare a couple o' gold coins to fix my damn roof!"

"You wound me, Mama," Eryk said, standing from the table. "And here I brought you a whole bag of gold coins to fix up this place." He grinned as he held out the small leather purse, shaking it for effect, and then gasped as the woman suffocated him with another giant hug.

"Now that's my boy," she said, beginning to cry. "That's my boy! You sure you don't wanna forget about your skinny li'l lady friend outside and maybe give old Mama Bear some lovin'?"

"Maybe next time," he said, kissing her on the cheek. He refilled his cup, nodded toward the door, and said, "Now, who wants to meet some fairies?"

As they walked across the muddy yard, Hillian made a connection. "So this is the secret haven you mentioned to King Loe?"

"One of them," his friend acknowledged. "This colony is just for the bee fairies, who live in hives, not in flowers or trees, and are organized in a monarchy, so they don't mix well with the more free-spirited types."

"And they produce honey, which makes amazing mead," Mona noted.

"Yes, which, along with the minotaur pirates, makes the bee fairies one of the few rescued races that generates me some revenue!"

"How many different varieties are there?" Hillian asked.

"The larger colony is home to the butterflies and dragonflies," Mona explained.

"In Ard Shaab," Ora added, "we share the forest with firefly fairies."

"The dwarves of Tyr are constantly harassed by mosquito fairies," Dobyn offered, not bothering to conceal his disgust.

Just as Dobyn finished speaking, Hillian spied Adia Varani in the moonlight, standing in a tangled excuse for a flower garden, smiling and talking with a cloud of bee fairies amid a cluster of hives. She was happy, Hillian noticed, and peaceful and relaxed. Most of all, she was alive.

"Adia!" Hillian cried in excitement. His heart expanded, filled with relief and joy, until he was suddenly surrounded by a swarm of angry bee fairies, the little females threatening him with their shiny black stingers and the males brandishing miniature spears and swords. Menacing as they were, the Vingish lord could only marvel, seeing them up close for the first time. Their tiny bodies, none taller than the length of his longest finger, were thin and delicate, proportioned very much like the elves of Ke'Andara and Dath'Duine.

In fact, they resembled the elves a great deal, with the same pointed ears, the same grace, and the same ethereal beauty, but the colors were far different. Instead of white with patches of green or blue, the skin of the bee fairies reminded the nobleman of the darkest ebony, smoothed and polished. Yellow or orange eyes shone from the dark faces behind their pointed helmets, none of which revealed any sign of hair on males or females. The gold of their helms, as well as the armor, sparkled in the moonlight, forcing Hillian's imagination to construct the unlikely image of a bee-fairy blacksmith shop somewhere in the hive.

"No, he is a friend," Adia said, amusement in her voice. "Yes, that's right; these are the friends I told you about." She was obviously conversing, presumably with the fairies, but Hillian could hear only one side of the discussion. The militant fairy folk did, however, withdraw from their threatening positions, for which the nobleman was grateful.

"Yes," Adia replied to a silent question, "right there, yes, that is your friend, Rook."

The swarm exploded, buzzing in all directions before converging on Eryk, the females covering him in kisses, while the males patted him in greeting or saluted him while hovering nearby.

Adia's brow furrowed as she cooed, "Oh, Eryk, they love you! They love you so much."

The master thief laughed, perhaps in response to her comments, or perhaps due to the tickling of fairy kisses, replying, "Yes, Adia, I can hear them."

Hillian could hear only the light buzzing sounds as they mingled with Ora's soft, musical voice. "Adia, you look well," the elf maid noted, and Hillian smiled in agreement. The sorceress had always been beautiful, he recalled, in a fierce and fiery sort of way, but her darkness had faded, replaced with a bright joy. Smiling and laughing, surrounded by fairies and garden flowers, she seemed reborn, brought back from the dead an entirely new person.

"You look…different," he said, finally, a statement that was not, perhaps, as complimentary as he felt.

Fortunately, Adia received it in the spirit it was intended. "Thank you, Hillian," she replied, her previously rare smile having become a permanent fixture on her face. "I feel different." She stepped forward and embraced him, almost nervously. As she released him, she kissed him gently on the cheek. "Sabar has blessed me with new life and new purpose," she declared, "and I see now that it is bigger than the Gifted."

"I am pleased to hear it," the pious Jalidin replied, returning her friendly kiss. "Jalidus has graced me with the same."

As she proceeded to embrace each of the others in turn, Hillian Drake marveled at the family they had become. He gave silent thanks to the Almighty, Jalidus or Sabar or perhaps even both, for delivering her safely. For, while it may have been true that his holy mission was not restricted to the Gifted, it was equally true that one particular Gifted, *his* Gifted, represented the key to his ultimate success.

As they returned to the Piss and Moan, their shadows growing longer as Numinos edged toward the horizon, Adia was attended by two bee fairies. Both armored warriors, the male carried a spear and a sword, while the female was armed with her stinger and a tiny dirk.

"Prince Htan is Captain of the Queen's Guard," Adia explained, "and Eoh is the leader of the Screaming Stingers, the most daring company of warrior princesses in the Hive."

"All the females are princesses and all the males are princes," Eryk noted with a smirk, "in a society where only the queen produces offspring."

The two tiny warriors buzzed in response, and the master thief was forced to eat at least a portion of his words. "Very well, my friends," he replied to their insistent buzzing, "perhaps the current queen is not the mother of all, but all are children of a queen, past or present, which proves me right, nonetheless."

"How do you understand them?" Hillian asked. "Do you speak their language?"

"It's Mind Magic," Mona replied.

"Like humans, fairies are capable of both Mind Magic and Spell Magic," Ora added.

"Though, unlike humans, none are born with Gift Magic," Adia clarified.

"I was thinking that these two would make a valuable contribution to our cause," the master thief declared. As Hillian's face betrayed his surprise, Eryk put the proposal to his leader. "What say you, Hillian? Have we any seats at our table for two bee fairies?"

Excited, Hillian glanced at his companions, finding dissent only on the face of the dwarf. "Dobyn?" he prodded.

The snort of derision was met with angry buzzing, and the nobleman guessed that the two races were not overly fond of each other. Finally, Dobyn shrugged. "It's not as if they take up much space," he joked, his deadpan delivery eliciting chuckles from all the humans in attendance. "I suppose our table can accommodate them."

"Then it is done," Hillian declared. "Htan, Eoh, I welcome you, and I regret only that we have no time to thank your queen, for we must be on our way." He spoke to them as equals, looking them in their eyes, but expecting one of his other companions to relay their replies. Thus, he was pleasantly surprised to find he could, in fact, hear them when they wished it.

*It is an honor to join your company,* the female said in his mind.

*Eoh speaks for us both, Lord Drake,* Htan added. *And Queen Tarala knows what we know. Such is the way of the Hive.*

They spoke little as they journeyed back to the stone road and into the heart of Calimygna. Assuming that the cathedral would be deserted at such a late hour, Eryk and Mona guided their friends to the very edge of Cardinal Cauda's property, an expansive estate rivaling the president's, with fountains and gardens and an enormous manor house, encircled by a wall of red and orange brick. Eight guards were visible at the main gate, but Hillian was certain there were more.

"Ora, how close must you be to read his mind?" the nobleman inquired as he and his companions huddled in the shadows.

"It is not a question of distance. He is unreachable."

"Protected by a Mind Magic shield, as we are?" Hillian asked.

"Perhaps, but I am afraid I do not know," the elf maid said apologetically.

Hillian nodded, his mind as sharp and crisp as the night air. "Htan, can you scout the premises and report on the numbers and locations of all the guards?" The small warrior nodded and was gone. "Eoh, we need to know what is protecting the cardinal from Ora's probing."

*I shall not fail you*, she replied, buzzing away into the darkness.

As they waited for the fairies to return, Hillian was not idle. "Ora, I want you to scan for thoughts nearby. I do not wish to be surprised by random citizens or patrolling constables." She nodded, and he turned to the dwarf. "In Porvatis, the king often employs Spell Mages to enchant an object such that it amplifies his voice when addressing a crowd. Have you experience with such spells?"

"I do," the dwarf replied.

"Do you think you could modify such a spell to amplify thoughts rather than voices?"

"That would be a useful spell, indeed," Dobyn observed, the stony surface of his face cracking with the hint of a smile. "Allow me some time to prepare."

"Of course," Hillian replied before turning his attention to the master rogue. "Eryk, do you have any agents in Cauda's household?"

"At one time, but no longer. He replaced nearly all of his guards and servants after his excommunication."

"Mona, what do you know about Cauda, the man? Family, friends, investments, anything that might be used as leverage."

"There is nothing, I'm afraid," said the Severlandi president, shaking her head. "We have launched several investigations into his personal affairs, his connection with various crimes that were credited to the Order of the Dawn, and the mysterious deaths of his wife and daughter, but no evidence has ever been found against him."

"Who replaced him as Severlandon's cardinal when he was removed?" Hillian asked.

"No one. The post remained open and his seat on my Interfaith Advisory Board rotated among various gadrinals."

"As if the prime cardinal always planned to reinstate him," Eryk suggested.

Hillian nodded, frustrated but resolute. He was certain Cauda was the key, the link that would prove his father's corruption, and he trusted that his certainty was a gift from Jalidus. Hillian had been chosen and had been graced with the knowledge, the vision, and the resources to make things right, so he was determined to earn the blessings he had been given.

"Adia," he said, turning to the one resource he had yet to tap, "did you learn anything from the merfolk that might be of use?"

"The merpeople are watchers, listeners," the sorceress replied, her eyes drifting to the ocean. "They know much, yet share little."

"Did they share anything with you?" Hillian asked after a short silence, carefully restraining his irritation at having to prompt her at all.

"The magic of the merfolk is unique. Their mages can cast only upon themselves, allowing them to change their shape. They become small fish, swimming through the underground rivers to the wells and fountains of our cities. They watch and listen, learning of our ways. They become men and women and walk among us, or birds to fly above, but they must always return to the sea, for their spells, like those cast by humans or fairies, are temporary."

Fascinated by her story as much as by her demeanor, Hillian listened as Adia continued, her voice far away, as if yearning for a forgotten dream. "Only a handful have learned to speak the modern tongue of Crozada, and they told me of dangers. They do not understand names as we do, and their language is difficult to understand, but they told me of men who seek to destroy magic, who plan and plot and speak of nothing else. I assumed they spoke of Ixodis, but perhaps this Cauda is one of them as well."

"And perhaps the prime cardinal," Eryk added.

"And perhaps my father," Hillian said simultaneously. The two men shared a look that spoke volumes. The young lord's trust in the master rogue had certainly grown, and while it was not absolute, such trust was a welcome relief. "I wonder," the Vingish nobleman pondered aloud, "if the merfolk could be of use to us, to spy on Cauda from places we cannot reach."

"And what places can we not reach, with the help of our new fairy friends?" Eryk reminded him.

"Valid point," Hillian acknowledged, just as one of those fairy friends returned from his mission.

*Lord Drake,* Htan greeted him mentally, *I am prepared to report.*

"Htan, do you make it a general practice to shield yourself from Mind Magic probes or attacks?"

*Yes, of course,* the fairy warrior replied.

"Good, and now, as you deliver your report, could you allow all of us to hear it?"

*If you wish.*

"I do. Please proceed."

*There are four gates on the wall, with a watchtower located at the midpoint between each. Eight men guard each gate, and two men are posted at each watchtower. Inside, twenty men roam the grounds, organized in military sweeps that leave no area unsupervised at any given moment. There are eleven potential entrances to the manor: three doors and eight windows on ground level, none guarded. Finally, there are four guards inside the home: two at the foot of the staircase and two outside the door to the cardinal's chambers.*

"Sixty guards outside and only four inside?" Eryk asked, incredulous. "This is too easy. Cauda is wasting his money."

"Perhaps you can give him a lesson in financial planning once we're inside," Hillian quipped. "First, would you please share with the rest of us exactly how we are going to accomplish that?"

"We fly, of course!" Eryk replied, the wicked superiority in his voice finally exhausting what little patience remained in Hillian after Adia's interesting, but overly long and fruitless, description of the merpeople. He chose to ignore his friend's condescension, for a moment at least, so he returned his attention to the fairy prince.

"Thank you, Htan, for a most thorough report."

Before the nobleman could begin to guess the details of Eryk's flying plan, the other flying member of his company returned.

*I am prepared to report, Lord Drake*, she said, demonstrating a consistency in training among the bee warriors.

"Thank you, Eoh. Htan delivered his report such that all of us could hear it. Could you please do the same?"

"I did not hear it," Dobyn grumbled, "though I doubt I would have found it useful. I gathered enough from Eryk's response."

The nobleman frowned, chastising himself for forgetting the dwarves' natural resistance to Mind Magic. "My apologies, Dobyn. I will relay it to you. Eoh, please begin."

*I could not read the cardinal's thoughts, but I was able to read the guards posted outside his chambers. Cauda wears a ring enchanted to protect against Mind Magic, and the guards permit one of two Spell Mages to enter the chambers every four hours to refresh the enchantment. The Spell Mages serve as the cardinal's personal attendants, so they are with him always.*

"So if we remove the ring, Ora can read his thoughts," Dobyn concluded after Hillian relayed the fairy's report to the dwarf.

"Only until the Spell Mages discover its absence," Mona noted.

"Dobyn, could you remove the spell from the ring and then protect it from further enchantment?" Hillian inquired.

"I could cleanse it, certainly, but Spell Magic cannot be used to make an object resistant to Spell Magic."

"Four hours is plenty of time for us to drop in from above, eliminate the four guards, and remove the ring," Eryk insisted.

Hillian shook his head. "No, there is no need to alert Cauda by killing his guards," he said. "Eoh, could you remove the ring without waking the cardinal?"

*With Htan's assistance, yes,* replied the warrior princess.

"So the fairies remove the ring, Ora reads Cauda's mind, and then the ring is returned, and the cardinal is unaware of our imposition," Hillian summarized.

"Or," Mona interjected, "since the cardinal wears many rings, the fairies could remove a different one, and Dobyn, whose spells are permanent, could enchant it to amplify thoughts, canceling out the first ring's protection spell. In this way, we would have access to Cauda's thoughts for more than four hours, while he would still believe himself protected."

Hillian smiled. "Now that is a brilliant plan, my dear president!" He kissed her in his excitement, earning a chuckle from the master thief and an expression of surprise from the Gift Mage.

"Oh, I am so happy for both of you!" Adia rejoiced, embracing the lord and the politician in turn.

Embarrassed, Hillian quickly returned to the planning. "Dobyn, are you ready with that spell?"

"Yes," replied the dwarf, "though it is untested and I cannot know if its strength will be sufficient to override the other spell."

"A risk I am willing to take," the nobleman replied. "Eoh, Htan, bring us a ring from a different finger on the same hand," he commanded.

The two fairies nodded and zipped through the shadows toward the manor.

*Chapter 18*

# INQUISITION

"Hillian Drake, Lord of Nydia, delegate of member-nation Vinglandon, please rise."

Sweat beaded on his brow, but he was not nervous. His heart raced, and his extremities tingled, but he was not nervous. Blood rushed to his head as he stood, creating a dizzy euphoria. "Mister Chairman," he managed.

"Lord Drake, you stand before this tribunal representing yourself and Mona Kesler, president and delegate of member-nation Severlandon, both of you accused of undermining the World Council. This court would hear your statement."

"Mister Chairman, if it pleases the tribunal, President Kesler and I respectfully request details regarding the grounds upon which these charges are leveled against us." He knew the details, as the chairman well understood, but Hillian needed the charges spoken aloud, heard by all the delegates and spectators in the courtroom.

The chairman nodded. "You are both accused of interfering with an event defined by the World Council as a protected international collaboration: the public execution, held by member-nation Mbúso, of the woman Adia Varani, convicted of Giftwitchery by member-nation Ard Alabia. Further, you are both accused of assisting the fugitive Varani, who is known to be a danger to safety and security, thereby endangering the health and welfare of all World Council member nations." The chairman looked up from his parchment, indicating that he was finished.

Hillian nodded, suppressing a smile. His defense on the first charge was clever and creative, so he was eager to present it, and his defense on the second charge represented his opportunity to change the world. Yet, he was forced to ask the chairman one more question. "We thank you, Mister Chairman. Would it please the tribunal to describe the potential punishments involved, were it to render a verdict of guilt?"

"Lord Drake, if you are found guilty of either charge, you will be banned for life from participation in the World Council, and the nation you represent will lose its council vote for a period of three years. The same applies to President Kesler."

"Thank you, Mister Chairman," Hillian responded, nodding at the old Ukbawan, whose silvery hair was pulled back from his wrinkled, reddish-brown face in a tight tail that reached just beyond his shoulder blades. Gawonii Chatima was an elder in the Church of Itam and a key adviser to Alom Qaletakwa, the high priest and ruler of Ukbawa. Having served two years as council chair, Chatima would serve one more before the position would have rotated to the other Itami theocracy, Tuskawa, had that nation's alom not chosen to withdraw from the World Council after suffering great losses in the early days of Severlandon's spellportals.

Instead, the chairmanship would rotate to the autocratic nation of Mbúso, whose head of state, Premier Mwambá, served as its delegate. Seated to Chairman Chatima's left, the premier observed the proceedings in angry silence, his dark face nearly always scowling, often punctuated by flaring nostrils that bounced the thin gold ring that hung from the center of his nose. Following Premier Mwambá in the rotation, and seated to his left, were Cardinal Poole, the Jalidin high priest of Grolandon, and Al'Awwal Nassi Diir, the high priest of the Sarim branch of Sabarism and the leader of the Akhdirian theocracy.

"My fellow delegates," Hillian called, carefully reminding each of the World Council representatives that he remained one of them, even though his seat, to the right of the chairman, was temporarily occupied by his monarch, King Ragnall of Vinglandon, a fair and just ruler whose brown hair had begun to gray at the temples. Seated to the right of the Vingish king were Dalil Rami Jaser, Ard Alabia's delegate, and King Kanoa, monarch of Xenrali, whose hair, skin, and eyes reflected the bronzing effect of the sun in the Pangerean Sea. At the far end of the table, participating as Mona's temporary replacement, sat Bryce Emory, the arrogant Vice President of Severlandon who, being a descendant of a noble house of Vingish colonists, spent most his waking hours trying to discredit the lowborn commoner he reluctantly served.

"Honored guests," Hillian added, finally, scanning his audience. Domus Viho was, perhaps, the newest major city in the world, and the Grolandi High King's castle reflected the city's youth. The great hall, designed to accommodate all of Grolandon's city-state kings at enormous feasts, was a perfect venue for a World Council tribunal. The overly large dais, meant for kings and great lords, served for the chairman and council delegates. The elegant mezzanine afforded an excellent second-level view of the proceedings for the most notable spectators, including the three heads of state not already sitting on the dais: Commander General Eyad Qawi of Ard Alabia, Alom Qaletakwa of Ukbawa, and High King Lynden Brook of Grolandon. Also seated on the second level were the high priests who did not have seats at the council table: Malini Galen Ziraili of the Kila Maháli faith, Al'Awwal Mukhtar Rahim of the Ghafari branch of Sabarism, and Prime Cardinal

Hydronimus Drake of Jalidinity, who sat with Cardinal Cauda of Severlandon.

The rest of the hall was filled with people of various classes and stations, from various parts of the world. Hillian spied Captain Ida Wadógo, standing with a cluster of her Golden Knights of Mbúso, and even Foster Branch, the master innkeeper and burglar who had led the prison break in Chayl.

Satisfied with the attendance, Hillian launched into his defense. "In the first charge against us, President Kesler and I are accused of interfering with an international collaborative event. Now, as my fellow delegates will certainly know, the World Council does not officially declare an event as having achieved this designation. Rather, council policy defines an international collaboration as any activity that involves the joint participation of two or more member nations. President Kesler and I, as delegates of our respective member nations, simply exercised our rights to participate in this international collaboration event."

They had expected him, he was certain, to argue that a witch burning was inappropriate on the eve of a World Council vote regarding the criminalization of public executions. Some may have expected him to argue the finer points of the word *interfere*, but none of them, not even Mona, had expected him to use the international collaboration policy against itself.

In the silence that followed, the Vingish nobleman stole a moment to congratulate himself. It would be extremely difficult for Dalil Jaser, or any of the accusers, to argue against one aspect of the policy without suggesting the fallibility of the other. As the silence evolved into a swarm of whispers and murmurs, Hillian was rewarded.

"Mister Chairman, I move to drop the first charge." The speaker was King Kanoa of Xenrali, a man whose famously open mind had led to the elimination and criminalization of organized religion in his island nation for the sake of spiritual independence, a concept that, though Hillian had studied it in university, suddenly became far more relevant to the Vingish nobleman.

"I agree with King Kanoa," added King Ragnall of Vinglandon, to which several others nodded.

Jaser, of course, voted against it, as did Vice President Emory of Severlandon, but the motion carried. A smile appeared on Hillian's face as the chairman announced, "The first charge is dismissed." The Lord of Nydia's smile grew as the gavel dropped, and the chairman asked for a statement regarding the second charge.

"In the second charge against us, President Kesler and I are accused of endangering the safety and security of council nations by assisting a fugitive known to be extremely dangerous. Now, I would like to point out that assisting a fugitive, particularly in times of war or political upheavals, has a great deal of historical precedent and would not, in and of itself, be enough to bring us before this tribunal. In fact, such an activity, engaged in by two member nations, would qualify for protection as an international collaboration."

The smile appeared, unbidden, as he used his success from the first argument to strengthen the second. That had not been planned, but Hillian's talent in public speaking allowed him to extemporize, to make impromptu adjustments. He had found the flow, the current, and his confidence expanded as he continued.

"The true charge, then, is that we threatened the safety and security of member nations. Now, this accusation is wholly dependent upon the definition of the fugitive, Miss Adia Varani, as extremely dangerous, which has not been demonstrated."

"Of course, it has been demonstrated!" Jaser exclaimed, pounding his fist upon the table. "She is *Gifted.*"

"Indeed, she is, a fact that makes her powerful, much like the Golden Knighthood of Mbúso or the Royal Navy of Vinglandon. Are you suggesting, Dalil Jaser, that these nations, simply through the existence of their formidable military strength, present threats to member nations, in violation of World Council policy?"

"If they use that strength to attack a member nation, yes," the dalil replied.

"Actually, even a military attack does not violate World Council policy unless the attack is deemed unprovoked and unfounded, which requires a formal vote by council delegates. Were you aware of that stipulation in the policy, Dalil Jaser?"

"Yes I was, Lord Drake," Jaser replied, frustration and irritation apparent in his voice, "but this tribunal is not concerned with military attacks. You have established nothing regarding the fugitive Giftwitch."

"What we have established is that the mere existence of power does not, by itself, qualify as a safety and security threat. Therefore, the fact that Miss Varani is Gifted is not enough to consider her an international danger."

"Lord Drake, this tribunal considers Miss Varani a danger not simply for being a Giftwitch but for using her Giftwitchery to attack," Jaser declared.

Hillian was immensely pleased that he had not killed Rami Jaser in Akhdiria, because the dalil was unwittingly playing his part to perfection.

"Mister Chairman, if it please the council, who is Miss Varani alleged to have attacked with Gift Magic?"

The old Ukbawan shuffled through leaves of parchment before answering, "It would seem that she attacked the Angel of Mercy in Rashida, a village in western Ard Alabia; several prison guards in Chayl, a city on the east coast of Grolandon; and a unit of Búso knights in Grolandon, just east of Domus Viho."

"Thank you, Mister Chairman, but it was my understanding that the knights encountered what they described as an invisible wall but saw no sign of Miss Varani on the scene and therefore could not claim, with any certainty, that she was responsible for their misfortune. Is that in your report?

"Similarly," Hillian rolled on, "the prison guards were attacked by something, by someone, but there were no living witnesses capable of describing the attack or the attacker. My fellow delegates, you *have* read these reports, have you not?"

As the murmuring and whispering spread throughout the great hall, the Vingish nobleman was chastised by his monarch. "Take care, Lord Drake," King Ragnall warned. "It is you and President Kesler who are on trial this day."

"With all due respect, Your Majesty, I believe that is precisely the problem. Being that the only incident with witnesses involves the Angel of Mercy, and being that those same witnesses describe the Angel of Mercy wielding Gift Magic as well, who is to say that *he* is not responsible for the other two attacks?"

"The Angel of Mercy is not a Giftwitch!" shouted Hydronimus Drake, standing in rage on the mezzanine. "He wields the power of God!"

Glancing only briefly at his red-faced father, Hillian returned his attention to the council table. "Mister Chairman, I was not aware that the prime cardinal had been invited to give testimony at these proceedings."

The old Ukbawan frowned, whispered with his colleagues, and then responded, "Prime Cardinal Drake is a known expert on the topic, and this tribunal will hear him."

"Will I be permitted to present expert testimony, as well?"

"Lord Drake," the old man replied in a tired voice, "you may call whatever experts you wish."

"Very well," Hillian responded, a smile clawing its way onto his face. He joined the rest of the assembly in turning, attentively, to the Jalidin high priest.

"The Angel of Mercy is a heavenly being, not a man, thus he could not possibly be Gifted."

"Well, if he is not a man, then the council should drop this charge, given that only four of the eight member nations recognize the existence of angels, and Miss Varani could certainly not be considered dangerous for attacking an imaginary being."

"Hillian, you know that the power of heaven must be granted to a human in order to be wielded in the world of men," the elder Drake said to his son, "just as the power of hell must be wielded by humans, like your Giftwitch."

"So, in your expert opinion, Miss Varani's opponent in the village of Rashida was, in fact, a man."

"Yes, but…"

"Does this man have a name?"

Hydronimus Drake paused. "He is the Angel of Mercy," the high priest insisted.

"He is *host* to the Angel of Mercy, but he is a man, as you have testified. What is his name?"

With hundreds of eyes upon him, the prime cardinal frowned, nervously shifting from one foot to the other. Finally, he said, "He is known to some, chiefly nonbelievers, by the name Ixodis."

Hillian nodded. His father was as easy to manipulate as Rami Jaser. "Father, I have one more question. In your expert opinion, would the powers of Ixodis be capable of the same marvels as the powers of Gift Magic, including fireballs, energy blasts, invisible shields, and lightning storms?"

"All that and more, my son. His is the power of God."

Turning from his father to his king, Hillian brought the conversation back to the point at hand. "As you can see, King Ragnall, President Kesler and I are accused because we assisted Adia Varani, who is said to pose a danger to all World Council nations not for being Gifted, but for battling Ixodis. However, through the prime cardinal's expert testimony, we have learned that Ixodis wields the same dangerous power. And, unlike Adia Varani, who is not known for killing anyone, Ixodis is well known, even celebrated, for killing citizens of every nation while channeling the Angel of Mercy persona. It seems to me that Ixodis is the danger, and Prime Cardinal Drake should stand accused for assisting him."

Hillian had intended to stun his audience, and his efforts met with great success, the great hall groaning from the weight of the silence. Before the moment had passed, before Dalil Jaser or the elder Drake could voice a retort, Hillian called his witnesses.

"Mister Chairman and my fellow delegates, I now introduce two experts on the topic of Ixodis: Dobyn, of Clan Varmingar, representing the dwarven kingdom of Tyr, and Queen Safeda, monarch of the elven nation of Ke'Andara."

Disregarding the gasps, whispers, and shocked faces, Dobyn strode proudly into the great hall, followed by four of his clansmen, all of them unarmed. Behind them came the graceful queen of the elves, resplendent in a shimmering gown of emerald green, accompanied by two of her green Andari elves and two of King Uli's blue Dathin elves, one of whom was Ora Fen.

"Two hundred years ago, in the time before the Great War," Queen Safeda began, speaking with a regal authority that commanded both respect and attention, "the elven nation of Dath'Duine occupied the territory you know today as Akhdiria and was populated with blue elves from the River Tyria to the River Drozza, from the Rachis Mountains to Keras Bay. But humans, led by Ixodis and his Gifted brethren, invaded from Ard Alabia, through Khada's Pass, slaughtering the blue elves and driving the survivors into the Forest of Ard Shaab."

Pausing momentarily to allow the humans in attendance to process the information, the elven queen continued, "The Dathin king, Uli, traveled through the Portal in Tantahir Lake, a magical gateway established centuries before to link Dath'Duine with my kingdom of Ke'Andara, located across the Kaoric Ocean on the continent of Otica. Joined by our allies, the Otica minotaurs, my army returned with King Uli to battle the invaders."

When Safeda stopped speaking, Dobyn picked up the narrative. "In the mountain nation you now call Ukbawa," Dobyn continued, as the humans in attendance struggled to process the information, "King Loe, of Clan Avishgar, ruled the dwarven kingdom of Tyr. The elven monarchs sent to King Loe for help, and the dwarves of Tyr streamed down the mountainside to join the elves and minotaurs in defending Dath'Duine. With the Spell Magic of the dwarves added to the Mind Magic of the elves, the human Gift Mages no longer enjoyed a clear advantage."

"In fact," Safeda said, "our combined strength had begun to force the humans into a slow retreat, so the Gifted generals were growing desperate."

"Mister Chairman," Vice President Emory shouted, slapping the table angrily, "I demand—" His outburst stopped abruptly as Ora Fen turned to face him. His eyes grew wide in fear, and he completed his sentence with an entirely different expression. "I demand to hear the rest of this evidence," he said, his voice a quiet mumble.

As the chairman frowned, Ora turned and smiled at Hillian, who smiled in return, wondering what the elven beauty could have done to change the Severlandi vice president's attitude so quickly and so completely. The Vingish lord had little time to ponder, though, for his dwarven friend continued the historical account.

"Ixodis was one of the less powerful generals," Dobyn explained, "until he began using the forbidden spells of necromancy, absorbing the strength and power of the elves and dwarves he killed. The other Gifted leaders tried to stop him, so he betrayed them."

"Yes," the elven queen agreed, "he struck a bargain with us, gaining our help in defeating his comrades in exchange for ending the war and withdrawing from Dath'Duine. But then he betrayed us as well, absorbing the other Gift Mages and gaining an enormous amount of power."

"Armed with that power," Dobyn spoke again, "he resumed the attacks."

"After a crushing defeat, in which King Uli and many more were killed, Ixodis offered us terms for peace." Queen Safeda paused, sadness, and perhaps regret, apparent on her face. "We were to remain hidden, invisible to human eyes, indefinitely."

"And if we did not," Dobyn added, "Ixodis would hunt us down."

"We believed that these conditions would not last long. We are elves and dwarves, after all, with life spans three or four times those of humans, so all of us expected to outlive Ixodis." She paused, her eyes sweeping the great hall before she concluded, "We were wrong. Two hundred years later, and Ixodis still lives."

"And still hunts us whenever we dare come out of hiding," the dwarf noted, "and murders Gifted infants to prevent any threat to his power."

"How could a human live over two hundred years?" King Ragnall asked.

"Our Spell Mages have studied the ancient scrolls and spell books of necromancy, those that survived the war, but have found very little about this phenomenon," Dobyn explained. "The prevailing theory holds that the absorption spell grants the necromancer not only the power and knowledge of his victim but also a portion of the victim's life force."

"How can you know for certain that Ixodis still lives?" the King of Xenrali inquired. "How do you know that it is not a different man today, carrying on the tradition of the original?"

"Because I knew him two hundred years ago," Queen Safeda responded, "and I see him sitting among you in this very hall."

On cue, six minotaurs and Gillis the satyr, led by Captain Lorcan, appeared on the mezzanine. Hillian silently thanked Eryk for arranging it, for six enormous minotaurs, armed with their enormous swords, and a crazed, bouncing satyr with a cutlass in each hand, would never have succeeded in quietly eluding the castle guards without assistance from the master rogue. Lorcan pointed his massive sword and gave the order. "Kill him," the minotaur captain rumbled, and the hall was consumed with chaos.

As the pirates moved purposefully toward their target, amid the screaming and shouting of frightened dignitaries, Hillian Drake had second thoughts. Perhaps his plan had not been so wise, after all. He stole a glance at Mona, whose terrified expression did little to relieve his concerns. But the move had been made, the pieces set in motion, and all he could do was wait to see how his game played out.

Ixodis backed away from his death, as any man would, and Lorcan kept his promise. "Harm no one," Hillian had told him, and the pirate captain stayed true to his word. The pirates shoved several people out of their way but encountered no significant resistance until Cardinal Cauda stumbled as he attempted to scramble from their path. "Throw one of them over the rail," Hillian had commanded, but he could not have guessed it would be the Severlandi cardinal, Luminary of the Order of the Dawn, nearly as much a threat as Ixodis himself.

As Cauda flew through the air, his squeal was almost amusing, and a good portion of Hillian's heart wished he could watch the wretched man splatter upon the polished marble. Alas, Adia Varani was prepared. Cloaked and hooded, standing hidden in the crowd, she activated her Gift Magic, illuminating the hall as her hair blinked to white and her eyes drained to a deep black. She caught the cardinal with an energy shield and dropped him safely, if a bit roughly, on the delegate table, as if presenting him as evidence to the tribunal.

As Adia crossed the hall to join Hillian and Mona, surrounding the three of them with a glowing energy shield, Ixodis activated his own Gift Magic. Like Adia, his hair blinked to white, standing on end as crackling energy danced from strand to strand, and his eyes became as pitch, staring coldly at his assailants. By the time the minotaurs reached him, he, too, was protected by a Gift Magic energy shield.

"Mister Chairman, fellow delegates, honored guests," Hillian declared in a loud voice, motioning to the mezzanine as he continued. "Behold the Slayer of Souls and Murderer of Millions. Behold the false Angel of Mercy, who is not an angel at all but a Gifted man. Behold Ixodis!"

*Chapter 19*

# GUIDANCE

The sharp pain in his gut grew like a weed, driving its roots into his bowels and twisting its vines around his heart. When Ora's probing of Cardinal Cauda had confirmed Hillian's suspicion that Hydronimus Drake was not only in league with Ixodis, but that he did, in fact, direct and coordinate the monster's brutal murders, neither Hillian nor his companions had been surprised. But Cauda did not know the identity of Ixodis. So, when a similar probing of his father yielded no results, the Lord of Nydia had been forced to wait for the elven queen. He had remained optimistic that Safeda's Mind Magic talent would succeed where Ora's had failed, but he had not been prepared to learn that his father and Ixodis were one and the same. He harbored doubts, in fact, until his plan had provided the proof.

Hillian felt sick, just as he had on the roof of the Rat's Nest Tavern, but one look at Mona and the nobleman knew that he could not succumb to illness or guilt. He nodded at Lorcan, signaling him to stand down, and the minotaurs positioned themselves at either end of the mezzanine, blocking the exits. With their withdrawal, all attention settled upon the elder Drake, still crackling with raw Gift Magic within his energy shield.

"I am not Gifted. I am the chosen host to the Angel of Mercy," the prime cardinal said, hubris in his voice and anger in his midnight eyes. "And why not? I am the high priest of Jalidinity, chosen to guide the sheep of men to the Almighty Shepherd."

"You are a fraud and a murderer," Hillian replied, the bitterness sharp and painful on his tongue, "and to-day all the world has seen the truth."

"You have no idea what burdens I have assumed for the sake of that very same world, nor how many lives I have saved with a handful of necessary deaths," Hillian's father insisted, vehemently. "We do not call it murder when a soldier slays an enemy in the midst of war. Make no mistake, Hillian, I have been fighting a war to save us all from the evils of Gift Magic."

The World Council delegates seemed to have forgotten the tribunal, watching and listening in stunned silence as father and son presented very different perspectives regarding the safety and security of council nations. Cautiously, the Vingish nobleman continued to bait his father, ironically attempting to herd the self-proclaimed shepherd to ever more damning admissions.

"Every nation in the council has laws against murder, even if that murder can be justified," Hillian replied calmly. "Kill a sick woman to prevent the spread of a deadly disease? Murder. Kill a man who has raped and butchered fifteen young girls in order to prevent fifteen more? Murder. Kill a Gifted infant to prevent him from growing into a dangerous threat to the world? Murder."

"But you cannot possibly comprehend the enormity of the threat!" the prime cardinal shouted. "Gift Magic is far too powerful for humans to manage. It corrupts everything and everyone it touches."

"Except you," Hillian taunted.

"Including me," the prime cardinal replied. "But I had no choice! I saw what had to be done, and I was strong enough to do it. I was stronger than all the other Gift Mages, stronger than the Mindwitches of the elves and the Spellwitches of the dwarves. And I am strong still, stronger than all these fools on the council, stronger than your Giftwitch whore, stronger than you, *boy*!"

Hillian flinched at the term, one his father had only ever used in anger, invariably followed by a stern hand and, later, his mother's warm, protective embrace. But the Lord of Nydia would not be intimidated. "That was twice," he said in a quiet, determined voice.

"Twice? What was twice?" his father raved.

"Just now, twice, you admitted to being Gifted. You said that the corrupting effect of Gift Magic affected everyone, including you, and then you referred to the Gift Mages in the Great War as 'all the other Gift Mages,' which can only mean you are one, too."

Hydronimus Drake was silent, and Hillian could not help notice the look of defeat on his father's face, but the young lord pushed ahead relentlessly. "So you have admitted to being Gifted and corrupt, as well as murderous—"

"*I* am corrupt?" the prime cardinal interrupted, his voice growing in pitch and volume. "I have *never* allowed my purpose to be corrupted, not by my wife, not by my king, not by my church, and I will certainly not allow it to be corrupted by the likes of *you*. I brought this world back from the brink, single-handedly, and you dare to stand in judgment of *me*?" As the prime cardinal's rage increased, it was matched by the intensity of his Gift Magic. Lightning danced along the edge of his energy shield, arcing to the walls and the vaulted ceiling. An ornate candelabrum exploded dramatically as Hydronimus Drake reached a breaking point. "You ungrateful, insolent *boy*, what have you accomplished here today? *What?* You have destroyed three lifetimes of growth! You have destroyed safety and security! You have destroyed peace! You have brought back war, *boy*, and sentenced the world to death."

Struggling to remain calm, Hillian Drake spoke to his dwarven friend, but his eyes never left the swirling blackness of his father's. "Dobyn, it is time for the prime cardinal to go."

The dwarf began to chant:

Light as air and fast as wind,
on to Ixodis I send
dust and dirt to stick like glue,
stretch and grow and cover, too.

Make a shell around the man.
Spellport him across the land
to a place away so far:
the capital of Tuskawa.

Hearing the chanting, which had grown louder as Dobyn reached the climactic ending, Ixodis turned his head just in time to see the dwarf blow a mighty breath into his hands, sending a swirl of dirt into the air. As it hurtled toward Ixodis, increasing in speed, the villain released his protective shield and clapped his hands together toward the dwarven Spell Mage. With a deafening crack that shattered three windows, a bolt of energy blasted toward Dobyn, ripping through the cloud of dust and scattering it in all directions.

Hillian experienced a moment of panic as he realized he had neglected to remind Adia to be ready, but his anxiety was unfounded. The sorceress redirected her energy shield to protect the dwarf. As the prime cardinal's blast glanced off Adia's shield, tearing into the ceiling and dropping stones and rubble upon unfortunate spectators, the spellcasted particles adjusted their paths, flying at Ixodis from all directions.

In a flash, Ixodis restored his protective shield, but the spell was not to be thwarted. The dirt attached itself to the surface of the energy dome and began to grow, each particle stretching out, joining with another, forming tendrils that wrapped around the shield in mere moments.

And then he was gone.

━━━

Just after sundown, the Pegasus Room was closed, highly unusual for the dining area of Domus Viho's Unicorn Palace Inn. The doors were closed for a private party, the innkeeper told her guests, but she would be glad to send food and drink to the guest rooms. Meanwhile, the Pegasus Room rang with sounds of drinking, singing, and celebration. Hillian wanted to be merry, to share in the success of the day, but he could not ignore the doubts that had been festering in his chest since leaving the World Council tribunal.

His plan had worked beautifully, even flawlessly. His friends and allies had all delivered masterful performances and even his enemies and accusers, particularly the prime cardinal and the Alabian dalil, had unwittingly played their parts to perfection. Hillian's strategy had succeeded at every level: exposing his father as Ixodis; introducing the nonhuman races to the world; and, of course, exonerating both Mona and himself of all international charges.

He should have been celebrating with the others. He should have been singing with Mona, laughing with Eryk, and drinking magical mead with Dobyn. Instead, the Lord of Nydia sat by the hearth, alone, staring into the fire.

"So, why Kewu?" he heard Adia ask.

"Because there are no spellportals there," Dobyn answered, "and it is in Tuskawa, which is surrounded by mountains."

"For a dwarf who lives underground, you certainly know a great deal about the human cities on the surface," Mona noted.

"As Chief of Clan Varmingar, I am ultimately responsible for preserving the secret of the dwarves from the humans above. To fulfill that duty, I must know more about humans than anyone else in Tyr." He swallowed another mouthful of Mama Bear's mead, adding, "Though it would seem I have no more secret to protect."

"So by sending him to Kewu, you would delay his return," Adia concluded.

"If he even survived," Dobyn said.

"Is that in question?" Eryk inquired.

"Well, I have never casted such a port," the dwarf admitted, "where the passenger was not willing and the destination was not expecting to receive."

"Yes," Mona agreed. "In the early days of my portals, many spellcasters offered spellportation services outside of our established network. By sending passengers to locations unprepared to receive them, many people materialized in spaces that were already occupied by furniture, animals, or other people, resulting in hundreds of deaths."

"And if those passengers were unwilling to be spellported, it is unknown if they would have traveled to the intended destination at all," Dobyn added.

"If the possibility exists that Ixodis could have been injured or killed in the process of porting, why not do it intentionally?" Eryk suggested.

"Indeed, that thought did cross my mind," Dobyn acknowledged. "I thought perhaps I should send him into the center of a mountain, killing or trapping him. But then..." The dwarf broke off with a rare chuckle before concluding, "But my home, my nation, is squarely in the center of a mountain."

Eryk laughed heartily. "Imagine how old King Loe would react if you sent Ixodis into his throne room!"

They all laughed, and even Hillian was not immune to the humor, smiling at the image. His somber expression returned, however, as he imagined the devastation that his father would have wrought on the kingdom of Tyr in such a scenario.

As he stared into the dancing flames, Hillian's thoughts grew ever more morose. If Hydronimus Drake had been truthful about his motives, if a new generation of Gifted might become corrupted by power, perhaps the Angel of Mercy's approach was necessary. Instinctively, Hillian knew that such a thought was merely an intellectual justification for evil actions, and his solid moral principles and strong faith in Jalidus prevented him from subscribing to the same self-manipulating philosophy that his father had adopted. Still, the anxiety remained, and the Lord of Nydia feared the future he was championing.

"Hillian," the voice of Ora said behind him, as the elf maid placed her hand gently on his shoulder, "Queen Safeda requests a word."

He heard her, despite the noise from a table of arguing minotaurs, despite the unending boasting of Dobyn's clansmen and their new satyr friend, and despite the incessant buzzing of the bee fairies. Hillian heard her and nodded, but his eyes remained transfixed by the fire. Ora paused, certainly waiting for him to stand and follow her to a small table occupied by the queen and her elves. When he did not rise, she departed, presumably returning to the queen.

After several moments, a hush fell on the common room. The minotaurs and dwarves paused in their activities, Eryk and Mona halted their laughter, the fairies seemed to have stopped flying, and even Gillis was silent. When Queen Safeda seated herself in a chair opposite the hearth, the Vingish nobleman understood. In the course of his association with Ora Fen, Hillian had often found himself noticing the graceful way she moved and carried herself, not to mention her ethereal beauty. The elven queen sitting before him possessed the same qualities, but they were bolstered by her age and station. Safeda was the embodiment of grace and elegance, of regal confidence and quiet power, of wisdom and experience. Yet she had come to him, deferring to him, and that had captured everyone's attention.

"Lord Drake," she greeted him, "I wish to congratulate you on your victory today."

"My thanks, Queen Safeda," the Lord of Nydia replied, acknowledging her with a glance before his eyes drifted back to the flames. The common room remained silent, ears of all races straining to hear the fireside conversation, and Hillian was painfully aware of their attention.

"You have given us great hope," the elven queen declared.

"I was graced with many wonderful friends and allies who contributed much to bring that hope to life."

"As one of those allies," Safeda began, "I am thankful for the invitation to participate."

"As I am thankful that you accepted."

The elven queen sighed. *Lord Drake,* she said in his mind, *I wish to give you counsel.*

Hillian's eyes abandoned the fire and fixed upon the elven queen. What sort of counsel, he wondered, would require the secrecy of Mind Magic?

*The human world is in shock*, she told him. *In the confusion that follows, they will yearn for direction and guidance and will eagerly follow whosoever steps forward to lead.*

The Vingish nobleman frowned, considering her unspoken words, but Safeda did not grant him time to ponder. *You must act, Lord Drake, before lesser men like Rami Jaser or Bryce Emory take the opportunity from you.*

*What would you have me do?* he asked, sending his thoughts to the elven monarch as Ora had taught him.

*You must lead*, she insisted. *First, you must lead the celebration this night, to show that you appreciate all of us who have already chosen to follow you. Then you must deploy us, as you did at the tribunal, to help you lead the rest of the world.*

*I have no ambition to rule the world*, Hillian responded.

*Not rule it, but lead it*, Safeda clarified. *You must guide the rulers, Lord Drake. You must complete what you began today, unraveling the knots your father used to bind them as prisoners and providing a new vision that will hold them together as willing participants.*

Hillian nodded, his mind already developing strategies, drawing up plans, but the queen was not finished.

*And you must put an end to Ixodis, lest he put an end to all of us.*

Hillian frowned. Only death would bring an end to the powerful sorcerer, but the younger Drake possessed none of his father's murderous instincts.

*I do not think I could kill him*, he thought to the elven queen.

*You need only neutralize him,* she replied. *Keb is filled with those who would be more than willing to finish him.*

The noble leader nodded. Her confidence in him was contagious, and he felt stronger knowing he had her support. *You will stand beside me?* he asked.

*Not beside you, Lord of Nydia. You must lead.* Suddenly, she switched from Mind Magic to audible speech, adding, "I stand behind you, with the strength of Ke'Andara behind me."

"And the Dathin elves?" Hillian asked aloud.

"King Uli will stand with me, eventually," the elven queen replied with quiet confidence, "or he will lose all but his eldest subjects to me. You will have Dath'Duine."

"And the kingdom of Tyr," Dobyn added, standing at the table just behind the Vingish lord.

"And Kiriti," Lorcan rumbled, supported by a bleating satyr and six minotaurs slamming their fists upon the tables.

*And the Hive,* declared Htan with Mind Magic, buzzing into the air.

"You have Severlandon," Mona insisted, smiling as she stood to join Dobyn.

"You have my guild," Eryk said, also standing, "and the malini will stand behind you, as well."

Five nonhuman nations, two human nations—assuming he could count on his own king—one world religion, and the largest network of spies and rogues on the continent...Hillian had much, and he would find a way to convince the rest.

Lord Drake looked at the faces of his friends and allies. They would follow him to their deaths, if necessary, so the responsibility to keep them safe, to use their talents and resources appropriately, to lead them to victory...that responsibility was his alone. Then his eyes fell on Adia Varani. She had not declared for him, he realized, and he could see the indecision written upon her face. She had changed while she was away, her anger and fiery vengeance softening into measured resolve. Yet, observing her from across the tavern, Hillian detected only doubt.

"Adia," he called, hoping he knew how to reach her. "Ixodis is my father. I cannot kill him."

"Hillian," she responded after a moment of hesitation. "You know he must be stopped."

"Yes, and if we do not kill him, he will return," the Lord of Nydia replied, calmly glancing at Eryk. "When you fail to kill an enemy, he always returns."

The sorceress frowned in confusion. "You said we cannot kill him," she said.

"I said *I* could not kill him, which is why *you* must do it."

She stared at him for a long moment before she nodded. Her amber eyes glowed with trust, as they had on the shore of the Iigra River just before he had lost her. "Then I stand behind you," she promised.

## Chapter 20

# REFORMATION

The Lord of Nydia arrived with a full entourage, bursting into the great hall of Domus Viho in dramatic fashion.

"Lord Drake, this is a closed council meeting!" Chairman Chatima shouted in aggravation, as the hall was filled with dwarves, elves, fairies, minotaurs, and a single satyr.

"Mister Chairman," the Vingish delegate replied with a calm confidence, "were you not present at the tribunal yesterday? Did you fail to understand that the most powerful Gift Mage in history has declared war on the world?"

"It was not proven that he is Gifted," Dalil Jaser vehemently interjected.

"You may yet harbor doubts, Rami, but consider this: if even one nation believes and puts an end to the genocide of Gifted infants, an entire generation of Gift Mages will be reintroduced to the world. Imagine the advantages that such a nation will enjoy, both in commerce and in military power."

Hillian paused to allow the delegates to ponder. Even Jaser was speechless, for the concept was profound. Finally, the Vingish lord added the final ingredient to the dish he was serving. "You might also imagine," he suggested, "how this new generation of Gifted will feel about any nation that rejects them."

Jaser's eyes widened, but it was the chairman who first spoke. "Are you threatening us, Lord Drake?" the old Ukbawan asked, not bothering to hide his suspicion.

"Of course not, Mister Chairman, but we are World Council delegates, charged with protecting the interests of our respective nations, regardless of our own personal or religious viewpoints. What happened yesterday was not a dream. Elves and dwarves, minotaurs, satyrs, fairies, and merpeople, an entire continent across the ocean, and Gifted children growing to adulthood alongside our own...these things are real. The landscape of our society is not *about* to change; it has already begun, and the World Council cannot avoid the decisions these changes have presented."

"What decisions, Lord Drake?" inquired King Kanoa of Xenrali.

"I move that the council accept the kingdom of Tyr into its membership, assigning Dobyn of Clan Varmingar as its voting delegate."

"I second the motion," Mona declared, stepping forward to stand beside Hillian.

"Neither of you are voting delegates," Bryce Emory noted from Severlandon's seat at the council table. "You can neither motion nor second."

"Actually, Mister Emory," Mona said, stepping onto the raised dais and walking toward her vice president, "you were Severlandon's delegate only for the tribunal, which has concluded." When she reached him, she added, "Now, if you will excuse me, I believe you're in my seat."

"Your Majesty," Hillian greeted, looking at his king, "of course you have the authority to retain your status as our nation's delegate. Is that your wish?"

"It is not," King Ragnall responded, standing to vacate his seat. "I shall remain to observe these proceedings, and I trust that my thoughts will be heard if I choose to voice them, but Vinglandon's vote is yours." Hillian sighed in relief as his monarch's vote of confidence reinforced his assumption that Vinglandon would be with him.

Despite Emory's grumbling and Jaser's consistent vote to the contrary, the World Council approved many of the motions brought by Hillian and Mona that day.

"The World Council admits to its membership the kingdom of Tyr, governed by King Loe and represented by Dobyn of Clan Varmingar, and having as its territory the underground caves, tunnels, and caverns beneath the mountain ranges of the Tyrenese and the Orbalese," the chairman read, summarizing the council decisions. "The World Council admits to its membership the nation of Ke'Andara, governed and represented by Queen Safeda and having as its territory a specific region of the continent of Otica, details of which shall be provided by the delegate at the next council meeting."

The mood at the table was tense, but the tension seemed to have spawned new excitement within some of his fellow delegates. Predictably, King Kanoa was chief among them, but the Premier of Mbúso was a distinct surprise. After the admission of Tyr and Ke'Andara, Premier Mwambá pushed to admit Dath'Duine, Kiriti, and the Hive as well but was successful with only one of the three.

As the chairman described the third admission, the Vingish lord's attention was already consumed with plans to facilitate success for the remaining two. "The World Council admits to its membership the nation of the Hive, governed by Queen Tarala and represented by Prince Htan, and having as its territory an autonomous region within the borders of Severlandon, details of which shall be provided by the delegate at the next council meeting. The World Council does *not* admit to its membership the nation of Dath'Duine, governed by King Uli, as its territorial claims conflict with those of council member-nation Akhdiria. The World Council does *not* admit to its membership the island of Kiriti, whose lack of an established government prevents it from qualifying for member-nation status under council guidelines.

"Finally," the chairman declared, and Hillian glanced at Mona excitedly, "the World Council adopts as policy the proposal submitted by Severlandon outlawing mob justice and public executions. It has been noted, however, that private executions by hanging, burning, etcetera, are still permitted, depending on the respective laws of each nation, if and only if a trial has been conducted and guilt determined."

"And what of Ixodis?" Hillian asked, almost before the chairman had finished speaking. "We cannot know the nature of the war he intends to wage, but we have a small window of opportunity to stop him before he truly begins."

"What do you propose, Lord Drake?" King Kanoa inquired.

〜〟〟

Hours later, as they stood upon the circular platform of the Domus Viho spellportal, Adia voiced her dissatisfaction. "I do not think it was enough," she complained.

"I understand," Hillian acknowledged, "but we accomplished a great deal. At the next council meeting, we shall have Tyr, Ke'Andara, and the Hive aligned with us, at which time we will pursue the elimination of laws that criminalize Gift Magic."

"But you had the momentum today, Hillian, and the climate of the council may be far different at the next meeting," the sorceress pointed out.

"With King Kanoa and Premier Mwambá squarely behind us, we control seven of the eleven votes in the council."

"But you cannot be certain that either of them will vote with you next time."

"Adia, we are on our way to destroy Ixodis, to realize your lifelong goal, with the support of the World Council. Let us focus on this today."

She argued no further, but her glare, even without the fire of Gift Magic, reminded Hillian of the time in Mbúso when she had struck him. The damage had been healed, and the bruises had faded, but the memory remained clear.

After porting to Chayl and riding for most of a day, they arrived at Norwood Marsh. Leaving behind their mounts, they trudged through the muck to the target location, where the darkness was thick and overbearing and carried a wet, offensive smell that served to further suffocate the Vingish nobleman and his companions. They were linked by Mind Magic but, even mentally, all remained hushed, tense with anticipation. Hillian tried not to dwell on his plan or, more specifically, on the significant possibility that his plan would be an utter and complete failure, resulting in the deaths of all his friends and allies. No, it was not a healthy thought, so he forced himself to focus on a different topic.

For a moment, he thought about Adia. He wondered if he had, indeed, failed her at the council meeting. More thought of failure, however, was equally unhealthy, so Hillian pushed his mind in a different direction.

Predictably, his thoughts drifted to Mona Kesler. Since their night of intimacy in the Calimygna prison, they had both been consumed by trial, tribunal, and Ixodis, leaving little time to further explore their deepening relationship. Still, whenever his thoughts were not obsessing about plans, they invariably invoked images of the amazing Severlandi president, inspiring both excitement and anxiety. In his extremely limited experience, Hillian had only ever harbored romantic notions about two types of women: household servants and highborn ladies. Mona was neither, and the Lord of Nydia had absolutely no idea what to do with her.

As Hillian's thoughts of Mona began to drift toward the intimately personal, Ora spoke in his mind.

*Hillian, recall that we are all mentally linked.*

Hillian smiled. Well, Mona was not linked, thankfully, having grudgingly accepted that her skills and talents would be more useful aiding Eryk in Kiriti, working to establish a formal system of government, than in Norwood Marsh, waiting in the swampy darkness to ambush the most powerful sorcerer the world had ever known.

Time tended to pass differently in absolute silence, when the darkness seemed alive and hateful. Perhaps Lakis was not a fiery inferno, Hillian mused, but a quiet swamp, where unrepentant souls fought to retain their sanity while suffering an eternity of nauseating humidity. If that were true, then Himil need not be a golden city ruled by the Almighty Jalidus, for a cool bath would surely qualify as paradise.

In the midst of his imaginary hell, Hillian's doubts resurfaced. First, he doubted that his plan would succeed. Then, he noted that success was relative. Would he feel victorious if his friends died in the process? Would it feel like victory to kill his own father? That thought, of course, led him back to the ultimate doubt: Was it right and just to kill a man, even if that man was a murderer who had declared war on the world, and even if such an act was approved by the World Council? Would Jalidus approve? Certainly, he asserted to himself, the Almighty had given his blessing, for it was Jalidus who had put Hillian on the path. Yet...if he justified an evil act in the name of God, was he not the same as his father?

Distraught and conflicted though he was, the unlikely leader found no opportunity to seek the answers in his heart or mind, for the signal had been given. Ixodis had arrived in the marsh.

The Lord of Nydia reviewed the plan in his head. It was a simple plan, and it would succeed exactly because of its simplicity, if it succeeded at all. Either way, however, the blood would be on Hillian's hands.

As Ixodis came into view, trudging through the watery swamp, Hillian's plan began to unfold.

Rising from the shallows, a strange and horrible creature began to advance on the prime cardinal. As anticipated, the sorcerer, visible in the darkness of the swamp due to the two fireflies that flew above his head, stopped walking and activated his Gift Magic, the crackling energy lighting him up like a bonfire. As the creature, a strange hybrid of snake and crocodile parts, retreated from the blinding light, Adia Varani let loose, blasting from the shadows.

Hillian held his breath, hoping against hope that her initial assault would be enough, but his father was not to be taken so easily. Just before Adia's blast reached him, Ixodis erected his energy shield, forming a glowing dome around him, reaching down into the marshy muck. The sorcerer scanned the swamp, but Adia had deactivated her Gift Magic, allowing her to hide in the darkness, and Hillian was left to hope and pray that the second team had managed to swim into position.

The water rippled at Ixodis's feet, inside his energy dome, as another swamp creature entered the fray. As it broke the surface of the thick, marshy water, it appeared to be a harmless lizard with an overgrown head, but from its open mouth poured sixteen Screaming Stingers, led by Princess Eoh. The bee-fairy warriors flew directly to Ixodis's face and neck, each plunging her poison-tipped stinger into his vulnerable flesh.

With his assailants attacking from inside his protective shield, Ixodis was defenseless, but Hillian expected a counterattack at any moment. That was the plan, of course, for the sorcerer would be forced to release his protective dome to attack the fairies, but the Vingish nobleman was concerned the Screaming Stingers might not have time to fly clear. It was a calculated risk, one Eoh and her warrior princesses had been eager to accept, but Hillian's gut twisted nonetheless.

The lizard had retreated to relative safety underwater by the time Eoh impaled the prime cardinal's eye, eliciting a roar of absolute hatred from the besieged sorcerer. Channeling his rage, Ixodis exploded in a ball of fire, the flames so fierce that the Screaming Stingers were vaporized to the last.

Moments after the energy shield fell, before his flames had entirely dissipated, Ixodis was feathered with arrows from the elves. The sorcerer's pain increased as the arrows, spellcasted by Dobyn, burst into flames, just as dwarven bombs began exploding in his face. His head jerked back as Ora and Safeda attacked his mind. The final blow, a powerful force blast from Adia, nearly separated his head from his body. Ixodis sank into the muck and slime.

Time stood still. It had happened too quickly. Hillian was frozen, unable to move, a battle raging in his mind between exalted victory and tragic disbelief.

Dobyn was the first to reach the body, immediately checking for signs of life. When Hillian finally arrived, he choked at the sight of his father's corpse, its face destroyed, completely unrecognizable. Was it grief, he wondered, or guilt that constricted his throat? Straining, he forced his eyes to connect with the dwarf's.

"He is dead," Dobyn declared.

"It is finished," Adia breathed, cautiously, but she did not appear relieved.

Hillian also felt no sense of relief. His body remained tense, and he realized, as he scanned the faces of his friends and allies, that many others felt the same. The swamp creature and the lizard had reverted to their mermaid forms but stayed well back from the dead sorcerer, as did the firefly fairies, the elven archers, and the dwarves. Ora and Safeda had approached the body, and the younger elf's expression resembled Adia's, fear clouding her lavender eyes. The queen's emerald eyes contained no fear, but they did show concern and perhaps worry. Dobyn, too, seemed concerned, a frown etched into his stony face.

"If it is finished," Hillian asked, "then why are we still afraid?"

"Perhaps it is not fear, but sorrow," Ora suggested. "Seventeen lives have ended, even if one belonged to our enemy."

"Sorrow, yes," the Vingish nobleman replied, "but also fear."

After a period of awkward silence, Dobyn spoke. "Perhaps we fear what is to come," he suggested.

"The future is, indeed, unknown," Queen Safeda responded, "but it inspires hope as well as fear."

"Perhaps we fear that Ixodis will yet rise," Hillian proposed.

"Then we finish him," Adia said, activating her Gift Magic.

"Wait," the Vingish leader commanded.

"When you fail to kill an enemy, he always returns," Dobyn said, borrowing Eryk's words.

"You told me I had to kill him," Adia reminded. "You must allow me to be certain."

Hillian nodded. "Do what you feel is necessary," he said. The Lord of Nydia turned his back and walked away.

# EPILOGUE

She paced restlessly, her mind anxiously racing. "I should be in there," she complained. "With Ixodis gone, I am Last of the Gifted. How could anyone else represent the interests of the next generation of Gift Mages?"

"Hillian will represent your interests," Ora encouraged, "as will Dobyn, Mona, Htan, and Queen Safeda. Trust your friends, Adia. You are not alone."

Despite the soothing words of her elven companion, Adia Varani felt very alone. She had succeeded in destroying Ixodis, a fact in which she took great satisfaction, certainly; however, with her goal achieved, she was forced to find a new purpose, a new driver. She had spent her entire life, she realized, locked on a path with Ixodis, but with him gone, she traveled the path alone, and she no longer possessed a clear understanding of the destination.

"How am I to trust anyone to represent my goals when I no longer know what they are?" she asked, unwittingly voicing the source of her anxiety.

"Why should your goals have changed?" Ora asked. "You seek to destroy Ixodis, do you not?"

"Yes, and he is dead," the sorceress replied, her voice tinged with sadness. "I made sure of it."

"Yes, but until the magical and nonmagical live in peace once more, until his work has been reversed, the destruction of Ixodis is incomplete," Ora insisted.

The accuracy of the elf maid's statement was astonishing, and Adia was stunned by its simplicity. "Thank you, Ora," the sorceress said, feeling a genuine appreciation as she embraced her friend.

Smiling, Ora said, "You are not alone, Adia. United, we defeated Ixodis, and united, we will destroy his legacy."

A short time passed in which the two women were content to enjoy the famous gardens of Qadir in friendly conversation. Night had fallen, yet the air did not cool as the heat of the desert sun—absorbed and trapped during the day—radiated from the sands. She closed her eyes, but she could still feel the heat, could still hear the dalils chanting their priestly prayers to Sabar as darkness descended upon the desert, and she could still see the sand, the endless ocean of sand. The sand had killed her once.

Startling Adia from her dark thoughts, Ora asked the question that Adia had expected since her reunion with the group in Severlandon: "What happened to you after we were attacked in the Forest of Ard Shaab?"

The sorceress frowned. "I have no memory of hurtling down the river or spilling into the ocean. I have been told I was conscious for days, though completely erratic and nonsensical, but I have no memory of this either. My mind had been shattered, utterly," she explained.

Ora frowned in concern.

"My first memory was a taste so unique and so wonderful that I can very nearly taste it again every time I imagine it." Adia closed her eyes, remembering the tangy sweetness on her tongue, but Ora interrupted.

"What was it that you were tasting?"

"Quince," the sorceress answered cheerfully. "It is a wonderful, delicious fruit that is plentiful in the merfolk colony. They squeeze it into a pulpy juice and that, my dear Ora, that is what I was tasting—quince juice—when I finally began to recover."

"Did they say how they found and rescued you?"

"It took some time, but yes, they finally explained it to me. Though there were a few among them who spoke our language, they described events in ways I could not understand. Even reading their minds was not effective, perhaps because I am not overly skilled at Mind Magic, but also because their thoughts were constructed in pictures that seemed to be randomly organized."

Ora nodded, clearly intrigued.

"I finally found some success with one of their more experienced Mind Mages, and the two of us were able to piece together a coherent story," Adia continued. "Apparently, my broken mind was mentally crying out for help, attracting attention from nearby mermaids and mermen as I floated along with the ocean current. They brought me to their Mind Mages, who were able to see pictures in my scattered thoughts, specifically images of me being attacked while traveling with Master Rook. That was enough for them to consider me a friend—"

"And then they found me," Eryk interjected, emerging from the darkness of night into the relative brightness of the garden, illuminated as it was by several braziers and candelabras. Bounding up the steps to join the ladies, he added, "And I arranged to have you brought back to the mainland, safely and secretly, to meet us at the Hive."

"Yes, and I have never been so happy to see anyone as I was then," Adia responded, "until now. Where have you been? You've been gone for ages."

"I was waiting for good news," the master rogue answered, apologetically.

"But it is not good news," Adia guessed, her spirits falling as she read the look on Eryk's face.

"There is good news, and there is news that is not yet good or bad," he replied. "Dath'Duine has been admitted to the council after King Uli, with Queen Safeda's assistance, successfully negotiating with Akhdiria for territorial rights. Kiriti has been admitted to the council after Mona and I succeeded in organizing it into a monarchy, its first king elected from several families that had loose ties to the original minotaur royalty in Otica.

Public executions were banned at the previous session, but this session has gone a step further, banning execution by burning, whether public or private."

He paused just long enough for Adia to conclude that he was not simply taking a breath. "But no discussion of laws protecting Gift Magic?" She felt herself getting angry, the heat and the sand of Ard Alabia adding to her anxiety.

"They have been discussing it for hours, but there is a great deal of disagreement."

"Disagreement over what?" Adia exclaimed. "Haven't we proven that Gift Magic isn't evil?"

"Only Jaser is still talking about evil," Eryk replied, his face clearly showing the distaste he harbored for the Alabian priest. "The larger conversation is about danger. The council may ban laws that criminalize *being* Gifted, but they are unlikely to ban laws against the *practice* of Gift Magic."

"Even if it's used for good?"

Eryk sighed. "I think the potential danger is looming larger than the potential benefit."

Of course. They were right, Adia realized immediately. Gift Magic was dangerous. She, herself, was dangerous. Somehow, in focusing on eliminating the threat of Ixodis, Adia Varani had demonstrated herself as an equivalent threat. Her chest tightened, and the anxiety returned.

Ora tried to comfort her. "It is but one meeting," she said, placing her hand on Adia's arm. "Today is only the beginning, and much progress has been made. Have faith that our allies will continue to seek even more."

"Our allies?" Adia scoffed. "And who would that be? With Dath'Duine and Kiriti added, there are thirteen members of the World Council. You say I should trust Mona, Hillian, Dobyn, Htan, and Queen Safeda to represent my interests, which would make five. And Hillian said I should trust that King Kanoa and Premier Mwambá are still behind us. Well, that makes seven, which is already a majority. So, if Dath'Duine and Kiriti are with us, too, which I think is reasonable to expect, the conversation should be over. So just who are these allies?"

Too late, Adia realized that she had directed her frustration at Ora, the kindest, gentlest soul she had ever encountered. "I'm sorry," she said, "but how can you be so positive?"

"As I understand it," Ora replied in her soft voice, "you met Hillian because he was arguing to have you burned, and now he has helped to ban burnings across the world. That is a great victory to add to your defeat of Ixodis. How can you feel anything but positive?"

"And the nations of the world have accepted that being magical is not a crime or a threat," Eryk added. "You have accomplished much, Adia Varani, Last of the Gifted."

"Last, but also First," Ora corrected him. Then, to Adia, she added, "The new generation of Gift Mages will look to you as their teacher and mentor."

Adia nodded as she pondered the words of her friends. She recalled the overheard conversation between Malini

Ziraili and Knight Captain Wadógo. The old priest had described how Mona Kesler's spellportals had not simply made change *in* the world, but had truly *changed* the world.

"We changed the world," she said, smiling at her companions.

"We did indeed," the master thief replied, his lips curling into a roguish grin.

"But there is still much to be done," the sorceress added.

"And we will do it together," Ora said, "with our current allies as we work to make more."

The sorceress was satisfied, finally able to relax for nearly an hour before a horn sounded, indicating that the World Council meeting had adjourned. Almost before the high note of the horn had settled into the hot sands, Hillian and Mona arrived to relay the news, accompanied by Dobyn and Htan. They confirmed Eryk's information about Dath'Duine, Kiriti, and execution by burning, but the remainder of their report was more disappointing than Adia had hoped.

"We succeeded fairly easily in banning laws that criminalize being Gifted," Mona reported. "However, the nations that opposed us have threatened to leave the council."

"Ard Alabia and who else?" Eryk asked.

"Yes," Hillian said, confirming Eryk's guess. "Ard Alabia, Akhdiria, and to my surprise, Grolandon."

"I believe the threat of their defection influenced the outcome of our next proposal," Mona explained. "In any case, we were unable to ban laws that criminalize the practice of Gift Magic."

Even though Adia had expected such an outcome, based on Eryk's prediction, disappointment fed bitterness into her reaction. "You said we could trust them," she said to Hillian. "You were wrong."

Hillian's eyes met hers, and his own disappointment was apparent as he dropped his head in defeat, but it was the bee-fairy warrior who responded.

*It is still a great victory*, Htan said through Mind Magic.

"Yes, and now you can safely move about the world without fear for being who you are," the elf maid added with her quiet optimism.

"Except in Tuskawa, since it is not part of the council," Adia noted, stubbornly, "or in any of the nations that withdraw."

"Do you think any of them really will?" Eryk asked, directing the question to the small group of delegates.

"Cardinal Poole of Grolandon and Al'Awwal Diir of Akhdiria seem to be somewhat pacified after successfully blocking our second proposal," Mona answered. "Jaser, on the other hand, remained adamant that Ard Alabia would withdraw, but he does not possess the same level of authority in his nation as the other two delegates do."

"No, he will have to convince the commander general," Dobyn pointed out.

"Or the al'awwal who advises the commander general," Mona noted.

"Whether he does or not, we will proceed in exactly the same manner," Hillian declared. "We will continue to work on the laws, and we will continue to save those who are not protected by the laws."

"And Adia will educate the young Gifted to ensure their safety," Ora added, fixing her gaze on the sorceress.

As the conversation came to an abrupt halt, Adia stared out into the desert, searching internally for anger, hatred, fear, or any of the familiar feelings that had fueled her for so many years. It took no more than moments for her to realize, however, that her negative feelings had lost their strength. The positive energy she had found in the merfolk colony had been reinforced by the faith of her friends. "We will educate them together," she said.

"Very well," Hillian said, smiling. "We are all agreed. We will continue to push this world forward."

They were all agreed. So many years ago, in the sand, Adia had died and been reborn. She nodded, a smile beginning to tickle the edges of her mouth. Once again, she was reborn.

For more information about the book and the author—and for more stories of Adia Varani, Hillian Drake, their friends, and their world—visit:

www.TheMagicOfKeb.com

# GLOSSARY

**Akhdiria** (ahk-DEER-ee-uh): A political nation on Crozada, organized as a theocracy and led by a male al'awwal who chooses his successor. This nation is a member of the World Council and has a moderate climate. The national religion is the Sarim branch of Sabarism, and most natives have migrated from Ard Alabia (brown skin, dark-brown hair, and brown eyes).

**Akhdirian** (ahk-DEER-ee-uhn): Of, or pertaining to, Akhdiria.

**Al'Awwal** (AHL ah-WAHL): High priest of one of the two branches of Sabarism. In the Sarim branch, the al'awwal operates out of Waiid and is also head of state of Akhdiria. In the Ghafari branch, the al'awwal operates out of Qadir and is an adviser to the head of state of Ard Alabia.

**Alabian** (ah-LAH-bee-uhn): Of, or pertaining to, Ard Alabia.

**Alom** (uh-LAHM): High priest and head of state of one of the two Itami theocracies, Ukbawa and Tuskawa.

**Andari** (aan-DAHR-ee): Of, or pertaining to, Ke'Andara.

**Andyric Ocean** (aan-DEER-ihk): A large body of water to the east of Crozada.

**Ansabar** (AHN-suh-bahr): Heaven, an afterlife place of eternal salvation, and home of Sabar in Sabarism.

**Ard Alabia** (ARD ah-LAH-bee-uh): A political nation on Crozada, organized as a dictatorship and led by a commander general, whose succession is unknown. A member of the World Council, the nation has a dry, desert climate and natives with brown skin, dark-brown hair, and brown eyes. The national religion is the Ghafari branch of Sabarism.

**Ard Shaab, Forest of** (ARD shah-AHB): A large wooded area in central Akhdiria.

**Avishgar** (AH-vihsh-gahr): A clan of dwarves, including the royal family of the kingdom of Tyr.

**Ayawi** (ah-YAH-wee): The female goddess of good in Itam. She resides in Doya.

**Banyan** (BAAN-yuhn): A priest of Kila Maháli.

**Bates**: A male human. A Jalidin, he resides in Trigoti as Cardinal of Vinglandon.

**Branch, Foster**: A male human, twenty-nine years old, with fair white skin, green eyes, wild red hair, and a long, scraggly red beard. An atheist, he resides in Chayl as tavern master of the Wild Boar Tavern.

**Brook, Lynden**: A male human. A Jalidin, he resides in Domus Viho as High King of Grolandon.

**Burúji** (boo-ROO-zhee): Capital city of Mbúso.

**Buscade** (boo-SKAYD): A small city on the northern coast of Severlandon.

**Búso** (BOO-soh): Of, or pertaining to, Mbúso.

**Calimygna** (kaal-uh-MIHG-nuh): Capital city of Severlandon.

**Cardinal**: A priest of the highest order in Jalidinity, with responsibility for all lower orders in a nation. There are three cardinals: for Vinglandon (operating out of Trigoti), for Severlandon (operating out of Calimygna), and for Grolandon (operating out of Domus Viho).

**Carrion Crow Thieves Guild**: An international organization of rogues.

**Castlewood Distillery**: An ale-brewing business in Chayl.

**Cauda** (KOW-duh): A male human. A Jalidin, he resides in Calimygna as Cardinal of Severlandon.

**Chatima, Gawonii** (guh-WAH-nee CHAH-tih-muh): A male human with copper skin. An Itami, he resides in

Qoto as Ukbawa's delegate to the World Council and serves as Chairman of the World Council.

**Chayl** (CHAYL): A city on the eastern coast of Grolandon.

**Crescent Bay**: A large water inlet on the northern coast of Grolandon.

**Crescent River**: A river flowing from River Tyria, near Qoto, to Crescent Bay in Grolandon.

**Crozada** (kroh-ZAH-duh): A continent on Keb consisting of a large landmass and several islands bordered by the Kaoric Ocean on the west, the Andyric Ocean on the east, and the Pangerean Sea on the south.

**Dalil** (dah-LEEL): A priest of Sabarism.

**Dámu, Bay of** (DAH-moo): A large water inlet on the western coast of Mbúso.

**Dath'Duine** (DAATH doo-EEN): A political nation of elves from Crozada, living in hiding in the Forest of Ard Shaab and in Ke'Andara on the continent of Otica. Organized as a monarchy, the nation is led by a hereditary king or queen. The national religion is the faith of the One Spirit, and this nation is not a member of the World Council. Natives have white and blue skin, blue and white hair, and blue or purple lips and eyes.

**Dathin** (DAATH-ihn): Of, or pertaining to, Dath'Duine.

**Diir, Nassi** (NAA-see diy-EER): A male human. A Sabarist, he resides in Waiid as Al'Awwal of the Sarim branch of Sabarism, head of state of Akhdiria, and Akhdiria's delegate to the World Council.

**Dobyn** (DAH-bihn): A male dwarf, 232 years old (sixty-six in human years). He is three feet six inches tall and has light-tan skin, dark-brown eyes, dark-brown hair with gray at the temples, and a thick, long beard, sprinkled with gray. He resides in Tyr as Chief of Clan Varmingar.

**Domus Viho** (DOH-muhs VEE-hoh): Capital city of Grolandon.

**Doya** (DOH-yah): Heaven, an afterlife place of eternal salvation, and home of Ayawi in Itam.

**Drake, Hillian** (HIHL-ee-uhn DRAYK): A male human, twenty-five years old. He is five feet eight inches tall and has light-tan skin, blue eyes, light-brown hair worn short, and a clean-shaven face. He was born and resides in Porvatis, where he serves as Lord of Nydia. A believer in the religion of Jalidinity, he serves as Vinglandon's delegate to the World Council and is the son of Hydronimus Drake.

**Drake, Hydronimus** (hiy-DRAH-nih-muhs DRAYK): A male human. A Jalidin, he resides in Porvatis as

Prime Cardinal of Jalidinity and adviser to the King of Vinglandon. He is the father of Hillian Drake.

**Drozza River** (DROH-zuh): A river flowing from the Lyric Mountains to the Bay of Mirth that serves as the border between Vinglandon and Akhdiria.

**Duchy:** A region controlled by a noble duke or duchess in Vinglandon.

**Dwarf:** A singular person of the race of dwarves.

**Dwarven:** Of, or pertaining to, the race of dwarves.

**Dwarves:** A race of people on the world of Keb. They are characterized by a height of three to four feet, beards on both males and females, and an average life span of 280 years. They possess a native ability for high levels of Spell Magic but possess no ability for, and are naturally resistant to, Mind Magic. They also possess no abilities for Gift Magic or Shape Magic.

**Elf:** A singular person of the race of elves.

**Elven:** Of, or pertaining to, the race of elves.

**Elves:** A race of people on the world of Keb. They are characterized by a height of five to six feet, pointed ears, and an average life span of 360 years. They possess a native ability for high levels of Mind Magic but possess no ability for Spell Magic, Gift Magic, or Shape Magic. Subdivisions include Andari elves and Dathin elves.

**Emory, Bryce** (BRIYS EH-muhr-ee): A male human. A Jalidin, he resides in Calimygna as Vice President of Severlandon.

**Eoh** (EE-oh): A female bee fairy, twelve years old (twenty-one in human years), 1.6 inches tall, with golden eyes, ebony skin, pointed ears, and short black hair. She resides in the Hive as leader of the Screaming Stingers and is a low-level Mind Mage.

**Fahmori** (fah-MOHR-ee): The male god of evil in Jalidinity. He resides in Lakis.

**Fairies**: A race of people on the world of Keb. They are characterized by a height of two inches, pointed ears, wings, and an average life span of forty-five years. They possess native abilities for low levels of Mind Magic and Spell Magic but possess no abilities for Gift Magic or Shape Magic. Subdivisions include bee fairies, butterfly fairies, firefly fairies, and mosquito fairies.

**Fairy**: A singular person of the race of fairies. Also, of, or pertaining to, the race of fairies.

**Fen, Ora** (OHR-uh FEHN): A female Dathin elf, ninety-four years old (twenty-one in human years). She is five feet five inches tall, with lavender eyes and lips, powder-white skin accented with patches of sky blue, pointed ears, and long blue hair, accented with patches of white. She resides in the Forest of Ard Shaab and is a highly skilled Mind Mage.

**Gadrinal** (GAA-drih-nuhl): A priest of the second order in Jalidinity, with responsibility for all ordinals in a city or small region.

**Gift Magic**: A magic with the ability to harness the raw energy of the world. Low-level mages are capable of creating and projecting fire, force energy, and lightning. High-level mages are capable of creating and manipulating weather.

**Gifted**: To possess the talent of Gift Magic. Also, one who is Gifted.

**Gillis** (GIH-lihs): A male satyr, eight years old (seventeen in human years). He is four feet ten inches tall, with tan skin, light-brown eyes, brown hair and beard, and brown fur. He resides on Kiriti as a pirate.

**Great Smith**: A religion based upon the worship of Tyrigar, the Great Smith. Followers believe there are multiple gods but that following Tyrigar is the only certain way to reach the Great Smithy. They believe the Gifted possess powers from Tyrigar, but this belief has been overshadowed by cultural hatred of the Gifted. This is the national religion of Tyr.

**Great Smithy**: Heaven, an afterlife place of eternal salvation, and home of Tyrigar in the Great Smith faith.

**Grolandi** (groh-LAAN-dee): Of, or pertaining to, Grolandon.

**Grolandon** (groh-LAAN-duhn): A political nation on Crozada, organized as a monarchy and led by a hereditary high king. The nation is a member of the World Council. The national religion is Jalidinity. The country has a moderate climate and natives of fair white skin, blond or red hair, and blue or green eyes.

**Haggle Bay**: A large water inlet on the southern coast of Vinglandon.

**Heimdall, Warrick** (WOHR-ihk HIYM-dahl): A male Andari elf with green eyes and lips, powder-white skin accented with patches of forest green, pointed ears, and long green hair accented with patches of white. He resides in the Forest of Ard Shaab as lord of the Tantahir Portal Protectorate.

**Himil** (HIM-uhl): Heaven, an afterlife place of eternal salvation, and home of Jalidus in Jalidinity.

**Hive**: A hidden political nation of bee fairies on Crozada, organized as a monarchy and led by a hereditary queen. The national religion is the faith of the One Spirit, and the nation is not a member of the World Council. The Hive is within Severlandon, and natives have ebony skin, black hair, and orange or yellow eyes.

**Htan** (huh-TAHN): A male bee fairy, fourteen years old (twenty-six in human years). He is 1.8 inches tall, with golden eyes, ebony skin, pointed ears, and a shaved head. He resides in the Hive as Captain of the Queen's Guard and is a low-level Mind Mage.

**Humans**: A race of people on the world of Keb. Characterized by a height of five to six feet and an average life span of eighty years, they possess native abilities for low levels of Spell Magic and Mind Magic. Some are born with a talent for Gift Magic, which comes with native abilities for high levels of Spell Magic and Mind Magic. They possess no ability for Shape Magic.

**Iigra River** (iy-EE-gruh): A river flowing from Tantahir Lake to the northern coast of Crozada. This serves as a portion of the border between Severlandon and Akhdiria.

**Intolla** (ihn-TAH-luh): A village in northern Ard Alabia, near Khada's Pass.

**Itam** (IH-tahm): A religion based upon the worship of Ayawi. Followers believe there are multiple gods but that following Ayawi is the only certain way to reach Doya. They believe any religion may be legitimate but that only Itam is certain. They believe the Gifted are threats to the chosen people of Ayawi and must, therefore, be put to death. This is the national religion of Ukbawa and Tuskawa.

**Itami** (ih-TAHM-ee): A follower of Itam.

**Ixodis** (IKS-uh-dihs): Also known as the Angel of Mercy. He possesses powers similar to Gift Magic and is known for visiting newborn Gifted at the time of their birth, killing each infant as well as his or her parents.

**Jalidin** (JAAL-uh-dihn): A follower of Jalidinity.

**Jalidinity** (JAAL-uh-dihn-uh-tee): A religion based upon the worship of Jalidus. Followers believe the soul is naturally evil and is made good only by a person's decision to side with Jalidus in the never-ending war against Fahmori. They believe Jalidus is the only god and Jalidins are the only ones eligible for admission into the presence of Jalidus. They believe any non-Jalidins who contribute to the war against evil will be spared the eternal pain and suffering of Lakis but will spend eternity in a lower level of Himil apart from the presence of Jalidus. They believe the Gifted are human bodies with demon souls and must be burned alive to return the demon souls to the fires of Lakis. This is the national religion of Vinglandon and Grolandon, but it's also practiced widely in Severlandon.

**Jalidus** (JAAL-uh-dihs): The male god of good in Jalidinity. He resides in Himil.

**Janni Lake** (ZHAH-nee): An inland body of water in Janni Wood near the source of the Drozza River.

**Janni Wood** (ZHAH-nee): A wooded area in Akhdiria, surrounding the northern side of Janni Lake.

**Jaser, Rami** (RAH-mee JAA-zihr): A male human, thirty years old. He has brown skin, brown eyes, dark-brown hair worn very long, a thinly trimmed mustache, and a separate trimmed beard on his chin. He is a believer in the religion of Sabarism and resides in Rashida as a dalil. He serves as Ard Alabia's delegate to the World Council.

**Kanoa** (kuh-NOH-uh): A male human. He is an agnostic and resides in Menuha as King of Xenrali. He is Xenrali's delegate to the World Council.

**Kaoric Ocean** (kay-OHR-ihk): A large body of water to the west of Crozada.

**Ke'Andara** (KAY aan-DAHR-uh): A political nation of elves on Otica, organized as a monarchy, led by a hereditary king or queen. The national religion is the faith of the One Spirit, and the nation is not a member of the World Council. Natives enjoy a tropical-forest climate and have white and green skin, green and white hair, pointed ears, and green or yellow lips and eyes.

**Keb** (KEHB): The world.

**Keras Bay** (KAYR-uhs): A small water inlet on the northern coast of Severlandon.

**Kesler, Mona** (MOH-nuh KEHS-lihr): A female human, twenty-seven years old. She has fair white skin, clear blue eyes, and long blond hair. She resides in Calimygna and is President of Severlandon. She is an agnostic and serves as Severlandon's delegate to the World Council.

**Kewu** (KEE-woo): Capital city of Tuskawa.

**Khada** (KAH-duh): The male god of evil in Sabarism. He resides in Nar.

**Khada's Pass** (KAH-duhz): A narrow stretch of non-mountainous terrain between the Rachis Mountains and the Tyrenese Mountains.

**Kila** (KEE-luh): The male god of good in Kila Maháli. He has no permanent residence or home but lives in all things and all people.

**Kila Maháli** (KEE-luh muh-HAH-lee): A religion based upon the worship of Kila. It believes all living things are part of an eternal, collective spirit connected to the life force of Kila himself. Followers believe all religions worship the same god, as Kila is known by many names, and that the Gifted are part of the same collective spirit and, therefore, are not inherently evil. Though illegal, this religion is practiced widely in Mbúso.

**Kiriti** (kih-REE-dee): An island off the east coast of Crozada, with no formal government. This is not a member of the World Council. Residents are largely minotaurs relocated from the continent of Otica.

**Kiritian** (kih-REE-shun): Of, or pertaining to, Kiriti.

**Kivúli Falls** (kih-VOO-lee): A large waterfall in the Riven Mountains near the source of the River Maish.

**Kuúma, Cliffs of** (koo-OO-muh): A natural formation of tall, vertical rock on the western edge of the Gulf of Kuúma.

**Kuúma, Gulf of** (koo-OO-muh): A large water inlet on the eastern coast of Mbúso.

**Lakis** (LAA-kihs): Hell, an afterlife place of eternal damnation, and home of Fahmori in Jalidinity.

**Loe** (LOH): A male dwarf. He resides in Tyr as king.

**Lorcan** (LOHR-kihn): A male minotaur, fourteen years old (twenty-three in human years). He is seven feet nine inches tall (eight feet ten inches, with his horns), with bronze skin, dark-brown eyes, and black fur. He resides on Kiriti as a pirate captain.

**Lumos** (LOO-mohs): The less bright of the two moons of Keb.

**Lynd, River** (LIHND): A river flowing from River Lyria to Haggle Bay in Vinglandon.

**Lyria, River** (LEER-ee-uh): A river flowing from the Lyric Mountains to Vanig Bay in Vinglandon.

**Lyric Mountains** (LEER-ihk): A mountain range in central Vinglandon.

**Madin, River** (mah-DEEN): A river flowing from Tantahir Lake to Waiid in Akhdiria.

**Mage**: A practitioner of magic. Variations include Gift Mage, Mind Mage, and Spell Mage.

**Magic**: A combination of natural talent and learned skill that allows the mage to perform extraordinary feats. The more difficult the magic, the more tiring it is to the mage. Variations include Gift Magic, Mind Magic, Shape Magic, and Spell Magic.

**Mahalist** (muh-HAH-lihst): A follower of Kila Maháli.

**Maísh, River** (mah-EESH): A river flowing from the Riven Mountains to Sóen Bay in Mbúso.

**Malini** (muh-LEE-nee): High priest of Kila Maháli, with responsibility for all other priests worldwide. He operates out of the Monastery of Kila on the Cliffs of Kuúma.

**Mbúso** (uhm-BOO-soh): A political nation on Crozada, organized as a dictatorship, led by a premier whose succession is unknown. This nation is a member of the World Council and has outlawed religion and religious expression. Natives enjoy a warm climate and have black or dark-brown skin, black hair, and brown eyes.

**Menuha** (mi-NOO-uh): Capital city of Xenrali.

**Merfolk**: An alternate term for merpeople. Also, of, or pertaining to, the race of merpeople.

**Merfolk Colony**: A colony of merpeople off the northeast coast of Crozada, living in underwater caves and grottoes with no formal government. They are not a member of the World Council. Natives have white skin, blond or light-brown hair, blue or green eyes, and green scales.

**Mermaid**: A singular, female person of the race of merpeople.

**Merman**: A singular, male person of the race of merpeople.

**Merpeople**: A race of people on the world of Keb. They are characterized by height/length of five to six feet; the head, torso, and arms of a human and the lower body of a fish; and an average life span of eighty years. They possess an ability to breathe in or out of water and possess a native ability for low levels of Mind Magic. They possess a native ability for high levels of Shape Magic but possess no abilities for Spell Magic or Gift Magic.

**Mind Magic**: A magic with the ability to control interactions between minds. Low-level mages are capable of protecting their own minds from attack or intrusion, projecting thoughts, and of hearing unprotected thoughts. High-level mages are capable of mind attacks, controlled projection of thoughts (such that only the desired recipient is able to hear), invasive mind reading, and possession.

**Minotaur** (MIHN-uh-tahr): A singular person of the race of minotaurs. Also, of, or pertaining to, the race of minotaurs.

**Minotaurs** (MIHN-uh-tahrz): A race of people on the world of Keb. They are characterized by a height of seven to eight feet; the head and two legs of a bull and the torso and arms of a human; and an average life span of fifty years. They possess extraordinary strength and endurance but no ability for magic.

**Mirth, Bay of**: A large water inlet on the western coast of Crozada, the northern side belonging to Severlandon and the southern side belonging to Vinglandon.

**Mwambá** (mwahm-BAH): A male human with black skin, a shaved head, and a nose ring. He is an atheist and resides in Burúji as Premier of Mbúso. He is Mbúso's delegate to the World Council.

**Nar** (NAHR): Hell, an afterlife place of eternal damnation, and home of Kahda in Sabarism.

**Necromancy** (NEH-kroh-maan-see): A subcategory of Spell Magic, criminal in all nations, focused on manipulating the death of a living or recently deceased organism.

**Nina, River** (NEE-nuh): A river flowing from the Iigra River to the Bay of Mirth. It serves as a portion of the border between Severlandon and Akhdiria.

**Norwood Marsh** (NOHR-wuud): A swamp in southern Grolandon.

**Nukpanii** (nook-PAH-nee): The male god of evil in Itam. He has no permanent residence or home but roams Keb.

**Numinos** (NOO-mih-nohs): The brighter of the two moons of Keb.

**Nyángo** (niy-AANG-goh): A large city on the eastern coast of Mbúso, located on the edge of Sóen Bay at the mouth of the River Maish.

**Nydia** (NIH-dee-uh): A duchy bordered by River Lyria, River Lynd, and the Kaoric Ocean in southern Vinglandon.

**Omanakwa** (ah-muh-NAH-kwah): A male human with copper skin. An Itami, he resides in Kewu as alom, head of state of Tuskawa and high priest of Itam in Tuskawa.

**Ómo Islands** (OH-moh): A chain of small islands off the southern coast of Mbúso.

**One Spirit:** A religion based upon the worship of life as one spirit though not personified in a god or deity. Followers believe all living things are part of this eternal, one spirit. They believe all religions are operating within the same one spirit but are choosing only to focus on one aspect of it, and that the Gifted are part of the same collective spirit and, therefore, are not inherently evil. This religion is practiced widely by elves, fairies, and merpeople.

**Orbal River** (OHR-buhl): A river flowing from the Orbalese Mountains to Norwood Marsh.

**Orbalese Mountains** (OHR-buhl-eez): A mountain range in northeastern Crozada. These serve as the longest portion of the border between Tuskawa and Grolandon.

**Ordinal**: A priest of the lowest order in Jalidinity.

**Otica** (AH-dih-kuh): A continent on Keb containing the elven nation of Ke'Andara.

**Pangerean Sea** (paan-JEER-ee-uhn): A large body of water to the south of Crozada.

**Poole** (POOL): A male human with white skin. A Jalidin, he resides in Domus Viho as cardinal and advisor to the

High King of Grolandon. He is Grolandon's delegate to the World Council.

**Porvatis** (pohr-VAH-tihs): Capital city of Vinglandon.

**Prime Cardinal**: High priest of Jalidinity, with responsibility for all other priests worldwide. He operates out of Porvatis.

**Qadir** (kah-DEER): Capital city of Ard Alabia.

**Qaletakwa** (kaal-uh-TAH-kwuh): A male human with copper skin. An Itami, he resides in Qoto as alom, head of state of Ukbawa and high priest of Itam in Ukbawa.

**Qawi, Eyad** (AY-yahd KAH-wee): A male human with brown skin. A Sabarist, he resides in Qadir as Commander General of Ard Alabia.

**Qoto** (KOH-toh): Capital city of Ukbawa.

**Rachis Mountains** (RAA-kihs): A mountain range in central Crozada. These serve as the border between Ard Alabia and Akhdiria.

**Ragnall** (RAAG-nuhl): A male human. A Jalidin, he resides in Porvatis as King of Vinglandon.

**Rahim, Mukhtar** (MOOK-tahr rah-HEEM): A male human. A Sabarist, he resides in Qadir as Al'Awwal of the Ghafari branch of Sabarism and adviser to the commander general.

**Rashida** (ruh-SHEE-duh): A village in western Ard Alabia.

**Riven Mountains** (RIH-vihn): A mountain range in western Mbúso.

**Rook**: Grandmaster of the Carrion Crow Thieves Guild, responsible for all guild masters and guild members worldwide.

**Sabar** (suh-BAHR): The male god of good in Sabarism. He resides in Ansabar.

**Sabarism** (suh-BAHR-ihz-uhm): A religion based upon the worship of Sabar. Followers believe the soul is naturally good but is constantly being attacked by the influences of evil. They believe life is a struggle to overcome the influences of Khada, but the true believers who remain vigilant will celebrate with Sabar in Ansabar. They believe Sabarism is the only true religion and Sabar is the only true god, but anyone can be accepted into Ansabar if he or she has been successful in overcoming the influences of evil. They believe the Gifted are human bodies with demon souls and must be burned alive to return the demon souls to the fires of Nar. This is the national religion of Akhdiria and Ard Alabia.

**Sabarist** (suh-BAHR-ihst): A follower of Sabarism.

**Safeda** (suh-FEE-duh): A female Andari elf with green eyes and lips, powder-white skin accented with patches of green, pointed ears, and long green hair accented with patches of white. She resides in Ke'Andara as queen and is a powerful Mind Mage.

**Satyr** (SAY-tehr): A singular person of the race of satyrs. Also, of, or pertaining to, the race of satyrs.

**Satyrs** (SAY-tehrz): A race on the world of Keb. Characterized by the legs of a goat and the head, torso, and arms of a human, they have an average life span of forty years. They possess extraordinary agility but no ability for magic.

**Screaming Stingers**: A company of female bee warriors in the Hive.

**Severlandi** (seh-vehr-LAAN-dee): Of, or pertaining to, Severlandon.

**Severlandon** (seh-vehr-LAAN-duhn): A political nation on Crozada, organized as a democracy and led by an elected president and vice president. There is no national religion. This country is a member of the World Council, and natives enjoy a moderate climate and have fair white skin, blond or red hair, and blue or green eyes.

**Shape Magic**: A magic with the ability to change the practitioner's shape. Low-level mages are capable of changes to similar shapes. High-level mages are capable of more complex changes.

**Sihu** (SEE-hoo): A priest of Itam.

**Sóen Bay** (SOH-ehn): A small water inlet on the eastern coast of Mbúso.

**Sorcerer**: A male practitioner of sorcery.

**Sorceress**: A female practitioner of sorcery.

**Sorcery**: An alternate term for magic, though commonly used only to describe Gift Magic.

**Spell Magic**: A magic with the ability to enhance the existing attributes of, or to assign new attributes to, nonliving objects. Low-level mages are capable of temporary results. High-level mages are capable of permanent results.

**Spellcast**: To perform Spell Magic.

**Spellcasted**: Enhanced or changed by Spell Magic.

**Surbal River** (SIHR-buhl): A river flowing from the northernmost edge of the Riven Mountains along the Surbalese Mountains to Norwood Marsh.

**Surbalese Mountains** (SIHR-buhl-eez): A mountain range in eastern Crozada. These serve as the border between Tuskawa and Mbúso.

**Taipa River** (TIY-puh): A river flowing from the Lyric Mountains to Trigoti Bay. This serves as the border between Vinglandon and Ard Alabia.

**Tantahir Lake** (taan-tuh-HEER): A large inland body of water within the Forest of Ard Shaab in Akhdiria.

**Tarala** (tuh-RAH-luh): A female bee fairy. She resides in the Hive as queen.

**Trigoti** (trih-GAH-dee): A large city at the mouth of the Taipa River that spans across borders, having portions in Vinglandon, Ard Alabia, and Mbúso.

**Trigoti Bay** (trih-GAH-dee): A large water inlet on the southern coast of Vinglandon, north of Xenrali.

**Tuskawa** (tuhs-KAH-wuh): A political nation on Crozada, organized as a theocracy, led by a male alom who chooses his successor. This nation is not a member of the World Council, and the national religion is Itam. The nation has a cold climate, and natives have copper skin, black hair, and brown eyes.

**Tuskawan** (tuhs-KAH-wuhn): Of, or pertaining to, Tuskawa.

**Tyr** (TEER): A hidden political nation of dwarves on Crozada, organized as a monarchy and led by a hereditary king. The national religion is the faith of the Great Smith, and the nation is not a member of the World Council. This is a nation of caves with natives of white or tan skin, brown or black hair, and brown eyes.

**Tyrenese Mountains** (TEER-ih-neez): A mountain range in central Crozada. These serve as the border around Ukbawa.

**Tyria, River** (TEER-ee-uh): A river flowing from the northernmost edge of the Riven Mountains to the northern coast of Crozada. This serves as the border between Ard Alabia and Tuskawa, between Ukbawa and Tuskawa, between Ukbawa and Grolandon, and between Akhdiria and Grolandon.

**Tyrian** (TEER-ee-uhn): Of, or pertaining to, Tyr.

**Tyrigar** (TEER-ih-gahr): The male god of dwarves in the Great Smith faith. He resides in the Great Smithy at the center of the world.

**Ukbawa** (ook-BAH-wuh): A political nation on Crozada, organized as a theocracy and led by a male alom who chooses his successor. This nation is a member of the World Council. The national religion is Itam. The nation has a cold, tundra climate with natives of copper skin, black hair, and brown eyes.

**Ukbawan** (ook-BAH-wuhn): Of, or pertaining to, Ukbawa.

**Uli** (OO-lee): A male Dathin elf with blue eyes and lips, powder-white skin accented with patches of dark blue, pointed ears, and blue hair accented with patches of white. He resides in Ke'Andara as King of Dath'Duine and is a powerful Mind Mage.

**Val Varen, Eryk** (AYR-ihk vaal VAYR-uhn): A male human, thirty-five years old. He is five feet ten inches tall with light-tan skin, brown eyes, dark-brown hair worn long and often pulled back in a clasp, and a scruffy brown beard. An atheist, he was born in poverty in Trigoti and now resides in Porvatis as a master innkeeper.

**Vanig Bay** (VAA-nihg): A small water inlet on the western coast of Vinglandon.

**Varani, Adia** (AH-dee-uh vah-RAH-nee): A female human, nineteen years old, with brown skin, amber eyes, and long dark-brown hair. She was born in Intolla and is a believer in the religion of Sabarism. She is a powerful Gift Mage and a low-level Spell Mage and Mind Mage.

**Varmingar** (VAHR-mihng-gahr): A clan of dwarves responsible for protecting the secret existence of dwarves from exposure.

**Ving** (VING): A resident of, or person claiming origin from, Vinglandon.

**Vingish** (VING-gihsh): Of, or pertaining to, Vinglandon.

**Vinglandon** (ving-LAAN-duhn): A political nation on Crozada, organized as a monarchy and led by a hereditary king. The nation is a member of the World Council, and the national religion is Jalidinity. Natives enjoy a moderate climate and have tan-white skin, brown hair, and blue or brown eyes.

**Wadógo, Ida** (EE-dah wuh-DOH-goh): A female human, thirty-four years old, six feet tall, with black skin, dark-brown eyes, and short black hair. An atheist, she resides in Burúji as a knight captain. She is the first female ever admitted to the Golden Knighthood.

**Waiid** (wah-EED): Capital city of Akhdiria.

**Witch**: An alternate term for mage, used as an insult. Common variations include Giftwitch, Mindwitch, and Spellwitch.

**Wukoa, Wall of** (woo-KOH-uh): A wall separating Tuskawa from Norwood Marsh. This serves as a portion of the border between Tuskawa and Grolandon.

**Xenrali** (zehn-RAH-lee): A political nation on Crozada, organized as a monarchy and led by a hereditary king or queen. A member of the World Council, this nation has banned organized religion, but residents otherwise have freedom of religious expression. Natives enjoy a tropical climate and have dark-tan skin, black hair, and brown eyes.

**Xenralian** (zehn-RAH-lee-uhn): Of, or pertaining to, Xenrali.

**Ziraili, Galen** (GAY-lehn zehr-RAY-lee): A male human, seventy-two years old, with black skin, dark-brown eyes, white hair, and a long white beard. He is a believer in the religion of Kila Maháli and resides in the Monastery of Kila on the Cliffs of Kuúma as the malini.